"JEANETTE,
THE CAPTAIN
IS WAITING . . ."

I knew I had no choice; I must obey.

While I dressed, I wondered with a hot blush if it had been Captain McCoy who had undressed me after I'd fainted and wrapped me in the blanket. Untouched by a man for nearly a year, the thought of Jamie McCoy's tanned muscular body and his easy grin were arousing a hunger in me I'd thought Hippolyte's perverted lust had killed for all time.

We'd been too close too long for my maid, Bliss, not to sense the direction of my thoughts.

"You need a real man, Jeanette." The top of her tongue circled her lips. "I'd have thought Captain McCoy would have taken you by now."

I turned my back to her. "Button me up!"

"Am I wrong? Did he?" Bliss asked.

"No. He did *not*."

My dress buttoned, Bliss clasped me against the soft warmth of her body, hands cupping my breasts for a moment. Then she let me go.

From her knowing smile when I faced her, I knew she guessed how much her brief caress had heightened my passion.

"Damn you," I said.

Bliss laughed. "Captain McCoy sent me to tell you that you're expected in his cabin, *now* . . ."

THIS
OUTLAW
HEART

Rosetta Stowe

A Dell/James A. Bryans Book

Published by
Dell Publishing Co., Inc.
1 Dag Hammarskjold Plaza
New York, New York 10017

Dell ® TM 681510, Dell Publishing Co., Inc.

ISBN: 0-440-08711-2

Printed in the United States of America

First printing—July 1978

PROLOGUE

Since 1667, when the French seized the western half of Hispaniola from the Spaniards, Haiti had been the diamond in the French colonial crown. But by 1803 its luster was stained with blood. Since 1791, escaped slaves based in mountain and jungle strongholds had fought regiments Napoleon could hardly spare and had decimated them.

But French white and mulatto planters had survived a number of bloody slave uprisings since 1667, defeating each one with more cruelty than the one before. Despite the smuggling of arms to Dessalines's maroons from Santo Domingo, the Spanish half of Hispaniola, the planters thought they could survive this revolt.

BOOK ONE

CHAPTER 1

LE ROI had been my home for a year, if one can call a virtual prison home. The great house on Isle Verlaine, across a narrow strait from Cap-Haïtien, the main port on the north coast of Haiti, was built in 1796 by Duc Raoul de Verlaine. It was a massive square block of granite on the highest part of the island, put there to resemble a moated chateau whisked from the south of France and set down on a West Indies island.

Le Roi is a gutted ruin now, patrolled by snakes and lizards. The slave quarters behind it

11

are crumbling, too, and miles of sugar cane no longer ripple in the trade winds.

I'm sure Isle Verlaine must be haunted. No living man or woman walks there today, and the bones of the unburied dead bleach in the sun. Across the strait behind Cap-Haïtien the rebel slave Henri Christophe is building San Souci, a mountain stronghold from which he can see Isle Verlaine. I understand he's rechristened himself Henri I of Haiti.

I wonder about his thoughts.

Bliss was my slave maid, a slender black girl from Senegal bought by my father off a slave ship when she was a child. We were the same age and had always been companions rather than mistress and slave. So I brought Bliss with me to Le Roi and Isle Verlaine after marrying Hippolyte de Verlaine a few weeks after my parents died.

Bliss and I were alone in the great house that afternoon. It was late in the year of 1803. The season of hurricanes had passed with the end of November, but it was extremely hot for that time of year. For the past few days, the trade winds had failed.

Because of the heat, Bliss had stripped to her thin white shift and was asleep on a mat near the door. Of the two of us, only I preferred a bed for my afternoon nap.

It was too hot and close under the cone of

mosquito netting drapped over my bed for me to sleep.

Except for those few slaves being punished in the stocks, forced to broil in the sun, the men, women and children were cutting sugarcane under the whips of mulatto overseers. Shouted commands were muted by distance.

I'd taken off my shift to lie on the bed naked, ankles and knees touching, arms crossed over my breasts, my sweat-moist body rigid. The early afternoon sun mottled the ceiling above my bed with unmoving leaf shadows. I stared up at them.

It had taken a month, but my plans to escape Isle Verlaine and Hippolyte were complete. How long would Hippolyte stay with his mistress in Cap-Haïtien this time? If Hippolyte stayed in Cap-Haïtien tonight, we could go. But if he didn't, if Bliss and I were caught by him, we'd both be murdered. She'd already endured one whipping I'd been forced to watch.

That had been for some fancied slight; an overbold glance in his direction, or what he considered a sullen tone of voice. If we were caught before we reached Philippe and his fishing boat, the flesh would be flayed from her bones.

I would die, too—I had no doubt about that. My usefulness to Hippolyte was nearly over.

Maroon drums had throbbed in the night for the past two weeks. Their sound drifted across the strait to us like the beating of an evil heart. We could only guess what messages they carried to the blacks in the slave compound.

The mixed-blood house slaves were more frightened than I'd ever seen them before. They had as much to fear from the blacks as we whites. They were as hated as we were. Their quarters, closer to Le Roi than the black compound, were barricaded every night, and they'd begged Hippolyte for guns.

I'd decided that Bliss and I could wait a few days more and was drifting off to sleep when I heard the first distant drumbeat. It came from far away deep in the mountain jungle, but was quickly answered by closer drums.

We'd never heard the drums before in the daytime. I was instantly wide awake, and so was Bliss. Her eyes were wide with fear.

"They talk to Damballa now." She'd cocked her head to listen. "They ask his help tonight."

"Can you get to Philippe without being seen?" I asked. Only Bliss knew all the slave paths through the cane fields. "Tell him to have his boat ready. We'll come tonight."

I prayed that Hippolyte would stay in Cap-Haïtien until tomorrow. By that time we'd be well on our way through the Windward Passage for Jamaica.

Bliss dressed hurriedly and was gone.

I locked and bolted the bedroom door, then looked to see if my small cache of gold coins was where I'd hidden it with my father's knife and my mother's crucifix on a gold chain. These small treasures were all I planned to take when we escaped Hippolyte and Isle Verlaine.

They were safe.

Jules DuBois was my father. His was a wealthy merchant family in Port-au-Prince. They owned only a few slaves. Ouida Fitzhugh was my English mother. I was their only child. They named me Jeanette after my father's favorite sister who died of the fever.

My blonde hair I inherited from mother, as I did my slender body. But my olive skin and gray-green eyes mark me as a DuBois.

"You have cat eyes," my father used to tease.

It was mother's idea to pack me off to England and a Sussex boarding school when I was nine.

Father wanted me educated in France.

"I won't have it, Jules," my mother told him. "I married you despite the fact you're French and distantly related—or so your mother claimed—to those royal fools who paved the way for Napoleon. But my Jeanette must know what it is to be half-English."

As usual, she had her way with my good-natured father, and I was put aboard a neutral Dutch ship for safe passage to England. Bliss sailed with me.

That was in 1790, a year before Toussaint L'Ouverture raised the banner of revolt against the

French and their mulatto favorites who dominated the planter economy of Haiti.

I don't know who mother's Sussex family considered more bizarre, Bliss or me. They called her "Jeanette's little blackamoor," and fed her sweets and petted her as if she were a puppy.

They were all good people, I know now. I can't blame them for not knowing what to make of a gawky girl-child who spoke better French than she did English.

"This is Ouida's child, you know," they'd say when introducing me to strangers.

"Oh, yes, poor Ouida" was the usual answer.

With some pride the Fitzhughs would explain Ouida had gone off to the West Indies as a governess and married a wealthy Frenchman. She was no longer poor.

I hated them all.

I also hated the other pupils and most of the teachers at Miss Wentworth's School for Young Ladies. In fairness, I must admit that having my own black body servant was a just cause for jealousy on the part of the other girls. My accented English when I first entered school was really atrocious. The fact I found the school's curriculum too easy after Mother's tutoring and made no bones about it; these things endeared me to no one.

When Mother's letter came in the midst of a dreary English winter calling me back to Port-au-Prince, I was delighted. So was Bliss. Mother's vague references to a marriage my father was arranging in the French fashion didn't bother me.

I would marry whom I loved when it pleased me.

Again we sailed aboard a Dutch ship. I'd left Santo Domingo a bewildered child. I came back a young woman as stubbornly English as I was French. I'd lived in a society that abhorred slavery. Port-au-Prince wasn't the pleasant Old World city I remembered.

The old churches were just as beautiful, its crooked cobbled streets were the same, the brilliant flowers with their fragrance were still a delight after the cold grayness of the English winter. But the atmosphere had changed. Bliss and I felt the change immediately when we stepped ashore on the old stone quay.

Father had come to meet us, driving himself. He said we'd have to send for our trunks in the customhouse. I remembered the quay and market nearby as thronged with blacks bargaining with each other for the food raised in their small garden plots. Today it was nearly deserted.

Father was older; his face was drawn.

Winding through the narrow streets to reach our home, we had to pass through the main square. Like the quay, it was nearly deserted.

It was Bliss who first saw what caused the smell of death and decay. She gasped, touched my shoulder, and pointed.

A wooden platform had been erected in the

middle of the square. Dangling from individual gibbets were five black bodies—three black men and two black women—suspended by their ankles. The broken and rotting bodies swayed slightly in the breeze, seeming to dance a macabre upside-down minuet.

"They were broken on the wheel the day before yesterday," Father explained in a toneless voice.

"What was their crime?" I asked.

Father shrugged. "Who knows? Leclerc likes to set examples." He gestured toward the bodies. "This sort of thing goes on all over Haiti these days. We French are becoming as cruel as the Spaniards ever were."

"It's hideous!" I exclaimed.

Father shrugged resignedly. "You'll get used to it."

Our home on a quiet side street in the upper part of Port-au-Prince was as Bliss and I remembered it. Behind the blank stucco wall facing the narrow street was the cool courtyard, its central fountain surrounded by flowers. We didn't notice at first that there was only the crippled old Mandingo woman who cooked for Mother, and an elderly black slave who lived in a hut behind the house in attendance.

"Your mother thinks it's too dangerous to keep slaves in the house," Father explained when I did notice and asked. "We've sold all but these two."

Mother felt safe with only the Mandingo cook and the old man.

"She may be right," he admitted and cited several instances in the past few years of slaves murdering their master and mistress before fleeing to the mountains.

Mother hadn't changed much. There was some gray in her hair, her step was a little slower, but she welcomed the two of us warmly, eager to hear about England. I was home two days before she mentioned the marriage father was arranging with Hippolyte de Verlaine.

"He comes from a very good and old family," she told me. "I want you to know it means a great deal to your father and me to see you make a good marriage."

We were sitting on a stone bench in the courtyard near the fountain.

"How old is he?" I asked.

"Forty, I should think. But he's a handsome man, Jeanette. You've heard of Isle Verlaine?"

"Something."

"You'll live there in the great house called Le Roi," Mother said. "I visited there once before I met your father."

"You surely can't expect me to marry a man I've never seen," I told Mother. "It's a ridiculous idea! And he's so much older than I am."

"Don't make up your mind until you've met him," Mother advised.

That evening Hippolyte came to the house for supper.

Slender and graying slightly at the temples, I suppose Hippolyte was a handsome man, and his manners were courtly.

Father treated him with deference. Mother was obviously charmed. I didn't like him. It may have been because I disliked the whole idea of an arranged marriage with an adequate dowry paid to my husband, but I like to think I sensed something evil about the man. At any rate, it was an awkward situation which I didn't improve with my acquired English frankness.

"Whatever you and my father may have decided," I told Hippolyte, "I'm the one who will say yes or no to any marriage."

We were alone together in the courtyard on the same stone bench I'd shared that afternoon with Mother.

"But of course," Hippolyte agreed. "There is no hurry." He kissed my hand. "I've waited long enough to find the right woman to share Le Roi; a week or even a month will make no difference."

"How can you be sure I'm the right woman?" I asked. "We've known each other how long? An hour? Two hours?"

"Long enough to satisfy me," Hippolyte said.

I suppose I should have been flattered.

"Of course in the end you will do as your father and mother wish in this matter," Hippolyte said then. "Santo Domingo isn't England, and you are a DuBois."

"I am also a Fitzhugh," I reminded him.

The next day, when I learned the marriage agreement had already been signed and sealed, part of the dowry paid Hippolyte, I quarreled with my father.

"I just won't go through with it!" I stormed at him. "I'm a woman, not your chattel."

"I've given my word, Jeanette."

"Damn your word! It's my body and future you're selling to this man whom I don't know and don't like."

My father was more angry than I'd ever seen him. He slapped my face. "You'll do as I say!"

"No!" It was a stinging blow and I covered my cheek with a hand, blinking back the angry tears. "I'm going back to England. You and Hippolyte can go to hell!"

Father had gone white. A pulse throbbed in his temple. But when he spoke again, his voice was even and controlled. "You don't yet understand the situation here on Haiti, Jeanette. You need the protection of a wealthy husband. Hippolyte is willing to give you his name and take you to Isle Verlaine, where you'll be safe."

"I'll be safer in England," I retorted.

Still flushed with anger, I dashed off a note to Hippolyte, who was staying with a cousin in Port-au-Prince until the marriage date was settled. It was a cruel note—I admit that.

I wrote I wasn't in need of his protection, that I'd soon be going back to England to choose my own husband if it was a husband I wanted. I stressed the difference in our ages. Then I sent Bliss to deliver the note before my mother could stop me.

To my surprise, Mother was frightened when she learned what I'd written to Hippolyte. "He's a very proud man, Jeanette, and you've insulted his honor. The Verlaines never forgive an insult. You should have consulted me. If you're so completely opposed to this marriage, we might have found a better way to avoid it."

"Whatever happens, it's done," I told Mother.

Strangely enough, when my father learned of the note, he accepted what I'd done with resignation. "But now we'll have to see you go back to England as soon as possible," he said. "Within the month, certainly, if we can get you aboard a Dutch ship."

When Bliss came back from delivering my note, she was shaken. She'd brought no reply. She didn't tell me how Hippolyte had reacted.

A week later, both my mother and father were dead—poisoned by the crippled Mandingo woman, the authorities said. She'd confessed the crime under torture, and she and the old man were both executed. I didn't have to see them broken on the wheel in the main square of Port-au-Prince. After the funeral, Hippolyte had taken me to stay with his aunt in Cap-Haïtien. I took Bliss with me.

Hippolyte never mentioned the note I'd sent. In those first stunned days, he was kinder to me than anyone had ever been. In my state of shock I accepted him as a surrogate father or the older brother I never had.

There could be no question of my going back to England now, Hippolyte pointed out. Napoleon would soon invade the island and bring the British to their knees.

He also said he loved me. Bliss was impressed by his kindness, too. She urged me to marry him.

It was a quiet marriage because I was still in mourning for Mother and Father.

CHAPTER 2

THE NIGHT Mother and Father died of poison, I ate the same supper they did. Bliss was away from the house on an errand for my mother. She was spared by accident. There was a good reason I wasn't poisoned. I should have guessed why, but I didn't until Hippolyte and I were married.

Gambling, Madame Leroux, his mistress in Cap-Haïtien, and successive crop failures because he'd neglected the plantation, made the liberal dowry my father had agreed to pay necessary to save Hippolyte from disgrace. When I threatened to return to England instead of going through with the arranged marriage, Hippolyte was desperate.

Under French colonial law, when I married Hippolyte, my inheritance from my father passed into his control. Despite being smothered by kindness and consideration after my parents died and until we were married, I was a fool not to suspect they had been murdered.

Our wedding night at Le Roi opened my eyes.

I wasn't completely innocent—Bliss had seen to that. She had had a whole series of sly sexual adventures when we were in England, but I was a virgin.

I confess I didn't love Hippolyte. I was frank with him about that before we were married, but I did promise him and myself that I'd try to be a good wife and hope time would nurture love.

Hippolyte came to the bridal chamber drunk on wine. Rape wasn't enough punishment for me —I was subjected to every indignity the man could devise. When I was fainting from pain, he brought in Bliss to have his way with her.

The next morning, I tried to kill him.

There was a knife among my father's effects— a dagger, really. When Hippolyte had finally spent himself and sent Bliss away, he fell into a wine-drugged sleep.

I was poised to plunge the knife into his throat when his eyes flickered open. A blow from his fist split my lip. He cut his hand, but finally wrested the knife from me.

I was still a spitting fury. Both of us naked, we wrestled. I was trying to blind him with my nails, but my strength was no match for his.

The struggle had aroused Hippolyte. I was raped again, then beaten nearly senseless. But Hippolyte had forgotten the knife. I hid it away before confronting him.

"If you so much as touch me again, I'm going to kill you," I promised.

Hippolyte laughed. "You'll lick my feet if I tell you to do so. No English bitch refuses to marry a de Verlaine. When I've finished with you, you'll have learned proper French manners."

"You killed my parents!"

Hippolyte laughed again. "Go tell your story to the authorities and see if they believe you."

They wouldn't, I knew. But I also knew in that moment that what I'd just said was true.

"Hippolyte, listen carefully to me. I failed to kill you this time. Next time I won't. I swear I won't. You've the strength to take me again, but if you do, you'd better kill me. A day, a week, a month—it doesn't matter. I'll manage to kill you."

Hippolyte jeered at my threat, but he never did touch me again. He used Bliss shamelessly, often in my presence, and finally had her whipped. But I was never again forced to submit to him.

* * *

When Bliss and I decided to escape from Isle
Verlaine and try to reach English Jamaica, she
had to find us a boat and pilot. House slaves kept
a close watch on me when Hippolyte was away
from Le Roi, which was often, but Bliss was
black. She soon found her way to a miserable
village of mixed-blood fishermen in a cove at the
west end of Isle Verlaine.

They sold their catch to Sabo, Hippolyte's mulatto steward, for the slaves. It was beneath Sabo's dignity to bargain with Philippe, the leader
of the fishermen. Bliss with her wiles and, I suspect, after allowing Sabo to seduce her, became
his agent in dealing with Philippe.

Over a period of time, we managed to smuggle
food from the great house kitchen and other small
comforts to these people. Philippe finally agreed
to take us to Jamaica in his boat. He'd sailed the
small craft to Kingston once to bring back a
young wife.

Philippe, his wife, Bliss, and I—the four of
us—would slip away from Isle Verlaine this time.

One dark night I slipped along the slave paths
through the cane to close our bargain with
Philippe. He was a thin old man with a tribal-
scarred face—part Carib Indian, I learned—a
proud man with wiry strength. Most of the north
coast of Jamaica was dominated by the maroons,
he told me.

These escaped slaves were friendly to him, he

said. They might accept Bliss, but I, as a white woman, could expect no mercy.

Philippe spoke a patois I couldn't understand. Bliss had to translate for me as we squatted on mats in his thatched hut.

"He says there is a *sect rouge* on Jamaica," she told me. "They are maroons, yes, but secret people who eat human flesh."

"Cannibals?"

Bliss nodded. "He doesn't expect me to tell you this," she said, "but he has joined their feasts as a special guest."

"I wish you hadn't."

"We can trust Philippe," she assured me.

"I hope so."

Philippe went on to explain why we had to avoid the north coast. Most whites captured in sporadic raids by the maroons on Jamaica plantations eventually found themselves turned over to the *sect rouge*. Philippe didn't want to see this happen to me. But helping us escape was a grave risk.

I agreed it was and parted with half my slender hoard of gold.

When we'd navigated the Windward Passage between Haiti and Cuba, there would be more than a hundred miles of open sea to cross before we reached Kingston's harbor. Philippe assured me we could make it.

Our only danger would be an out-of-season hurricane. Philippe and his wife were praying to the voodoo god of wind that such a catastrophy wouldn't overtake us.

I assured him that I'd be praying to my god and all the saints, too.

At dusk a drum on Isle Verlaine near the fishing village answered the Santo Domingo drums for the first time. It was beaten in carefully measured tones. We were at supper because we had agreed that everything should be as normal as possible before we slipped away in the night.

Hippolyte wouldn't be returning from Cap-Haïtien this late, but some of the house slaves—especially Sabo—might try to hold us until he returned.

We needn't have worried. The moment the drum on Isle Verlaine spoke, the house slaves vanished from the great house to their barricaded quarters.

"Tonight they will certainly come to Le Roi from the compound," Bliss told me. "Probably when the moon rises at ten o'clock. We must reach Philippe before then—he is very nervous."

Upstairs I changed to a split riding skirt I'd brought from England and the stoutest pair of boots I had. From a cord around my waist, I tied a small suede bag containing the remaining gold and the knife in its scabbard.

Water and food for the voyage were Philippe's responsibility.

In the sack with the gold I put the few pieces

of Mother's jewelry I'd brought to Le Roi from Port-au-Prince.

Bliss made me change the white blouse I'd selected for a dark one. She'd wear only a black cloth twisted around her waist; she depended on her dark skin to make her less visible in the night. Now we were finally ready to go, her spirits were high.

From one of the field slaves, she'd somehow gotten a razor-sharpe machete—the kind used for cutting cane. Now she flourished it with a wide grin.

"I'm remembering my father tonight," she said. "One time before the slavers captured us, I saw him cut off a man's head with one of these. I cried and he slapped me."

Leaving most of the lanterns in Le Roi burning, we circled around the barracaded quarters of the house slaves and set out to reach the fishing village. Bliss's high spirits buoyed me up.

It would be an hour before the moon rose.

At least one of the black field hands had been watching Le Roi, and it was Bliss who first heard the shuffle of his bare feet on the path behind us.

We hid in the tall cane, one of us on each side of the path. Bliss clutched her machete, I'd drawn my knife. We caught the whiff of raw rum before we saw the tall black trying to catch up with us. I remember saying thanks to God that the slaves were nerving themselves tonight with stolen rum!

When he drew abreast, it was Bliss who jumped behind him. She swung the machete with both hands, aiming for the junction of his neck and shoulder.

He was too tall. The machete struck his left arm above the elbow, severing it, but with a high-pitched scream he turned and lifted the machete he carried to chop down Bliss.

Blind with anger, spurred by fear, I drove my knife between his shoulder blades, felt my hand give his flesh a meaty smack as the blade severed his spinal column. He went down, a cry choking in his throat.

Bliss didn't miss with her second stroke.

I stood frozen with shock. Bliss knelt, and with a grunt jerked my knife from his body, wiping it on the cloth twisted around her waist, and handed it to me.

Without a word between us, she led off down the path, hurrying now.

We'd almost reached the fishing village when we heard the pounding feet of blacks coming after us. A moment before, we'd heard the first fusillade of musket shots from the direction of Le Roi. The slaves hadn't waited for moonrise.

This time we cowered in the sugarcane, weapons beside us, and waited.

At least a dozen blacks ran by flourishing their machetes. One paused in the path just op-

posite where we were hiding to fire off the musket
he carried. Then he was gone, pounding after the
others. We breathed again.

A woman screamed. A man shouted. Soaked
with rum, the blacks who had missed us were
attacking the mixed-blood fishermen and their
families.

We crept through the cane as close to the
doomed village as we dared. In the light from
the fired huts, we saw the blacks running amok.
Pinned against the cove, the people of the village
had no chance. Those who tried to flee across the
beach and into the surf were cut down as they
ran.

Even children and babies weren't being spared.

As he fell, each man was literally hacked into
bloody pieces. We saw a woman tossed back into
the smoldering remains of her hut, stabbed but
still alive. The slaughter was horrifying yet soon
finished.

Laughing and panting, the blacks started back
up the path, some carrying severed heads, their
blood lust not yet slaked.

But they'd evidently forgotten Bliss and me for
the time being.

That was good.

But the moon had risen now, and we saw the
sail of Philippe's boat clear the cove, headed out
to sea.

We were stranded on Isle Verlaine.

When she realized we were trapped, Bliss lost her nerve. For some reason, I was no longer afraid. There had to be a way to escape the island!

The Verlaine sugar mill was near a stretch of beach that faced Cap-Haïtien across the strait. A pier jutted out there. The water was too shallow for a ship of any size, but a ship's boats could load barrels of raw sugar at the pier and ferry the cargo out to the ship.

I'd come ashore at that pier when Hippolyte brought me to Isle Verlaine. Now I remembered a few skiffs had been drawn up on the beach.

Bliss cowered in our hiding place above the smoldering ruins of the fishing village, head buried in her arms, shuddering with sobs.

"Stop that now!" I jerked her by the hair and slapped her face. "I know how to get off the island." I told her about the beach and the skiffs I'd seen. "Stop blubbering! We have to be gone before the sun comes up."

It was too dangerous to cut back through the cane fields to reach the beach. Anyway, I was afraid we might get lost in the dark. We started skirting along the shore from the cove.

There was an orange-red glow from the direction of Le Roi. Evidently the blacks had fired the house. By morning it would be a gutted granite shell.

Moonlight helped us find our way through dense mangroves and along narrow beaches.

I led the way this time, Bliss meekly followed.

Huge land crabs clattered and scuttled out of our way. We drank brackish water from the few rain puddles we stumbled across.

Bliss fell twice. The second time, I had to kick her back to her feet, cursing her with words I didn't realize I knew. It was false dawn by the time we reached the pier and the beach.

I was afraid that the blacks would have come to burn the sugar mill. Smoke was already stinging our eyes from the cane they were firing. Had we hidden in the fields, they would have flushed us out like singed rabbits.

There was only one skiff on the beach, and it was drawn up above the high-tide line. Since it was ebb tide, we'd have to push it more than twenty feet down the beach to reach the water.

We'd lost our machetes, but I still had the knife strapped around my waist.

The skiff had a short mast. As we slogged toward it through the ankle-deep sand, I resolved to rig a sail from my skirt if there were no sail or oars in the skiff.

The skiff was larger and more sturdy than it had first looked. Both Bliss and I were near collapse from total exhaustion.

It was stuck in the sand, and our combined efforts couldn't budge it.

Bliss had collapsed in the sand, sobbing hopelessly. I was on my feet, legs braced, staring across the strait at Cap-Haïtien, fingers digging at the ache in the small of my back.

Over the lapping surf, I didn't hear him approach. I heard a grunting breath, smelled the musky odor of his body, whirled, and found myself face to face with Sabo. His eyes stared wildly from a blood-smeared face. One arm hung broken and useless. A deep wound in his side oozed blood.

"Sabo." I saw recognition in his eyes. "The boat." I aimed a kick at Bliss. "Help us."

We somehow dragged it down to the water through the sand and launched it. Sabo sprawled into the skiff to lie gasping on the bottom of it. Blood from his wounded side tinted the inch of water sloshing in the skiff.

There were two oars, but no oarlocks. Bliss and I paddled the skiff out through the surf toward Cap-Haïtien, but then our strength was gone. We were bobbing about a quarter of a mile from the beach.

I ripped strips from my blouse and tried to bandage Sabo's side but it was no use. His eyes went black, and after one last shuddering breath, he was dead.

There was no pulse, no heartbeat. Even the bleeding had finally stopped.

"Bliss, help me." We had to get his body into the water. She scrambled back from the bow. We nearly overturned the skiff doing it but finally I pushed his body away from the skiff with an oar. He was floating face-down, arms and legs spread wide.

Digging at the water with the oars, we managed to get a short distance from Sabo's body before the first shark struck it. Then the school of them was in a feeding frenzy as blood turned the blue water dark red. Neither of us could look away from the sight. Within minutes they'd torn Sabo's body apart and gulped it down.

A breeze was blowing offshore from Isle Verlaine—a breeze that could take us the few miles to Cap-Haïtien's harbor—but our next task was rigging a sail. Bliss was nearly naked, so we tried the dark cloth she'd twisted around her waist first. But it wouldn't hold the wind.

My divided skirt draped over the mast, Bliss holding the other end of it, did nicely, and I found I could steer with one of the oars. The skiff began closing the distance between us and Cap-Haïtien.

As much as possible, I kept my legs and the lower half of my body in the shadow of the sail. The sun seemed to burn right through the white linen pantaloons I'd worn under the skirt.

The Cap-Haïtien harbor behind its stone breakwater was usually busy with a least a dozen ships swinging at anchor, loaded with cargo for Haiti, or waiting to take aboard barrels of sugar.

On most days, fishing boats with their colored sails made the straits a festive sight, but today none were in the harbor or putting out to sea. And it was nearly empty of ships. The largest was a glistening black three-masted schooner anchored behind the breakwater near the entrance to the harbor. No flag flew from its foremast.

Black pillars of oily black smoke laced the morning sky behind the town and up and down the coast. Behind us Isle Verlaine was blurred with the smoke of the burning cane fields and the sugar mill had been set on fire.

Occasionally the rattle of musket fire came from the direction of Cap-Haïtien. The rampage of the blacks on Isle Verlaine last night must have been only a small part of a general uprising that would sweep away all white control of Haiti.

Bliss came to the same conclusion.

"We'll be no safer on Haiti than we were on Isle Verlaine," she said over her shoulder. "What can we do, Jeanette?"

I pointed to the black ship. "It probably has taken other refugees aboard," I told her hopefully. "Two more of us won't matter to the captain."

When we'd entered the harbor, I pulled on my skirt. Bliss and I paddled toward the black schooner. The ship was being prepared to sail. Crewmen in the rigging were responding to shouted orders from someone amidships.

As we approached, two black faces peered over the rail at us. I waved, and they called us to the attention of the man amidships shouting orders.

He tossed us a line, which Bliss caught. A rope ladder was lowered. Bliss scrambled up it first.

Then I came aboard to be helped to the deck.

Our backs to the rail, we stood facing a half-circle of grinning black seamen. The only white man in sight was the captain, judging from the cap cocked on the side of his head. It was he who'd thrown Bliss the line.

CHAPTER 3

I WAS a child again, and Mother was bathing my fevered body. But when I called out to her, there was no answer. Yet gentle hands were at work on my naked body. I heard the sound of water rushing along a ship's hull and opened my eyes.

"So you're finally awake." A man bent over me to pull a coarse blanket up to my chin.

His was a tanned face, satanic eyebrows arched over ink-black eyes, a grin showing even, white teeth. There was a livid scar across the bridge of his nose.

"Who are you?" My voice was a whisper.

41

A hand raised my head and he pressed a tin cup to my lips. "Drink." It was an order.

After what we'd been through to reach this ship only to find ourselves surrounded by blacks was too much and for the first time in my life I fainted. How long I was in a senseless stupor I don't know but when I finally awakened the ship had cleared Cap Haïtien harbor, I could tell that by the motion that rolled me slightly from side to side in the bunk and the sound of rushing water along the hull. I wasn't alone. A man crouched beside the bunk in the small cabin with a tin cup of rum and water he made me drink. It was strong dark rum and I choked.

"So it's finally awake you are now." There was a lilt to his voice, a rolling of the Rs.

When I tried to sit up, I found my clothes were gone. I fell back and clutched the rough blanket to me. "Who are you?"

"Jamie McCoy." He'd refilled the cup. This time I gulped the rum and water without choking. "You and the black lass are aboard the *Salem Witch*."

"What's happened to Bliss?"

"She's safe enough. You have my name, girl. What should I be calling you?"

"Jeanette."

"Aye?" Jamie cocked an eyebrow and combed fingers through his sandy hair. "How far did you come in the wee skiff?"

"From Isle Verlaine." I was feeling the rum.

It was lazy warm in my blood. For the first time, I realized that Jamie was bare to the waist. I was fascinated to see the play of muscles in his broad chest and heavy shoulders whenever he moved. "We escaped last night."

"Lucky you didn't try to go ashore in Cap-Haïtien, I'm thinking," Jamie said. "It's a bloody slaughterhouse since last night. I was ashore when it started."

"Your crew is black," I said.

"That they are, maroons too every last one—but from a different island." Jamie raised my left hand and saw the gold wedding band. "Where might your husband be?"

"I don't know. Hippolyte was in Cap-Haïtien on business."

"You could be a widow then. On the other hand, he might have shipped with the other Frenchmen who got away for Martinique yesterday, though it's doubtful he'd leave his wife alone on Isle Verlaine."

I didn't offer Jamie an opinion on that score! Instead I asked, "Is that where we're bound?"

"We're not reaching for there," he said. When he stood, Jamie had to duck his head beneath the low ceiling of the cabin. "It would be pressing my black Scots luck too hard to put in there with a price on my head."

Before I could ask another question, Jamie ducked out of the cabin, bolting the door behind him. I was alone to wonder what was happening to Bliss.

And to remember where I'd heard the name Jamie McCoy before. At supper one night aboard the Dutch ship that brought Bliss and me back from England, the captain entertained his passengers, telling us how Jamie and his Jamaican maroons boarded and sank a British privateer within sight of Kingston.

"*Ja,* that *verdammt* American—he's the devil's favorite son," he said with a hearty laugh.

Bliss and I had chosen to escape Isle Verlaine and Santo Domingo aboard a pirate ship! I was too tired and warmed with rum to feel fear. We were alive. For the time being that was all that mattered.

I curled up in the bunk with the blanket around my shoulders and slept.

The Golfe de la Gonâve is a gaping mouth of water gulping the current of the Windward Passage, with Port-au-Prince at the hinge of the jaws. In the mouth is the Ile de la Gonâve, an island that voodoo legend says is a sleeping whale with a woman on his back.

Bliss finally joined me in the cabin, bringing hot food from the galley, and told me that was where we were bound.

She was barefoot but wore a green silk dress with a white scarf on her head, loops of gold swinging from her ears.

"Refugees will be waiting for a ship there," she explained. "All the whites and mulattos not yet killed are trying to escape."

She'd brought me a change of clothes—another woman's but freshly laundered.

I dressed myself without asking Bliss any questions. She was more relaxed and at home aboard the *Salem Witch* than she'd ever been at Le Roi. I knew it hadn't taken her long to find at least one lover among the maroon crew.

While I dressed, I wondered with a hot flush if it had been Jamie who had undressed me after I fainted and wrapped me in the blanket. Untouched by a man for nearly a year, the thought of Jamie's tanned muscular body and his easy grin were arousing a hunger in me I thought Hippolyte's perverted lust had killed for all time.

Bliss and I had been too close for too long for her not to suspect the direction of my thoughts.

"You need to be taken by a real man, Jeanette." The tip of her tongue circled her lips. "I would have thought Captain McCoy would have had you by this time."

I turned my back to her. "Button me up."

"Am I wrong? Did he?" Bliss asked.

"No."

My dress buttoned, Bliss clasped me against the soft warmth of her body, hands cupping my breasts for a moment. Then she let me go.

From her knowing smile when I faced her I

knew Bliss guessed how much her brief caress had heightened my passion.

"Damn you!" I said.

Bliss laughed. "Captain McCoy sent me to tell you that you're expected in his cabin. You'll find it at the end of this passageway."

I drew back my hand but couldn't slap her face for impudence while she smiled with that wise and knowing look in her eyes.

It was my turn to laugh.

"Come along in" was Jamie's answer to my hesitant knock.

He was fully dressed in well-tailored black broadcloth jacket and trousers, a white stock at his throat. Supper for two was spread on a sideboard: cold lobster, roast pork, boiled fish garnished with red sauce, chilled wine.

"Madame de Verlaine."

"Bliss said you expected me." I hated blushing, but Jamie's sudden formality had taken me completely by surprise.

The twinkle in his eye told me Jamie knew my discomforture. He'd planned this second meeting well, damn him!

"So I did. Are you hungry?"

"Very hungry."

Jamie waved me to the set table in the center of his roomy cabin and began to fill a plate for me at the sideboard. After putting it before me, he went back for his own supper, then poured our wine.

Despite the food Bliss had brought, I was ravenous. There was no conversation because both of us were intent on our food. Jamie refilled my wineglass once, his own twice.

"You do well for yourself at sea, Captain McCoy," I said when we'd finished eating.

Jamie nodded with a wry lopsided grin. He lay back in his chair, an arm hooked over the back. It was dusk, and there were flickering shadows in the cabin caused by the movement of the ship.

"More wine?" Jamie asked.

"No . . . yes." My head was clear enough, or so I thought. I reached for the cut-glass carafe, but Jamie seized it first, rose from his chair, and came around the table to pour my wine. "Thank you."

His hands rested lightly on my shoulders as I drank. I didn't shrug away from his touch. All the sensual hunger within me that Bliss had heightened with her caress flooded back while I drained my glass.

When I rose from my chair, Jamie turned me toward him to bend his head and press his lips to the top of each breast above my bodice. Then he carried me to the square bunk in the darkening cabin and laid me on it gently.

I was dizzy and hot, eager to be naked as soon

Jamie handed me a glass filled to the brim. "Drink it, woman. You'll need strength tonight." When he'd filled his own glass, he said, "I'm thinking I will, too."

For both of us it was a night of unbridled passion, a search for new heights of feeling with only a few words spoken. My demands were as great as his and as hard to slake.

Wanton he'd called me. Wanton I was in ways I'd never imagined.

When the lamp had flickered out and the first rays of daylight filtered into the cabin, Jamie fell into exhausted sleep, his head on my breast. I watched the rise and fall of his chest, studied his face in repose, and felt a sudden tenderness for him—a feeling deeper than any I'd ever experienced before.

He'd called me a lot of woman. To how many other women had he said that? *Jean-ette*. At least that way of saying my name was all mine.

I touched his lips, his nose, that white scar on the bridge of his nose with a finger.

In a few hours, Jamie McCoy had reduced Hippolyte de Verlaine to a shadow of a man, more to be pitied than hated, cruel because he was weak. I worked the gold band off my finger and flung it through an open port hole into the sea.

CHAPTER 4

THE SMALL number of men and women refugees
from Haiti that were gathered on the nearest
beach had fired on the first boat Jamie tried to
take ashore. He'd hoisted the flag of Cartagena
from the forepeak of the *Salem Witch,* and also
a white flag of truce.

Cartagena was a port-republic on the north
shore of South America, fighting to throw off the
Spanish yoke and commissioning French and
American privateers to prey on Spain's sea com-
merce.

So he really is a privateer, I thought when I

51

saw the Cartagena flag. Then I remembered my father's comment.

"What do you expect me to do?" I asked Jamie when he'd told me what was happening.

"Go ashore and talk with those people in your good French. You're Madame de Verlaine." Today he was being gently persuasive. "They're afraid of my black crew, I'm thinking."

His crew was bunched on the forward deck, Bliss among them. "I am, too," I said, and I meant it. "Why shouldn't they be?"

"Jeanette, I control my men. They trust me." Jamie's earnest mood was a new experience for me. "Why were you anchored in the Cap-Haïtien harbor?" I asked.

"I had a bargain with Leclerc. I once served with the regiment of Irish mercenaries on Haiti, and he trusted me. We were supposed to reinforce his garrison, but we were too late."

What Jamie said rang of truth. Since Napoleon had stopped sending regiments to Haiti, General Leclerc had been hiring mercenaries wherever he could find them in the West Indies.

"I'll row you to the beach," Jamie said.

"And get us both shot dead!"

Jamie grinned. "Probably."

I was barefooted and in duck pantaloons wrapped nearly twice around my waist to keep them up. My sailor's jacket didn't fit much better. But the least of my worries was the costume.

The refugees had drawn back up the beach as we approached, except for one man. The sun was behind him, but there was no mistaking the pistol pointed at me.

"Bonjour," I said, wading ashore while Jamie handled the boat. "We have come to rescue you and those others."

"Madame de Verlaine." Hippolyte bowed from the waist, stuffing the pistol under his belt after he'd uncocked it. "So you've escaped Isle Verlaine."

I was shocked silent and staring.

Hippolyte's fine clothes were soiled and in rags, but I was ashamed of the way I looked; guilty to find him alive when I'd wished him dead, and certain he knew exactly how matters stood between Jamie and me.

"Who is your American brute?" Hippolyte asked.

We'd been speaking French, but Jamie understood the last question, if not what Hippolyte had called him. "Jamie McCoy," he said. "You and your friends are welcome aboard my ship. You'll be having a safe passage."

I translated for Hippolyte.

He gave Jamie a gracious bow and smile, but said to me in French, "You deserve an American pig like this one, Jeanette."

Jamie pushed off to bring the longboat ashore, leaving me stranded with Hippolyte.

"How did you escape Cap-Haïtien?" I asked.

Hippolyte shrugged carelessly. "Without too much difficulty."

From his clothes, bandaged hand and weary lines etched in Hippolyte's face, I suspected that he and the others had experienced as much of an ordeal as Bliss and I had been through. Isle Verlaine and Le Roi were lost to him; yet he wasn't a broken man.

He watched me with amusement in his dark eyes, a smile on his lips. I wondered if it was possible to hate and admire a man at the same time.

"Bliss got away, too?" Hippolyte asked.

I nodded.

"Fortunate."

The others were gathering around. I searched among them for Héloïse Leroux, the last of the mistresses Hippolyte had entertained at Le Roi, but she wasn't among the survivors.

Hippolyte understood my questioning glance. "I'm afraid she is dead," he told me.

"I'm sorry."

Hippolyte shrugged philosophically.

The anchors came up as soon as the refugees were aboard. Jamie had promised to land them on the French island of Martinique, and he assured Hippolyte there was no hint of a slave revolt there.

The *Salem Witch* was overcrowded now. Jamie ordered his crew to sleep on deck and assigned the forecastle to the Frenchmen. The few distraught women and girls were accommodated in the aft cabins near Bliss and me.

From the women and girls, I learned that Hippolyte had been the hero of their escape. When the streets of Cap-Haïtien boiled with Dessalines's maroons, he'd organized the men into a rearguard. They'd fought their way across the island to St. Marc and reached the Ile de la Gonâve in nearly swamped fishing boats.

He'd been confident they would be rescued.

"Such a brave and gallant man, your husband," a Madame Delacroix told me. "You should be proud."

I wondered how she would have reacted if I'd told her how he'd contrived to have my parents murdered and what I'd suffered at his hands.

It was Bliss who told me that Jamie's Jamaican crew planned to seize the ship before we reached Martinique. They were plotting to kill Jamie and the men in the forecastle.

"How do you know this?" I asked.

Food was in short supply and water was being rationed, but I hadn't noticed any unrest among the crew.

"I sleep with Amos."

From the way she shifted her eyes, I knew Bliss wasn't telling the whole truth.

Amos was Jamie's mate, a towering man, almost a full-blood Carib to judge from his bronze skin and high cheekbones.

I grabbed her by the shoulders. "Tell me the truth, Bliss. Why should Amos trust *you?* He knows you're my . . ." I nearly said "slave." "My maid."

"He will take me to The Cockpit and make me his queen." Bliss said.

It took me a moment to realize that she was talking about the remote mountains of Jamaica where runaway slaves had defied their British masters for generations. Jamie had been brave— or foolish—when he recruited his crew along the north coast of that island.

"Do you believe him?" I was scornful.

"Don't tell Captain McCoy." Bliss was defiant. "If you tell him, Jeanette, I'll have to kill you."

In her present mood, Bliss was capable of doing that.

I bolted the cabin door. "Why is the crew ready to mutiny?" I asked. "They haven't been mistreated."

"We hate Frenchmen!" Her hands balled into fists.

"What about French*women?* Haven't the ones on board this ship suffered enough, Bliss?"

Bliss licked her lips. "The men tell me what we will do with *them*." Her voice was cruel and gloating, and suddenly Bliss was a person I didn't know.

"What about me?" I asked in a quiet voice. My hands fell away from her shoulders. "Have they told you who will rape me first, and what other tortures they have in mind for Jeanette DuBois? Or will I be at your mercy?"

Bliss dropped her eyes and wouldn't answer.

"You little fool!" I didn't even sleep without my knife. Now I drew it from under my clothes and touched the point to the hollow of her throat. "Come along and tell Jamie your story."

"No!"

"Yes." I pricked her skin. "You've seen me kill with this."

Bliss drew a whimpering breath. "The crew will kill me, Jeanette." She was pleading.

"Not as surely as I will."

Bliss believed me.

Jamie was dining in his cabin with Hippolyte. I hadn't spoken to either man since the Ile de la Gonâve—I'd been too busy caring for the women.

Jamie listened quietly, drumming the table with his fingers, while Bliss stammered out her story. This time she didn't mention Amos.

I could tell nothing from his eyes or the expression on his face. "I think she's telling you the truth, Jamie," I said.

"That one's a lying bitch," Hippolyte said in English. Slouched across from Jamie, he was turning a wineglass in his hand.

Jamie had risen from his chair when I brought Bliss into the cabin; Hippolyte had not. Now Jamie was seated although Bliss and I were standing, and it was Hippolyte who came to his feet.

"I will have the truth from your little slut!" he snarled at me in French.

He took a knife from the table and held it in a candle flame.

Lost in thought, Jamie didn't seem to notice. Bliss cowered behind me. But when Hippolyte started around the table, the heated knife in his hand, Jamie rose. In doing so, his hip thrust the table against Hippolyte, knocking him off balance.

Hippolyte swore and dropped the knife when the hot point of it grazed his other hand.

Jamie didn't even glance in his direction. "You'll be coming with me," he said, taking Bliss by the arm.

He tucked a pair of loaded pistols in his belt. "You'll stay here with your wife," he told Hippolyte in very bad French.

"I'm coming, too," I said.

Jamie didn't answer. I followed them out into the passageway. Amos had just climbed down into the other end of the passageway. Our odd procession startled him.

Jamie stopped, hands on the butts of his pistols.

"Bliss didn't tell you, but he's the ringleader," I whispered to Jamie.

"Amos, assemble the crew amidships," Jamie said, as if he hadn't heard me. "I'll be having a word with them."

Hippolyte was in the passageway behind us.

as Jamie's deft hands finished stripping away my garments. Yet I shuddered as if freezing.

Finally I lay spread-eagled on my back when Jamie moved back into the shadows. I turned my head to watch him and saw his clothes heaped on the cabin floor, his broad back and narrow flanks toward me as he reached to light a lamp swinging from an overhead beam.

Jamie was over me then, staring down at my body, his lips twisted and his dark eyes hungry. I felt his weight then, the heat of his big body. With no will of my own left I arched my body hard against his.

"Aye, but she's wanton!" It was a whisper, his breath hot on my cheek.

A quick stab of pain—then pulsing pleasure and need that made me cry out—a wordless cry he stifled with his lips crushed hard against mine.

My response was as savage as Jamie's embrace, my need as great as his own, and we carried each other to a final explosion of passion that wracked us both.

Then my face was wet with tears. Raised on an elbow, Jamie was tracing them with a finger. I couldn't read the expression on his face.

"You're a lot of woman, Jean-ette," Jamie said with a heavy sigh.

Sliding from the bunk he padded to the table and brought back the wine decanter and our glasses.

"I've had enough," I told him.

Amos stopped where he was, bracing himself against the slight roll of the ship by touching the bulkheads on either side of him. "Aye," he said, surprised, and clambered back up the ladder.

We heard him shouting orders on the deck above us.

Jamie turned to Bliss. With thumb and fingers, he grasped her lower jaw, pulling her up on her toes. "What was it you were saying about my mate?" he asked.

Tears in her eyes, hands grasping his arm, Bliss stammered, "Not him. Another one."

Jamie released her. "Who?"

"The bitch is a liar," Hippolyte broke in.

We could hear the shuffling of feet as the men assembled on the deck amidships.

Jamie ignored him. "Who?" he asked Bliss again. "Which ones?"

"The mulatto," she stammered.

"Enoch?"

Bliss bobbed her head.

"Any others you could be naming?"

Bliss shook her head.

Jamie waved for the three of us to return to his cabin and started for the ladder at the other end of the passage. Hippolyte brushed past us to follow Jamie. He was armed with a single pistol.

"Jamie," I called, and he turned his head to look back.

I'd thought Hippolyte was tensing to shoot Jamie in the back, but now he shoved the pistol into his belt. "We face them together," Hippolyte said.

Jamie waved him to come on.

I'd shooed Bliss back into Jamie's cabin. Now I went down the passageway to climb the ladder to the deck. I arrived on deck to find Hippolyte beside me while Jamie faced his crew.

"I've heard the word 'mutiny.'" Jamie spoke carefully, staring down the crew except for Amos.

It was easy to pick out Enoch's lighter face among those of the black Jamaicans.

"I've been hearing a name," Jamie said.

The men close to Enoch began edging away from him.

"Amos." Jamie pointed. "Put that man in irons."

Amos took a step toward Enoch. The man shrank away from the huge mate. Hippolyte took a step, drew his pistol, fired.

Startled, Jamie jumped aside, staring at Hippolyte. Enoch had spun around when the bullet struck him in the face. Now he sprawled face down on the deck, his body twitching.

"You're a damned fool, man!" Jamie exploded. "One man isn't a mutiny."

Hippolyte blew across the muzzle of his pistol. Shoving it into his belt, he made his way forward, toward the forecastle. With a smile and wave, he ducked out of sight.

Jamie swore.

* * *

"Why did you lie to me?" I asked Bliss. "Why did you say Amos was talking mutiny?"

She wouldn't answer.

"Or was it a lie?"

"Yes."

"He wouldn't pay attention to you?" I asked.

From the expression on her face I saw she was going to be stubborn.

"Never mind, Bliss," I said. "You got your information from Enoch, didn't you?"

Bliss nodded.

I wasn't satisfied yet, but I let the matter rest.

We sighted Mount Pelée the next morning, and by noon were anchored in Martinique's harbor.

Hippolyte had cousins in Fort-de-France, and I expected he would go ashore to stay with them and plan for the future. I wanted no part of whatever future he might plan! I wasn't his slave.

I hadn't been especially happy at school in England, but now I missed Sussex and the Fitz-hughs. Perhaps I could convince Miss Wentworth to hire me as a French teacher. Word would soon reach the English of events on Haiti.

Since the near-mutiny, I'd stayed in my cabin and refused to talk with Hippolyte the few times he tried to approach me. I sent Bliss to make sure he'd gone ashore with the other refugees before I sought out Jamie. I found him in his cabin, stripped to the waist in the humid heat of Martinique, making entries in the ship's log.

"What would you be wanting?" he asked, pleasantly enough.

"I don't want to be put ashore here," I said.

Jamie raised an eyebrow.

"I won't go back to Hippolyte as his wife," I told Jamie.

Jamie sat back, hooking an arm over the back of his chair, linking his hands. "Where would you go then?"

"Somewhere I can write my English relatives for help. They will send me money for passage."

His smugness infuriated me. "You treated me like a whore, Jamie."

He grinned, then was serious. "No whore can do for a man as you did, Jeanette. And there's a compliment to make you blush, I see. When I lift anchor, I won't be touching English ports, but would New Orleans be suiting you? The Americans are there now."

"Yes."

"It can be arranged then—passage to New Orleans for you and your Negro girl—because we sail for there. But it will be a dangerous voyage. The French here on Martinique expect the British to come any day. We will carry gold for deposit in the American banks."

"I've noticed the cannon you're taking aboard," I said.

"Peashooters if we tangle with a British man-of-war or some well-armed pirate, Jeanette." Jamie frowned. "Amos is still my man, but some others . . ." He broke off that line of thought. "You should know that de Verlaine and some of his friends will be along this voyage."

This news dumbfounded me!

"Wouldn't you share his cabin?" Jamie asked.

"The man murdered my parents!"

"He's mentioned you believe that," Jamie said noncommittally.

"What else has he said about me?"

"You have a bit of a temper, but we know that, don't we?" Jamie was amused.

"As far as I'm concerned, Hippolyte de Verlain is no longer my husband," I said stiffly and felt like the young fool I probably was. "I won't be sharing his cabin."

"He's a proud man, Jeanette."

"You're a fool to trust him aboard your ship!"

CHAPTER 5

BEFORE THE *Salem Witch* sailed from Fort-de-France, bound for New Orleans, I spent a day ashore plundering the small shops for clothing. I bought for both Bliss and me, paying ridiculously high prices for shoddy merchandise. It was the British blockade, the shopkeepers told me.

There was very real fear that the British would soon invade the island, and they cursed Napoleon for leaving them defenseless. The frightening tales the refugees Jamie had brought from Haiti instilled a new fear. I wouldn't be sad when we sailed. I'd nearly exhausted my small hoard of gold, but I wasn't afraid of the future.

I had convinced myself that the escape from Isle Verlaine was the worst ordeal I'd have to suffer, that once the Fitzhughs knew my plight, immediate help would be forthcoming.

In my own mind, I was no longer Madame de Verlaine. My terrible marriage was now a nightmare from which I'd awakened. Since those first minutes on the beach of Ile de la Gonâve, I hadn't been alone with Hippolyte. I'd avoided him as much as I could aboard a small ship, and he'd made no effort to press matters.

Was I finally free of the man? By law I was still his wife, but with England and France at dagger points, my wishful thinking was that I could get a divorce as soon as I reached Sussex. By law I was a citizen of that country as much as I was a French citizen.

Jamie was a part of my life I would have to forget as soon as I was ashore in New Orleans, as much as I ached to be taken by him again. I owed him thanks for arousing the woman in me, but there would be other men in my future—perhaps a titled Englishman who would make me forget the wanton who lay in the bunk of a Scots pirate/privateer.

My dues were paid in full to Damballa, or so I thought before we sailed from Fort-de-France. It's God's blessing we can't read the future!

Just before Jamie lifted anchor, Hippolyte came back aboard, bringing two men with him. Olaf Anderson was a burly man with a full Viking's red beard and a cast in his right eye. His face was scarred by smallpox—what could be seen of it above the beard.

Antoine Frechet was a head shorter than Olaf, and his face reminded me of a ferret's. He was thin to the point of emaciation and had a hacking cough. I wondered in what sleazy waterfront dive Hippolyte had recruited this pair to help him guard the gold they carried aboard in a small trunk.

They stowed the trunk in the cabin Jamie had assigned them. Their cabin was across the ship from the one Bliss and I shared.

Jamie met me on deck. "No one except those three should be knowing we carry so much gold," he told me. "Don't confide in your Negro girl, Jeanette. That one has a loose mouth, I'd be thinking."

"You're afraid of your crew?" I said.

"It's a damned poor captain I'd be if I wasn't," Jamie said. "Verlaine killed Enoch too soon for me to find out who else planned mutiny. Keep your girl out of the forecastle."

"She considers herself free now," I said.

"And free she'll be entirely, with a knife in her ribs," Jamie told me. "My crew knows who it was brought me the word that killed Enoch."

"I'll lock Bliss in our cabin if I have to," I promised.

"And see to yourself when I'm busy tending my ship, Jeanette."

"I can take care of myself, Jamie."

"Aye, that you can, Jeanette. But I have a feeling in my guts and bones about this voyage. I haven't the second sight like my mother, but I glimpse the future now and then. Stay locked in your cabin as much as you can."

"I have my knife, but I'll be careful," I promised Jamie. I wanted to keep him talking to me. "How long will we be at sea?"

"Depends on the weather and wind." Jamie scanned the rigging. "Amos," he called, and pointed to a dangling line. Amos sent a seaman scurrying aloft. Turning back to me, he said, "You might pray for my soul."

He seemed serious, but I saw a twinkle in his dark eyes.

Hippolyte had come on deck. Lounging against the rail, he'd been watching us. His lips twisted into a gloating grin when he realized I'd seen him, and I can't describe the expression on his face better than that. I'd seen it before—the time he whipped Bliss and I was helpless to rescue her.

I consoled myself with the thought that I was safe from him aboard Jamie's ship. Once we reached New Orleans, I could find protection with the American authorities until I could sail for England.

I assumed that Hippolyte and the men he'd chosen to help him guard the gold were aboard simply because the *Salem Witch* was the first available ship to leave Martinique, bound for New Orleans.

I was wrong.

Bliss was no problem once I'd impressed on her that the crew knew she'd brought word to Jamie of the planned mutiny. She stayed in our cabin those first few days outward bound, unless I went on deck for air. Then she was always a step behind me.

I saw Hippolyte only once. Jamie wasn't on the quarterdeck. Hippolyte was having an earnest conversation with the black helmsman.

Twice I noticed Anderson and Frechet coming aft from the forecastle. Jamie wasn't on the quarterdeck either time.

The fourth day at sea, our following wind failed, and the *Salem Witch* wallowed in oily swells within sight of the Cayman Islands. Only occasional gusts of wind filled her sails.

It was sweltering hot that late afternoon. Heat haze hung over the water. Jamie was on the quarterdeck, anxious about a sail between us and the Caymans, to judge from the way he kept staring at her with a spyglass. I knew the Caymans were a pirate stronghold, and was a little anxious myself. But our ship's guns were rolled out and loaded, the crew lounging around on deck.

On deck for a breath of air, I was at the starboard rail, amidships, staring at the sail and the

Caymans. Clouds over the islands were building an air castle that faintly resembled Le Roi.

Anderson passed behind me, headed for the quarterdeck. Frechet lounged against the rail a few feet from me. He, too, seemed to be studying the Caymans, or perhaps he was more interested in the sail. I could smell the sweaty odor of his body.

I glanced around to see Anderson climb the ladder to the quarterdeck. Jamie was speaking to the helmsman. I became aware of a tenseness among the crew and saw all eyes were on Anderson's broad back.

In a terrifying moment, I knew what was going to happen, and screamed, "Jamie!"

A pistol seemed to spring into Anderson's hand. He fired at Jamie, point-blank. The report was like a loud handclap.

Jamie staggered back. Astonishment was printed on his face. Then he dropped to his knees, both hands clutching his chest. He fell forward on his face and lay still.

A crewman sprang up the ladder to take the wheel. Frozen with horror, I watched the helmsman and Anderson seize Jamie's arms and legs to drop him into the wake of the ship.

It was Frechet who'd pinned my elbows behind my back. "Over he goes, and food for sharks," he gloated in my ear. The foulness of his breath stifled me. "We'll just march his fancy piece along to meet the new captain."

His hands found the knife I'd concealed under my clothes. "I'll take your pig-sticker," he said. "We don't want Monsieur de Verlaine bloodied up, now, do we?"

I didn't struggle. I was too stunned.

Hippolyte was waiting in the cabin with the gold. On his bunk, fully dressed, with a spotless white ruffled stock at his throat, he sat with a pistol across his knees. Another was within easy reach on the table with a half-filled bottle of claret.

Hippolyte barely glanced at me as I huddled against a bulkhead, arms clasped in front of me, trying to control my shaking body.

"Do we have the ship? I heard only one shot," he told Frechet, his voice level and calm.

"Aye." Frechet's was a wolfish smile. "McCoy, the black Scottish bastard, is feeding the sharks."

"What about the mate—Amos?"

"I couldn't find him in time, but we'll lay the rascal by his heels soon enough."

"The crew?" Hippolyte asked.

"Olaf and I can handle them. They'll eat from our hands," Frechet said. "At least until we swing at anchor in the North Sound. After that, you'll deal with the greedy bastards."

Hippolyte nodded.

Frechet grinned at me. "I'll be leaving you with your husband, missy, while Anderson and me have a bit of sport with your black wench. Senegalese, ain't she?"

"Ashore at Georgetown she'll be for sale, part of my bargain with you and Anderson. She's a lively wench. Have your fun but don't damage the merchandise."

"Worry not, Frenchie." Frechet laughed. "We know how to tame our women, if you don't."

Hippolyte's pistol swung up to cover Frechet. "It tempts me." His voice was cold and deadly. "A hole in your stinking guts would leave more gold for me to share with Anderson."

Frechet's hand strayed to the pistol in his sash, but the click when Hippolyte cocked the weapon in his hand, and the look in my husband's eyes, froze Frechet.

"An apology to the lady, monsieur," Hippolyte said. "And to me, if you please."

Frechet was no longer laughing. Ducking his head, he touched a forelock to me. "My apology to you, missy . . . madame," he corrected himself. "No offense meant," he told Hippolyte.

"Satisfactory, Frechet. Leave us now."

When Frechet had scuttled away, Hippolyte waved to the bottle of claret. "Wine, Jeanette?" When I didn't answer, he poured himself a brimming glass. He drank thirstily, then said, "You remind me of a rabbit my brother and I cornered one time when we were just children." Hippolyte sighed. "So long ago. But we're no longer children, are we, Jeanette?"

Hippolyte wasn't drunk, but his face was flushed, his eyes fever-bright.

I settled on the edge of the bunk facing Hippolyte's, hands clasped in my lap to keep them from shaking. "Children don't murder," I said.

"Ah." Hippolyte smiled. *"Touché.* But one does what one must to improve his circumstances, don't you agree? Le Roi and Isle Verlaine, gone." He touched the small trunk containing gold with the toe of a boot. "Here is a fortune, Jeanette. A small fortune, only, it is true, once I've shared with Anderson and Frechet, but . . ." Hippolyte dangled a chamois sack for me to see. "Uncut diamonds, Jeanette. A very large fortune, once we've reached France. Enough to buy an estate— perhaps one of those titles the Corsican has for sale."

"What are you trying to say?" I asked.

"Was McCoy your lover?" Hippolyte's eyes bored into me. "Answer me!"

So he wasn't certain? "No." I prayed that I'd be forgiven the lie.

My eyes didn't waver when I met Hippolyte's stare. My God! After mistreating me as he had, and flaunting his mistresses, subjecting Bliss to his will, the man was jealous!

Bliss!

"Hippolyte, I'll make a bargain," I said. "Do you want me as your wife?"

"As my dutiful and obedient wife, yes," he said.

"I'll do your will, but only if you save Bliss from those men."

73

"She was part of our bargain," he said.

"They don't know about the diamonds, do they?"

"I'm not a fool," he said, with disdain.

"Buy her back for me. You can do it," I flattered, hoping that he could. "I saw you bring Frechet to heel."

Hippolyte hesitated before he said, "You have your bargain."

I crossed the cabin and stooped to kiss him on the lips. He rose, reaching for me, but I spun away. "Bliss, first, Hippolyte—I have your word. I'll be here waiting. You have my promise."

Hippolyte locked me in Jamie's empty cabin when he went to rescue Bliss from Anderson and Frechet. He brought her back, tearful, terrified, but unharmed, and she ran to me.

"It's all right, Bliss." I gathered her in my arms to pat her head. "You're safe now—you won't be bothered."

Over her head I could see the way Hippolyte was regarding us. Revulsion was mirrored in his face and eyes. With his upbringing, there was no way he could understand my affection for a black slave! But that would never stop him from using her as a pawn again.

There was a second, much smaller cabin that adjoined Jamie's—little more than a cubbyhole. It was for a cabin boy. I got Bliss to stretch out on the pallet in there and stroked her forehead until she was asleep.

I locked her in to rejoin Hippolyte.

He'd poured wine for us, and there was food on the sideboard.

I was too exhausted to feel the full, numbing effect of seeing Jamie die and be disposed of as so much garbage. Hatred still burned in me, but for the time being, its fire was banked.

I was still alive. Bliss was safe because I had a *hold* on Hippolyte! He wanted me on any terms. I'd have to exploit that with my body. It wouldn't be too hard, I thought, considering the difference in our ages.

The fool! Was it vanity that made him accept my answer about Jamie and me?

Hate I'd felt for Hippolyte had been nourished by fear, and he was as dangerous now as he'd ever been. But I was no longer afraid of him. The girl he had terrified and abused was a woman now, and vindictive. I hadn't been able to save Jamie's life, but I could avenge his death.

Hippolyte wanted a willing Jeanette in his bed, and he would have her—until the right time came for me to revenge not only Jamie, but also my mother and father.

"Thank you for saving Bliss," I said and smiled.

Hippolyte, a glass of wine in his hand, watched me. It was easy to read the expression on his face and the hunger in his eyes.

75

"What happened to Héloïse Leroux?" I asked.

Hippolyte drew a finger across his throat.

I began to undress. The sun was down, but moonlight streamed through the porthole, so I chose that spot, with my back to Hippolyte, to step out of my last undergarment. I turned slowly to face him, arms at my sides, but when he came to me, I lifted my breasts. He buried his hot face in their soft, cool valley.

Then he was on his knees, arms clasping my thighs. I moved away from the kneeling man, toward the bunk. Stretched on it, I watched Hippolyte shed his clothes and noticed how his hands trembled. The sight of him, naked and aroused, stirred me in spite of myself, so I closed my eyes.

It was no use. I couldn't be supine. My body betrayed me and engulfed his savage thrusts, welcomed them, my nipples hardening and breasts throbbing to his bruising touch.

Hippolyte was satisfied too soon! I punished him for that with busy hands and lips until he was aroused enough for *me* to take *him*—and reach my own shuddering climax.

We lay side by side on our backs in the moonlit cabin. For a long time neither of us spoke, but it was Hippolyte who finally said, "You're better than the Leroux woman ever was, Jeanette."

"And the others?"

Hippolyte raised on an elbow to stare down into my face. "I bought them— I own you."

"That makes a difference?"

His smile was cruel, and so were his eyes. "It makes a difference. What you learned from me our wedding night wasn't wasted effort on my part."

I tangled my fingers in his hair. "What, no horns?" I whispered.

"What did you say?"

I drew his face down and found his lips with mine.

He forgot the question.

Inside I cried for Jamie but let my body once again respond to Hippolyte. I understood for the first time what it is that makes a woman a whore.

CHAPTER 6

I CHERISHED no illusions about Hippolyte de Verlaine. So long as he could use my traitorous body, I'd be safe enough, but the time would come when he tired of me. I could play the whore until then. It shamed me to know how willingly.

Grand Cayman had always been a pirate stronghold. Below Cuba and on the western sea approach to British Jamaica, Blackbeard, Neal Walker and Thomas Anstis had sailed from there. When he'd paid off Jamie's Jamaicans and enlisted a fresh crew, Hippolyte planned to sail for Marseille. From there Anderson and Frechet would take the *Salem Witch* to some hospitable port on the Barbary coast of North Africa. Established in Napoleon's France, Hippolyte planned to sell whatever merchandise the pair of them could plunder along the Mediterranean trade routes. With Britain blockading most of the French ports, it could prove a profitable venture.

The *Salem Witch* wasn't anchored off Georgetown, but instead was sailed into the North Sound, a huge water-bite out of the small, almost barren island. Anchor was dropped among the sloops, ketches, and other schooners sheltering there. Georgetown was just across a narrow neck of land at the head of the sound. Tents and huts crowded the wide beach.

Small boats made for the *Salem Witch* as soon as her anchor chains stopped rattling. Half-naked girls and women offered themselves to the crew, climbing aboard despite the shouted orders of Anderson and Frechet, and coupling with the men on every part of the ship. Some were Chinese, others mulatto, with a sprinkling of white women. It was a wild scene, and one Bliss enjoyed as much as it shocked me. I discovered there were more ways to satisfy a man than I'd ever dreamed.

Hippolyte watched the saturnalia with an arm around my waist and a hand thrust inside my bodice. There on the quarterdeck we watched Frechet—and then red-bearded Anderson— spend themselves on a willing and eager Bliss.

As the shipboard orgy reached its climax, Hippolyte took me below and subjected my throbbing body to acts I hadn't experienced since our wedding night. But this time I was a willing partner. Slippery with our own sweat, we writhed and thrust, experiencing one nerve-shattering climax after another.

"No more!" he panted finally.

I was astride him. "Once again!" I gasped.

"No!"

"Yes!"

"My God!"

"You'd better pray." I furrowed his chest with my nails.

"You're a bitch!"

"No. Just a woman." I lowered my face and drew blood from his lips. "Once again?"

"My God, yes!"

"I'm your bitch."

"Yes!"

I finally exhausted myself, too, and fell away from his naked body, an arm over my eyes.

Hippolyte raised on an elbow to stare down at me. "Did McCoy teach you these tricks?" he demanded.

I lowered my arm to meet his stare. "He raped me," I lied. "You did, too. Remember?"

I covered my breasts with my hands, trailed fingers down my sides, smiled at the hunger I saw again in his eyes. "More?" I asked.

Hippolyte didn't have to answer me.

* * *

Hippolyte paid off Jamie's Jamaicans. He sent Anderson and Frechet ashore to enlist a new crew from among the beachcombers.

"You're now just a cabin boy," he told me.

I thought for a moment. "I suppose I can bind my breasts," I said. "What do we do about my hair?"

"Chop it off. These men won't ship out on a craft with a woman on board. We're dealing with The Brethren."

"The Brethren?"

"You're ignorant," Hippolyte said. "Piracy is a profession with rules and regulations."

"I'll get Bliss to cut my hair."

She did, and Hippolyte fitted me out from Jamie's sea chest. So when Hippolyte took me to the beach, I was Jean, his cabin boy.

Frechet admired me in my new garb. "Just don't let the vixen mix too much with our new crew," he advised Hippolyte. "Without a wench handy, they'd soon bugger the cabin boy." He gave me a lewd wink. "I'm sometimes so inclined myself, on a long voyage."

I had learned Anderson was a brutal but stupid man. Frechet thought for him. Hippolyte had saved them both from the hangman's noose back on Martinique, by a few discreet bribes. Anderson had strangled a woman. Frechet had killed two men.

* * *

On the beach I saw a girl and two women put up for sale. Stripped naked, they were exposed to the crowd of men and women there to barter for them. Every other shack on the beach was a grog shop or bordello.

The cowering girl, trying to cover herself with her hands, went first. She was flaxen-haired and Dutch, taken prisoner from a Dutch merchantman.

The women, each in turn, examined her before the bidding started. The men watched with avid interest. "This one is virgin!" was the surprised exclamation of the first blowsy madam.

That drew a shout from the men.

Hippolyte watched with an amused smile on his lips. "Do you want her?" he asked me.

"No. I have Bliss." I shuddered to think of the Dutch girl's fate, but there was no way I could help her. Aboard the *Salem Witch,* she would be at the mercy of the crew, unless Hippolyte decided to amuse himself with the girl.

He was entertaining that idea— I could tell by the expression on his face.

"You don't need another virgin," I whispered.

One of the naked women was a proud Spaniard, with coal-black hair streaming down her straight back. She submitted herself to intimate examination with a contempt that I admired. and spit in the face of the last harridan. She drew a better price than the virgin Dutch girl.

The second woman was a weeping half-caste

with fleshy thighs. The auctioneer, a tall Carib Indian, delighted and inflamed the watching men by putting her through a series of lewd postures.

I was sick to my stomach.

Hippolyte enjoyed the spectacle, before he hurried me back aboard the *Salem Witch* and into his cabin.

I soon learned that my masquerade as a boy added an extra fillip to Hippolyte's passion. He liked me in his bunk nearly fully dressed. I played this new role to the hilt. It added a startling new dimension to his lovemaking.

I have to admit that the girl-boy role added something to mine, too, a fact that disgusted me, but my damned body betrayed me again. I promised myself the time would come for me to rid myself of Hippolyte, as he'd done away with my parents and Jamie. Yet part of me knew I could never kill the man in cold blood, and I prayed he would force me to do it.

"Now that you're lying with him, we'll never get away," Bliss complained.

She was pouting and sullen. She felt that I was betraying both of us.

"Our time will come," I promised, "but it isn't now."

With a crew of twenty, we sailed from the North Sound of Grand Cayman, outward bound for France. It was Frechet whom Hippolyte appointed sailing master, with Anderson his second in command. One man, a towering light-skinned Negro, reminded me of Amos.

I never learned from Hippolyte what happened to Amos after Jamie was killed and thrown overboard. It was my guess that he'd taken his chance in the sea rather than face the mutinous crew.

Hippolyte and Frechet plotted a course far enough south of Kingston to avoid the British.

We'd sail up through the wide Anegada Passage between Danish islands to reach the horse latitudes in the North Atlantic, and from there veer toward Madeira and Gibraltar. The *Salem Witch* was becalmed in the horse latitudes when Anderson and Frechet quarreled over Bliss. Hippolyte suggested a duel with cutlasses. I know now that he needed to be rid of one man or the other.

(Bliss has told me since that it was Hippolyte who urged her to provoke the men.)

It was a hot afternoon when the hulking Anderson and slighter Frechet squared off amidships, in a circle of crewmen eager to see blood. Cutlasses rang and sparked as they circled each other warily. Anderson was stronger, Frechet more cunning, but the red-bearded Swede drew first blood when his cutlass nicked Frechet's shoulder.

Bliss watched the fight, huddled in the circle of my arm on the quarterdeck. Her hip pressed mine and her eyes sparkled with excitement.

Anderson tried to press his advantage when

Frechet slipped on the deck and fell to one knee. The ferret-faced man ducked his wild swing, then drove his blade up into Anderson's groin.

Anderson dropped his cutlass and went to his knees.

Frechet slashed Anderson's throat and ordered the crew to fling the still-twitching body over the side. Bliss watched avidly, shuddering against me, but it wasn't fear that put that wrapt expression on her dark face. Frechet beckoned and she followed him to his quarters.

Bliss wasn't the only one aboard whom the sight of a man's blood had excited. Hippolyte's eyes were glassy when he ordered me to follow him to our cabin, and once there, he threw himself on me. His hard flesh impaled mine, and his body felt fevered.

It was the next morning that we sighted the brig *Mary Evelyn*. Frechet and the restless crew urged Hippolyte to overtake and board her. She was laboring low in the water, her sails in tatters.

Within the hour, the *Salem Witch* overtook her. Her master, John Briggs of New Bedford, hailed the *Salem Witch*. "Stand away. We're not in distress."

His crew of ten men were huddled beside the foremast, none of them armed. Frechet ran up the black flag, confirming Brigg's fear, and the longboat was lowered. When I saw a swirl of skirt aboard the brig, I jumped down in the boat before the men pulled away.

The sight of the girl and women being sold to the highest bidders back on Grand Cayman was still fresh in my mind. I didn't know how I was going to protect the woman aboard the brig, but I had to try.

Frechet was at the tiller. I sat in the stern sheets beside him. "There's a woman aboard that ship," I said, "and I don't want her harmed."

"Tenderhearted, ain't you, missy?" His saturnine face mocked me.

We spoke in low voices so we'd not be overheard by the crewmen at the oars.

"I mean it, Antoine." I thought it was a good time to use his first name. I touched his bare shoulder. "Please?"

His grin was cynical, but I recognized the hunger lurking in his eyes. "What will you do for me if I see the woman's safe?" he asked.

We were close under the lee rail of the *Mary Evelyn*, so it was no time to be coy. One of the men had seen the woman and claimed he would be the first.

"Anything you want," I whispered.

Frechet stared at me, then ordered the men, "Leave any female on board alone. That's an order, and whoever disobeys will join Anderson."

The men grumbled among themselves, but I knew they would obey. Mary Evelyn Briggs wouldn't be handled and raped. I knew that some-

time I would have to keep the bargain I'd made
with Frechet, but I didn't care.

The sailors aboard the brig were a cowardly
lot, but it's true that they were outnumbered and
poorly armed. By not resisting, they bought their
lives, but lost the valuable cargo they'd been entrusted with. Gunpowder, muskets, and hardware
were in her hold. Hippolyte brought the *Salem
Witch* alongside, had the two ships lashed together in the calm sea, and began transfering the
cargo.

Mary Evelyn was Captain Brigg's daughter.
She was slender, with brown hair and a spray of
freckles across her pert nose. Pale and obviously
frightened, she managed to hold her head high.

Her father was a ruddy-face New Englander,
furious to find himself at the mercy of pirates and
afraid for his daughter until I told him, "She
won't be touched, but I'd keep her out of sight if
I were you."

"You're just a boy!" He stared at me. "Damned
if you'll give me orders on my own ship!"

"Father." It may have been my voice that gave
me away, or perhaps Mary Evelyn's eyes were
sharper than those of the men aboard the *Salem
Witch*. "She gives us good advice. Will you join
us?" she asked me.

"Yes." I was hungry to talk with another white
woman.

"You aren't a boy, are you?" Mary Evelyn said when we were below decks.

"No. I'm Jeanette, not Jean."

We could hear the voices of the men on deck and the heavy tramp of their feet.

Captain Briggs stared at me, astonished. "By the great God!" he muttered.

She touched my cheek. "I saw you speak to that man."

"Frechet?"

She nodded. "The one at the tiller. I somehow knew right then that my prayer would be answered." From its concealment under her voluminous skirt, she drew a pistol and laid it on the table. "I really didn't want to kill myself."

"A damned pirate *girl!*" Captain Briggs was having a hard time getting over his astonishment.

"Sir, I've killed a man because I had to. I've seen the man I loved murdered." It was a stilted speech, and tears stung my eyes. "My husband left me to be killed during the Haitian uprising. Now he commands that ship over there, and I can't escape him—not yet."

Mary Evelyn's warm embrace broke the floodgate, and I sobbed on her shoulder. "I'll pray for you, Jeanette," she said. "Father, how can we help her?"

"I don't know." He was gruff but not unkind.

I swallowed my sobs and dashed the tears from my face. "There's no way without endangering your crew and your ship," I said. "Also your daughter."

Captain Briggs nodded agreement.

"Who was the man you loved?" Mary Evelyn asked.

"Jamie McCoy. He owned the *Salem Witch.*"

"Do we know him?" she asked her father.

Captain Briggs scratched his head. "There was a McCoy who sailed from Boston, I seem to remember. A big Scottish lad, handy with his fists and the ladies."

"Is that your Jamie?" Mary Evelyn asked.

"Yes!" I was going to cry again.

"Don't, Jeanette," Mary Evelyn said in a soft voice. "Are you sure that he's dead?"

"Yes." I told them what had happened.

Mary Evelyn was thoughtful. "You can't really be sure he was killed, can you?"

"I'm sure," I said, but she'd lighted a tiny flicker of hope.

"Don't torture the poor girl with doubts," Captain Briggs told his daughter. "From what she's told us, the poor devil is dead and gone. It's best she lives with that fact." He furrowed his brow. "Now, what we can do for you, Jeanette, is tell the American authorities your situation. Where is your ship bound?"

I told him.

"Aye." Now he was thoughtful. "We've heard the United States Navy has a flotilla in the Mediterranean, now, based in Malta. You wouldn't know it from the lily-livered men aboard my ship, but Americans are too proud to pay tribute to Barbarossa and his scurvy Barbary pirate scum. Maybe you'll be rescued."

Captain Briggs was only being kind and trying to light a flame of hope within me.

Mary Evelyn kissed me good-bye, and Captain Briggs wished me god-speed with a catch in his voice and tears in his eyes.

Back aboard the *Salem Witch*, I found Hippolyte drunk and pleased with his haul. Frechet was worried about the weather. He'd learned that the *Mary Evelyn* had barely survived a near-hurricane. Now the glass was dropping, the sky was brassy, and sullen swells rocked the *Salem Witch*. Frechet set the crew to work battening down hatches and strengthening the rigging.

It was sundown. Black clouds to the west seemed to kiss the ocean. Lightning laced them. It was then I saw a terrifying sight.

CHAPTER 7

ONLY A few miles away, a giant snakelike water-spout dropped from a sullen black cloud and hit the surface of the ocean like a huge, mailed fist. It came directly at the *Salem Witch,* which was barely underway with all sails set. I stood frozen on the port side of the quarterdeck, my knuckles white as I grasped the rail.

Hippolyte was drunk in our cabin. Frechet saw the waterspout when I did, and he shouted an order at the helmsman. There was no time to take in canvas. I felt the slight list of the ship beneath my feet as the helmsman spun the wheel and she started to come around. I sensed that our only hope was to meet that twisting water tornado head-on. Watching the thing, for the first time I realized why a snake immobilizes its prey! I couldn't move—or even blink. It left a path of froth and surging waves as it approached. Its roar was as terrifying as its appearance.

Somehow the *Salem Witch* did come around, just far enough not to be lashed amidships, and probably capsized. The waterspout grazed the starboard side with a terrific suction that tore away a mainsail as if it were a handkerchief, and left another on the aftermast slashed to ribbons. Still grasping the rail, I watched over my shoulder and saw the helmsman literally torn away from the wheel, to disappear, spinning like a thrown rag doll, into its maw.

My grip on the rail saved me. Frechet, arms locked around the binnacle, managed to save himself before a solid wall of water, churned up when the waterspout passed, engulfed the *Salem Witch*. Knocked off my feet, finally torn from the rail, I was washed along the quarterdeck. As the ship staggered drunkenly, I found myself bruised and half-drowned, plastered against the stern rail.

What approached now looked like a solid wall of wind-driven water. On my hands and knees, I scrambled for the hatch that would take me below decks.

Down the ladder, I found the passageway half-flooded, and pitch-black. Bliss was screaming. The ship pitched, then rolled, but I somehow kept

94

my balance long enough to reach the cabin she was sharing with Frechet.

"Jeanette!" I could see the whites of her eyes. "We're all right."

We were. clinging to each other then, breast to breast, thigh to thigh, bracing each other against the madly lurching ship. Frechet found us in each other's tight embrace.

Braced in the cabin entrance, he took in the sight, then grinned to show rotting teeth. "How often do you and the black wench make love, missy?"

The ship was settling back on an even keel, now that the squall had blown through, and I tried to brush past him, but an arm captured me. His mouth covered mine and his fingers dug into my buttocks, but I wrenched free.

"We still have our bargain, missy," he reminded me with a leer. "Full payment next time."

Bliss was on his back, clawing at his face like a cat. With a roar of rage, Frechet flung her back across the cabin. She struck her head and was dazed, but conscious.

I couldn't help her.

Perhaps Hippolyte could, as he had once before, so I ran to the cabin we shared. I found him sobered by the beating the *Salem Witch* had just taken, but groggy and unsure of exactly what had happened.

"I think Frechet will kill Bliss," I told him, trying to stay calm and lucid. "You can save her."

"What has the black wench been doing?" His voice was thick, his eyes bleary and bloodshot.

He'd taken my knife, but I knew where it was supposed to be hidden. Dodging past Hippolyte, I snatched it from its hiding place—a locker under the bunk—and started back to help Bliss.

Hippolyte came after me. He'd snatched up a pistol.

In the shambles that had been a cabin, Bliss was fighting for her life against the enraged man whose face dripped blood from a dozen deep scratches. He had her cornered and was reaching for her throat, but he spun around when he heard me.

His eyes insane, Frechet dashed at the blood on his face with the back of his hand. A foot shot out to kick the knife from my hand. It was then that Hippolyte knocked me aside, to be framed in the cabin entrance, the cocked pistol leveled at Frechet.

Frechet's face changed. "Now, captain." He cringed, speaking in a fawning voice. "I come below to find your fancy piece and the black slut making woman-love." He spread his hands. "What would you have me do?"

Hippolyte gasped. The pistol swung in my direction.

"No!" I cowered back against the bulkhead.

My eyes were fixed on the gaping muzzle of the pistol, so I didn't see Bliss spring past Frechet to snatch up my knife. The pistol exploded, but her lunge knocked off Hippolyte's aim. He staggered back into the passageway.

Bliss raised the knife, only to plunge it into his exposed throat. Then they both were down!

Stunned by the muzzle blast, I stared as Frechet twisted the knife from Bliss's hand before she could stab Hippolyte again. He knocked her off Hippolyte. As she crawled away down the passage, Frechet stared down at Hippolyte.

Ignoring Frechet, I knelt beside my husband. Blood spurted from the wound in his throat, and his eyes were glazed. He couldn't speak. Blood bubbled from his lips, a strangled sound broke out of his mouth, and he died.

Frechet caught me under my armpits and lifted me to my feet.

Someone shouted down the hatch for Frechet to come back on deck.

For the first time I saw fear reflected by the man's ferretlike face, but a cunning half-smile was his next expression.

Grabbing Hippolyte by the heels, he dragged him into the wrecked cabin and slammed the door.

"We'll not let the crew know the black wench killed him, missy. You keep her out of sight until I'm rid of the body. They'll hang her by her heels and cut her to pieces." He screwed his face into a scowl, then said, "It's our little secret, eh?"

I didn't have to answer. "I'll go to Bliss," I said.

Beside the helmsman, the *Salem Witch* lost a forward lookout when the waterspout swept by. Thus there were no questions from the crew when Frechet swore that Hippolyte had been washed overboard, too. He had his own reasons for saving Bliss from the wrath of the crew, of course. They would certainly kill her if he told them she'd stabbed Hippolyte to death, but suspicion would fasten on him.

Frechet couldn't afford that.

Bliss had saved my life, and by so doing she'd brought us closer together than we'd been since childhood, when we had our secrets. I found she'd retreated to the cabin Hippolyte and I had shared —to me it was always Jamie's cabin—and I found her in the small cabin where she'd slept on a pallet.

Naked, shivering, she was trying to bathe her cuts and bruises. Her swollen face made me want to laugh and cry at the same time.

I sank down on the pallet beside her. "Let me, Bliss." I took the sponge from her hands.

"I killed him, Jeanette!" Her eyes were wide with fear.

"I know."

Most of her clothing had been ripped to shreds. I stripped her and made her lie face down, so I could bathe the welts on her back and flanks.

"Frechet won't tell the crew." I cleaned the cuts on her shoulders, where she'd been thrown against something sharp, and winced to see the lash scars that Hippolyte had caused. "They can't kill us, Bliss."

There was a nasty cut in one sleek buttock. Bliss had winced when I'd bathed it. Now I touched it lightly with my fingers.

"Lie still, Bliss."

She buried her face on her arms.

I rose long enough to bolt the door. Then I placed my hands on the small of her slender back. "Are you hurt here?"

"No, Jeanette." Her voice was muffled.

I finished by bathing the backs of her legs, then said, "Turn over, darling."

There had never been terms of endearment between us before, and I sensed our whole relationship had changd the instant I did because Bliss dutifully rolled onto her back, knees drawn up, thighs parted slighted, her swollen eyes fixed on my face.

Bliss no longer shivered at my touch. Eyes wide, her hands rose to cup my head, fingers in the hair that she'd cropped, pleading.

Responding to her shy pressure, I let Bliss draw my face to her own, met her lips with mine, and it bcame a lovers' kiss.

"A minute, Bliss," I whispered, and rose to strip off my boy's clothing. Then I rejoined her on the pallet, and we embraced.

I'd nearly forgotten. When we were children, one night I'd taken her into my bed during a thunderstorm, and we'd explored each other's bodies, giggling. We were women, no longer girl-children, and there was no laughter. My hands strayed down Bliss's back, found her flanks, and she moaned.

Her faltering hands began exploring my body, and I gasped, "My God!"

She'd cupped my intimate woman-flesh!

When her face, and lips, and tongue, followed her hands, I nearly fainted.

"Jamie!" His name screamed, soundless, through my brain, but for the moment I gave my whole body to Bliss. Who we were, what we were—did it matter?

The Dutch girl. The haughty Spaniard who'd spit in her tormentor's face, the half-caste with the fleshy thighs.

The Dutch girl. Hippolyte had promised to buy her for me, but I told him that he didn't need another virgin.

I cried inside for her!

"Jeanette?" Bliss raised her face, swollen as it was, and I couldn't deny her.

"Lie still."

"Yes, Jeanette."

"Turn over."

"Oh, yes!"

Mother had bathed us as children in the same tub, and I knew her dimpled black flesh as well as I did my own, but when my hands pressed apart her

100

thighs, and Bliss whimpered a half-protest, I snapped, "Lie still!"

"Jeanette . . . oh!"

Frechet shouldered open the door, to say, "Well, I'll be damned!

He took me for the first time, there on the pallet while Bliss watched. When he'd spent himself, Bliss was banished to the forecastle, and Frechet moved into the cabin I'd shared with Jamie and then Hippolyte. I was to be a prisoner there until the ship reached port at Marseille.

To make sure I was, Frechet took all my clothes except a brief shift.

Frechet treated me reasonably well and demanded less than Hippolyte. His lovemaking was mechanical, almost absentminded at times.

For days on end, with jury-rigged sails, the *Salem Witch* beat toward Madeira. She neither sighted nor overtook any other ships. It was a time for me of excruciating boredom, and I missed the company of Bliss.

Frechet told me the crew was treating her well. The crew shared an unprotesting, usually quite willing, Bliss, passing her nubile body from one to another during the long days and nights at sea.

"She's good for the crew's morale," Frechet told me. "I may keep her aboard when we cruise the Mediterranean. You'd miss her hugs and kisses, wouldn't you, missy?"

My interrupted interlude with Bliss had Frechet convinced that I was basically a lesbian, and I didn't trouble to disabuse him of the notion. Instead of stimulating him, it seemed to inhibit his pleasure with me. Or maybe he would have preferred me to be a strippling cabin boy. The crew was certain Frechet spent off-duty hours toying with Hippolyte's *pretty boy*. And some of the men had sailed with Frechet previously.

He promised I'd be set ashore when the ship had reached Marseille. I'd found the pouch of diamonds that Hippolyte thought he'd concealed so well and put them in a better hiding place. I wore them on a thong around my neck and convinced Frechet it was a *gris-gris* bag. I'd discovered he was deeply superstitious, well-versed in *obeah,* or voodoo. He was convinced that nothing but disaster would occur if he should tamper with my *gris-gris*.

I think the reason Frechet planned to give me my freedom when the *Salem Witch* reached France was influenced by the bad luck that had dogged the *Salem Witch*.

The jury-rigged ship was hard to steer and could run well only ahead of a stiff following wind, so Frechet was nervous. He was afraid another pirate craft would overhaul us before we reached Funchal.

This was a well-based fear.

* * *

Cloudy days and nights, as well as faulty dead reckoning, let us pass Funchal in a rain squall, and Frechet was on deck, cursing the crew, trying to tack the ship back into a headwind. They'd broken out a rum cask the night before and let Bliss entertain them with her naked African dances (at least they considered they were African!), so Frechet had his problems.

I was below, in my shift, bored and drowsy. I couldn't think much beyond Marseille, selling a few of the diamonds once Bliss and I were ashore, a bed all my own, covered with silken sheets (black ones, if I could find them), behind a locked door. I'd have chests and closets brimming with the latest Paris fashions.

It was a really beautiful daydream.

I was aware of the sound of increased activity on deck and alarmed shouts, but I paid no attention.

Maybe I would be the bride of a rich and handsome nobleman. Children? Maybe two, a boy and a girl. Jamie was my lost love. I ached for him, but only dully now. We'd had each other such a short time!

I'd convinced myself that Jamie really loved me. Somehow that helped assuage the grief I'd felt.

Hippolyte? I felt only relief that he was dead, and thankful it was Bliss, not I, who had killed him.

*　*　*

My daydream ended when something struck the *Salem Witch* a shuddering blow. Cries of *Allâh!* mixed with the scared profanity of our crew. The porthole on the starboard side was blocked by the red hull of another ship.

The fighting on deck was finished quickly. I cowered in the cabin, certain that Frechet and his crew had been overwhelmed, wondering what new fate Bliss and I faced.

A man screamed. He sounded like Frechet. I had to go up on deck. Waiting alone was too much torture!

A tall ship of strange design with blood-red sails was about to take the *Salem Witch* in tow. Frechet dangled, still kicking, from a forward yardarm. Bliss and none of the *Salem Witch*'s crew were in sight, but the decks were puddled with blood.

Dark-skinned men, wearing ankle-length pantaloons, sashes, and tight jackets, with turbans on their heads, thronged the ship. Moors! The *Salem Witch* was a prize of Barbary pirates.

I finally saw Bliss. A towering man as black as she was was carrying her to the other ship.

"Bliss!"

"They're all dead, Jeanette," she called back.

That's when the pirates saw me. A strapping red-bearded man strode toward me, a scimitar in his hand, but other glances in my direction were strangely uncurious.

"I am called Barbarossa.'" He spoke perfect

English and seemed amused to find me in my shift. Barbarossa's voice was deep, even for such a giant of a man, but strangely gentle. "We are Moors," he told me. "You haven't fallen into the hands of savage dog-Christians. You are Christian?"

I nodded dumbly.

"Too bad. But you'll make a lovely slave for the man who can pay your price. The blackamoor —does she belong to you?"

"Yes."

"You'll be sold together then. It's my custom. We sail for Tripoli where you'll be kept and groomed aboard an American ship my men have captured. Where are your tears?"

I laughed bitterly. "I'm sorry to disappoint you, but I cried them all a long time ago."

His hand lifted my chin, a hand that was heavy with jewel-crusted rings. Gray-blue eyes stared into mine from over his flowing beard. "It usually takes a touch of the whip to make Christian women stop crying when they know they'll be sold as slaves. I notice, from her back, that you've whipped your slave."

"No." I shook my head. "Someone else did that."

Barbossa beckoned a nearby Moor, and spoke to him in Arabic. "You'll be taken to my cabin," he told me. "So will your slave."

CHAPTER 8

WHILE IN England, I'd heard of Barbarossa, the most infamous of the Barbary chiefs. His name meant Redbeard. His dhow, with its high pop-deck, and open area amidships, dwarfed Jamie's *Salem Witch*. I found when I was carried aboard the dhow, however, that I'd exchanged one ship's prison for another.

Bliss and I were locked into an iron cage, deep in the ship, our wrists and ankles shackled, my shift and Bliss's garments removed. This was done, I learned later, so that we couldn't harm ourselves; but at the time I felt like a caged animal.

Our jailer was a huge Nubian eunuch, a mute because his tongue had been removed.

The Senegalese who'd carried Bliss aboard came down and tried to converse with her in that African tongue, but it was no use. She'd been torn from her family and shipped to Haiti too young to remember her native language. But we both realized the tall black man had come to comfort her.

With smiles and gestures, he seemed to be telling us we'd come to no harm aboard the dhow.

Bliss told me what had happened aboard the *Salem Witch*. "This ship came from a cloud," she said.

"Cloud? You mean a fog or mist?"

Bliss bobbed her head. "Those white men were too drunk to fight much."

It had been a quick slaughter, with the bodies tossed over the side, except for Frechet.

"The man—the one with red beard? You saw him?"

"Yes. Barbarossa."

With gestures, Bliss demonstrated how Barbarossa had emasculated Frechet before hanging him, and now I understood that scream. I sickened just thinking about the cruel streak Barbarossa's gentle voice and manner concealed. But at least he'd shortened Frechet's agony.

Underway, the dhow was a steady ship, and to judge from the rush of water along the keel, a fast one. I told Bliss we were bound for Tripoli.

"Where is that, Jeanette?" she asked.

"In the Mediterranean, on the north coast of Africa, near the island of Malta," I explained.

"What will they do with us there?"

"Sell us into slavery, so Barbarossa says. We'll be sold together—he's promised."

Bliss regarded me thoughtfully. Then she tossed her head and giggled. Pointing a finger at me, she said, "You are a slave now. How do you like to be one?"

It was a rueful thought. "I don't think I'm going to like it," I told her candidly. "But Barbarossa promises we'll be treated well."

"Your husband made promises, too," she reminded me.

The chains between our ankle and wrist shackles were light enough to give us some freedom of movement, and there were clean pallets for sleeping. Simple food—some sort of a meat stew—was served us, with a flagon of spicy wine. Each morning our Nubian took us above for fresh air and exercise.

The attitude of the Moors toward our naked parade was puzzling. They simply ignored us almost completely. Twice I saw Barbarossa braced on the high poopdeck, but he ignored us, too. His red turban that matched his beard sparkled with gems.

Torches stuck in brackets along the passageway gave us reddish light in our cell, and it was a strangely comfortable inferno, once we were used to our light shackles.

On the third day, an elderly man wearing a fez came below. "I am Suleiman Bey, a physician," he told us with a friendly smile. "I am here to examine you both."

He called our Nubian jailer and asked him to remove the shackles. "I don't believe they are necessary any longer," he explained. "You are healthy young women and not inclined to harm yourselves."

Suleiman Bey spoke excellent English, and when he learned I was half-French, we conversed in that language, too. It was an impersonal, but very *complete* examination, with satisfied grunts when he was finished.

"Neither of you is diseased, I'm delighted to report," he said. "There is no reason you can't be put up for sale."

"What if we had been diseased?" I asked.

"The strangling cord," he said in a pleasant voice.

I heaved a sigh of relief, and so did Bliss. Sitting cross-legged on my pallet, his hands tucked into flowing sleeves, Suleiman Bey told us what we faced once the dhow anchored in Tripoli's harbor.

"There is an American ship on a reef near the mouth of the harbor," he said. "It is named *Philadelphia,* for an American city of that name. Aboard it you will be groomed and schooled in the art of pleasing Moorish and Arab men. Pay close attention to what you will be taught there," he cautioned. "Moors and Arabs are not patient with women—even Christian slaves."

When our tutors were satisfied with our progress, Barbarossa would have us offered for sale in the main square of Tripoli.

"He has many Christian slaves ready for the market," Suleiman Bey told us. "Chief Barbarossa is a very great man. You are fortunate to be in his hands. Who knows? With your hair and eyes and your fine body, you might find favor with Barbarossa," he told me. "That would be most fortunate for you and your blackamoor."

"Jeanette will please any man in bed," Bliss volunteered.

Suleiman Bey laughed. "Were I a few years younger, and didn't have three jealous wives, I might buy her as another concubine."

One thing that might reduce my price was the length of my hair, he told me. "Barbarossa may keep you until it's long again."

Before he left, Suleiman Bey ordered the Nubian to bring us warm, scented bathwater, and said to send for him immediately if either of us fell ill.

"You must stay healthy," he warned, then added, "And get fat, too. Arabs and Moors like their women fat."

As soon as the dhow anchored in Tripoli's harbor, Barbarossa sent his Senegalese for me, but I was to come only after I was bathed and scented.

111

The only garment he brought was filmy silk pantaloons that reached my ankles but revealed more than they concealed.

The lights of Tripoli twinkled in the clear, warm night air as he led me along the deck to Barbarossa's spacious cabin. The man sat cross-legged on an oval bed, arms crossed on his chest, and he was entirely naked except for the jewel-studded turban.

I'd entrusted my diamonds to Bliss, and now she wore a *gris-gris* bag.

Barbarossa watched me with heavy eyelids, smoking a water pipe, and seemed half-asleep, but his voice was normal.

"Show yourself to me, woman," he ordered.

I stepped out of the pantaloons.

With an arm, I modestly covered my breasts, and a hand shielded me elsewhere, as I met his stare. It was obvious that my modest nudity hadn't aroused the man, so I raised my arms and turned around, then faced Barbarossa again.

He sucked on his pipe impassively.

"Do you dance?" he asked.

"No."

"You will be taught." He studied my body with a critical eye. He approved it with a nod, then put aside his pipe. "Come and please me." It was an order.

Barbarossa *still* wasn't aroused! But the sight of his impassive body was a challenge, and a new sexual experience for me. Before the Senegalese brought me to Barbarossa, he'd had me drink a cup of highly spiced wine. From the way my blood was singing, there must have been more than wine in that cup!

Barbarossa lay back, fingers combing his beard, and waited.

Finally, he was aroused, and I was panting from the effort it had cost me. Once aroused, the man was a bull! I was handled roughly, but not abused, and experienced one shattering climax after another until my face was wet with tears and sobs were catching in my throat.

Barbarossa laid me aside as if I was an exhausted flesh doll, one big hand absentmindedly exploring my spent body. Again he smoked the pipe and I recognized the smell of a drug when he exhaled. Hashish?

"You've still much to be taught," he said in a calm, almost disinterested voice, "but you'll be a most willing pupil. Is it well with you and the blackamoor?"

"As well as we can expect."

Barbarossa nodded gravely. "You have spirit, and I like that in my women; but your new master may not, so be careful. Some prefer a submissive and cringing concubine. Their eunuchs know many ways to accomplish the breaking of a woman's spirit without disfiguring her face or body. Do you believe this?"

"Yes."

"Good." He clapped his hands, and the Senegalese appeared from nowhere. "Take this one back and bring me the blackamoor," Barbarossa ordred.

I wondered if I'd had a predecessor that night!

I meekly followed the Senegalese back to my cage. "Now it will be your turn," I whispered to Bliss while she bathed.

"Will he hurt me, Jeanette?" she whispered back.

"I don't think so."

Had I disappointed her? It was hard for me to tell.

When the Senegalese brought Bliss back, she was as exhausted as I had been.

The frigate *Philadelphia* had been abandoned by her American crew when it struck and was hung up on a reef in Tripoli's large harbor. As soon as Barbarossa's dhow was moored, Bliss and I were taken to it and turned over to the fat eunuch in charge of prisoners. He took us to Madame Phyrigia.

Partly Greek, but mostly Moorish, she had garish henna-dyed hair, kohl-smeared eyes, and a grossly fat body. Her luxurious cabin was curtained and dim. She lounged on a bank of pillows, dipping fingers into an enormous bowl filled with some sort of sticky sweetmeat. We stripped for her inspection and examination.

"You have a name?" she asked me, her voice husky and harsh.

"Yes. It's Jeanette."

We spoke in French.

"How many men have had you?"

"Four." The plaited whip with its ivory handle that lay close to her hand prompted my meek answer.

Madame Phyrigia carefully licked the sticky fingers of each hand, reminding me of a cat, and I almost expected her to purr. Instead she touched the whip, saying, "I like to use this."

Bliss and I found ourselves among a group of Christian girls and women captured by the Barbary pirates, some of whom had been aboard the *Philadelphia* for more than a month. From them we learned that Madame Phyrigia truly *did* like to use her ivory-handled whip with its plaited leather lash.

We were confined together in a large cabin and served our meals there, invoking memories of my English boarding school—but how different this curriculum was! Ahmed and Mohammed, a pair of lusty Arab boys, were our instructors, under the watchful eye of Madame Phyrigia. The officer's wardroom was where classes were held.

The boys coached each of us the intricacies and perversities (to our Western minds) of Oriental love. We had to learn a wide variety of positions, while the others looked on, and Madame

Phyrigia was always present, with her whip. If she thought anyone wasn't fully participating, or unwilling, that girl or woman quickly learned that a flick of her whip always reached the most sensitive flesh.

Our body hair was plucked with tweezers, a most painful procedure! We were fed only the richest foods and highly spiced wines. Except for Bliss and me, the others were resigned to their fate, and a few actually looked forward to seraglio life as a concubine. This was more true of the women than the girls, something I found strange.

Huddled together as we were, daily stimulated, lesbian activity was commonplace, and even encouraged by Madame Phyrigia. It was a natural outlet, we were told, for the bored and sometimes sex-deprived women in a harem.

There had been a sale of slaves that day, and all but Bliss and me had been taken to the marketplace in front of the grim castle. We had only been aboard the *Philadelphia* a week, and evidently Madame Phyrigia didn't consider us well enough versed in the erotic arts to take our place on the auction block.

Our quarters weren't locked, for there was no way we could escape the ship without drowning in the swift harbor currents.

Bliss was asleep beside me, but I lay awake praying to the Blessed Mother and every saint I could remember for deliverance. My mind must have been weakening because I remember wondering if I wasn't already dead and delivered to hell.

We could hear the crew of Moors aboard the ship conversing on deck in the quiet, warm darkness. One called out, hailing what he thought was a passing boat. It was a ketch, familiar to all the crew, because it had passed outward bound just that morning.

There was no way for us to see what was happening, but the sudden sharp cry, "Americanos!" jerked Bliss awake and electrified me.

The crashing sound of two ships coming together was familiar to us now. There was a pounding of feet above us, shouts, the clash of cutlasses. Then a young voice cried out, "The bastards are going over the side, mates!"

There was excited, delighted laughter. Then another young voice said, "There's no way to pull her off the reef. Remember your stations. We'll burn her to the waterline!"

That's when Bliss burst out of our cabin, and bumped into a whiskered but young American sailor. He nearly dropped the torch he carried. I'll never forget the startled expression on his face!

"We're prisoners aboard," I said.

The sailor quickly gained his composure. "Get on deck. Ask for Stephen Decatur, ladies. We'll take you off when this hulk is well alight."

Wisps of smoke seemed to come from every corner of the ship when we'd clambered up the ladder to the deck. Standing near the rail was a slender young man, a cap cocked on the side of his head, arms crossed. Behind him were the masts of the ketch.

"Prisoners?" he said when he saw us.

"Yes."

Turning, he peered down over the rail. "You Catalano," he called. "Steady on the rope ladder. Two ladies coming your way." Turning to me, he said in a matter-of-fact voice, "Be careful and don't fall to the deck of my ketch."

He took Bliss's elbow, then mine, to help us over the rail. His men were gathering now from all parts of the ship, their well-rehearsed work done, and Stephen Decatur was calmly calling the roll.

Catalano, the swarthy Sicilian pilot, greeted us both with a hug and kiss. His delighted grin was something to see.

"Saved you from the *renegados*, eh?" he said in strongly accented English. Slapping his thigh, he roared with laughter. "We've signed paid to Barbarossa this time, no? Singed the scoundrel's beard, yes?" Catalano was suddenly contrite and struck his forehead. *"Madre mia!* My manners. We see you below," and he took my arm. "Such a night's work!"

Decatur's bold raid had caught the Moors so completely by surprise that we aboard the ketch sailed out of the harbor to join the two other

118

American ships before the guns ringing the harbor could be brought to bear.

Our destination was Valletta on Malta, a port the British shared with American warships, far from their home ports to protect American shipping against the Barbary corsairs. Stephen Decatur told me this.

"The ship we burned was once my father's command. You're very tired, Miss Jeanette, but there are questions I must ask for my report."

There, in the small aftercabin of the ketch, the whole story poured out of me while Decatur listened intently, with only an occasional question. Once started, I couldn't stop. When I'd finished, my face was bathed with tears, and I was utterly drained.

"You're finally safe after a terrible time," Decatur said. "Whatever your plans are now, I'm at your service, and so is the United States Navy," he added with pride. "We haven't finished with that Tripoli scum yet."

It was stunning to realize that there was now a future for Bliss and me that I could plan! My prayers had been answered, but I wept again, this time for what might have been with Jamie Mc-Coy.

Dawn was breaking over the harbor of Valletta when our ships entered, and I saw both British and American flags whipping in the morning breeze. I couldn't swallow the lump in my throat.

BOOK TWO

CHAPTER 9

MANY TIMES I wonder what my future might have been if I'd sailed from Malta to England with my cousin, Cedric Fitzhugh. Maybe a cottage in Devon, or a town house in London. It would have been a quiet life, with children of my own, and a husband who cared for me and my comfort. There wouldn't have been a Thomas Townsend or an Edith Radcliff.

Africa's grim Skeleton Coast wouldn't be a memory, nor Table Mountain at Capetown. And I wouldn't be remembering those long nights that the stars burned down while we crossed the Indian Ocean.

Perhaps my sons and daughters would have borne me grandchildren who would listen to my stories when young, but patronize Grandma when they grew older, and disbelieve much of what I'd told them.

Would that have been a good life for me?

Malta, with its green hills and terraced farms, was heaven for Bliss and me, a place we could heal and rest. Tired as he was after the Tripoli raid, Stephen Decatur insisted on escorting Bliss and me to the Palace of the governor, Sir Richard Godwin.

When we were announced, Sir Richard came from having luncheon with Lady Godwin and Cedric Fitzhugh. We must have been a queer sight, fitted out in sailor cast-offs given us aboard the ketch, but Sir Richard didn't raise an eyebrow when Stephen introduced us.

"Sir Richard, this young women tells me she is a British citizen," he said about me. "We rescued her last night in Tripoli harbor." Stephen paused, and his face flushed. "Jeanette, you've told me everything but your last name."

"It was de Verlaine," I said, "and before that DuBois, but my mother was Ouida Fitzhugh before she married in Haiti."

Sir Richard was a tall, thin man, with slightly stooped shoulders and a craggy face. Now his eyes widened with surprise, and both bushy eyebrows shot up.

"My word! I do believe your cousin is lunching with Lady Godwin and me right now," he said. "Your name was mentioned, and the poor chap thinks you were done in during the slave revolt."

He'd staggered me. I'd met him only once while I was in England, but I remembered Cedric well because he took me to tea when he visited the school.

"Do forgive me." Sir Richard steadied me on my feet. "You must be very tired. I'll call Lady Godwin for you and your servant."

Cedric hurried to the marble-floored anteroom of the palace with Lady Godwin. He was older than I remembered, with less hair, but his loud voice was the same.

"Jeanette! I do say!" There was an echo in the spacious anteroom, and he'd aroused it. "Where the devil have you been?"

Lady Godwin was a matronly woman, with a kind face, but she had a sharp tongue. "Cedric, you fool! Can't you see the poor girl is about to faint?"

"I never faint," I told her, and promptly did.

It was Stephen who caught me in his arms.

I was in a bedroom when I revived, with Lady Godwin fussing over me, and a bustle of activity in the background. Bliss was gone. "Where is she?" I asked.

"Your servant?"

"Yes."

"She's being cared for in the servants' rooms," Lady Godwin said. "Is Bliss a slave, dear?"

"Yes." To the look of disapproval on Lady Godwin's face, I said, "But I intend to set her free as soon as possible."

She patted my hand, then felt my pulse. "You do seem to be all right now. I'd imagine it was the excitement, and the relief. The American naval officer told us something of what you've been through before returning to his ship. These Maltese girls are my personal maids," Lady Godwin said, indicating with a nod the pair in long black dresses. "We'll get you bathed now, and then you'll want to sleep. I know how anxious you must be to talk with Cedric, but you really are exhausted." She paused, then said, "My, but doesn't he have a foghorn voice."

There was a twinkle in her eyes.

I laughed. "He certainly does."

"I imagine he got it before he left the army to join the foreign office," she said. She patted my cheek, then bent to kiss my forehead. "In just a little while you'll be right as rain, dear, and then we'll see."

When she was gone, the maids took over.

Sir Richard and Lady Godwin treated me as if I was royalty, and I enjoyed every minute of it. She called in her seamstress, a wrinkled little Maltese woman, to fit me out with a wardrobe. A carriage and driver were at my disposal. The third day I was on the island, Sir Richard held a reception in my honor. The Americans were invited, as well as the British, and that was the last time I saw Stephen Decatur.

Cousin Cedric had arranged passage for me to England within two weeks. Word had gone to the Fitzhughs that I was coming. "They are killing the fatted calf," he assured me. "They bloody well should, you know. The family never treated Ouida right. But then she could be cheeky herself."

It was at the reception I met Thomas Townsend. I particularly noticed the tall, spare man with a streak of gray in his hair because he wasn't in uniform. Nearly all the other men were. Yet Thomas was tanned and looked uncomfortable in civilian clothes. He was either shy or rude, I decided, because he didn't join the line of men and their wives waiting to meet me. Instead, he stood across the room and stared at me, pretending that he wasn't.

I caught his eye and smiled. He quickly glanced around, to make sure I was smiling at him, then grinned and winked.

Look at us, he seemed to be saying. *We shouldn't be here, but they don't know it.*

I winked at him.

The collation had been served, and the guests were leaving the palace, when I stepped out on the terrace overlooking the harbor. Thomas stood with his back to me at the stone railing, smoking a cigar as he studied the ships. When he sensed my presence, he turned and threw away the cigar.

"Hello," I said.

"Yes." Far from being a handsome man, with his beaklike nose, and large mouth, there was humor as well as strength printed in his face. "Hello."

"You don't like to stand in line, do you?"

"Did too much of it when I was a kid. You stood in line for everything at the orphanage. I can't get the habit again." His eyes admired my dress—or was it my figure? "I have a daughter back in Liverpool nearly as old as you," he said. "She's a pretty thing, too."

"Why didn't you bring your wife to my reception? Like all the other wives, she must wonder how many times I've been raped."

That bold remark didn't make him wince. "My wife died two years ago," he said. "But she wouldn't have wondered, she would have asked. You'd have liked my Gwen."

"I'm sorry about your wife."

"I am, too."

"You miss her terribly, don't you?" I said.

"Yes." Thomas sighed. "My ship doesn't quite take her place." He pointed out a proud, four-masted ship, painted as black as the *Salem Witch* had been, but nearly twice as large. "From here I'm bound for India and points east with a mixed cargo and some passengers. It's going to be a very long voyage."

"I can imagine it will be."

Thomas bit the end off another cigar, and carefully lit it, not bothering to ask my permission, because he knew I wouldn't object.

"Her name is the *Nancy Freeman,* out of Liverpool and well-found. I own two others in the Atlantic trade," he said. "I'll be sailing in a week."

"I'm bound for England," I told him.

Thomas nodded. "I know."

I stood beside him to view the harbor. Lights twinkled aboard each ship and were reflected by the dark water. When I reached England, I was going to miss the sea.

"One of your Barbary pirates is in the dock tomorrow," Thomas told me. "A big Senegalese, one of Barbarossa's men. Came sailing here in a dhingy, and someone recognized him."

The one who'd carried Bliss from the *Salem Witch,* and later tried to console us!

"How do you know this?" I asked.

"I've talked with him." Thomas watched me closely. "It was yesterday. No one else spoke his native tongue."

"Why did he take such a chance?" I asked.

"Your servant."

"What will happen to him?"

"He'll be hanged, probably."

"That can't happen! He was good to Bliss and me. Do you know his name?"

"Ishmael. He was a king once, before the slavers got him." Thomas smoked quietly for a moment. "Does your servant love the man?"

"I don't know. I'll have to ask her."

"If she does, you have the ear of Sir Richard," Thomas said. "I'd advise you to act quickly."

When Bliss heard that Ishmael had come to Malta to find her, she cried. "He's a good man, Jeanette," she said. "A slave like me."

I went to Sir Richard and told him of our experience with Ishmael. When he'd turned the matter over in his mind, he agreed to talk with the man and asked Thomas to interpret. I went with them.

Ishmael was chained to one stone wall of a narrow, damp dungeon, shackled hand and foot. But he hadn't been tortured, and he immediately asked about Bliss through Thomas.

I told him she was well and had asked about him.

"This one is a very proud man," Thomas said, after they'd spoken in Ishmael's language for some time. "He came to take Bliss back to Senegal and risked his life. Before he dies tomorrow, he wants to see her again."

Sir Richard had been quietly watching and listening. "Who gave the information against him?" he asked the jailer, hovering in the corridor outside the dungeon.

"Captain Joshua Roberts, Sir William."

"I see." Sir Richard fingered his lower lip. "Do you know the man?" he asked Thomas.

"I do, but we've never been friendly."

"Would you care to state a reason?" Sir Richard asked.

"He commands a slaver," Thomas said. "I've no use for the black ivory trade, and never have had. I belong to the Emancipation Society."

"Hmm." Sir Richard studied Ishmael for a moment, and the black man's eyes didn't shift. "I've quite a bit against the institution myself, Townsend. What do you suggest we do here?"

"Well, a friend of mine from Liverpool, Captain Jenkins, lifts his hook tomorrow to coast down the African continent, and he could use a good hand."

"What about Bliss, if she wants to go?" I asked.

"Jenkins could be persuaded to take her," Thomas said. "He's a member of the society, too."

Sir Richard frowned. "Whitehall thinks I'm too lax in my administration of this island, as it is. If I release this man without a trial, Roberts will tattle to the foreign office." He glanced at me, with a twinkle in his eyes. "Your cousin Cedric came down to slap my wrist again."

"Joshua Roberts won't tattle." Thomas smiled grimly. "Smuggling is a serious crime against the crown."

"So it is," Sir Richard agreed, "but we get devilish little cooperation from your captains as to which ones of you do and which don't."

"I didn't just tell you Roberts is a smuggler," Thomas said. "I simply state two unrelated facts."

"So you did." Sir Richard chuckled, then made up his mind. "We'll free this man, and Captain Townsend will make the arrangements for him to leave Malta. In the meantime," he told Thomas, "Ishmael is in your custody."

"Agreed."

"If your servant wants to join him in his exile from the British Empire," Sir Richard told me, "that can be arranged, if you'll set her free."

"I've done so once, but it didn't work out," I said. "As far as I'm concerned, Bliss is as free as the wind, if she wants to be."

When Sir Richard and I got into his carriage, Thomas and Ishmael were walking side by side down toward the harbor.

Bliss wasn't too easily persuaded. "I will always belong to you, Jeanette," she said with tears in her eyes.

"Don't you like Ishmael?"

"He's from my tribe," Bliss said.

"He was once a king, Bliss."

"Ishmael came here for me." Hers was a self-satisfied smile, but then she frowned. "Maybe he has other wives in Senegal."

"You can ask him."

"He's on a ship. Will you go with me?" she asked.

"Certainly I will."

I'd arranged with Thomas, before we parted, for a boat to be waiting at the wharf that evening, so Bliss and I were rowed out to the *Nancy Freeman*. Thomas and Ishmael were waiting on the deck.

Thomas told Bliss, "He says he no longer has any wealth, and that there is a new king. He doesn't know how his tribe will receive him after all these years, coming back empty-handed. The Senegalese are great traders," he explained. "Ishmael says times will be hard at first, and that he may have to become a farmer."

Bliss had listened intently, her head to one side, eyes shifting from Ishmael, to Thomas, and back again, with side glances at me. She fingered the pouch of diamonds suspended around her neck, absentmindedly, I thought, but it gave me an idea.

"Ask him if his people trade in diamonds," I said to Thomas.

He asked my question, and Ishmael nodded.

"Bliss wears her dowry about her throat," I said. "Do you want to go with Ishmael, Bliss?"

"Has he more wives?" Bliss asked Thomas.

"No, he hasn't," Thomas said, without asking the question. "We've talked about that."

We embraced, I kissed Bliss good-bye, and she went to Ishmael. Thomas waved a hand of dismissal, and they disappeared down a gangway. Bliss didn't even have a backward glance for me!

"We'll go ashore and I'll walk with you to the palace," Thomas said. "We have something to discuss."

It was a long walk, through narrow, twisting streets, and Thomas smoked a cigar and was quiet most of the way. There was a fountain in a small, cobbled square, with a bench beside it, and we sat there to rest a few minutes. In one of the small, shuttered houses surrounding the little square, someone played a lute, singing a Maltese song.

"That's a love song," Thomas said.

"Do you speak Maltese, too?"

"No. You'd have to be tone-deaf not to tell by the sound of it." His strong hand covered mine that I'd clasped in my lap. "I sail sooner than I thought, the day after tomorrow," Thomas said. "The Miss Radcliff I waited for arrived from Italy sooner than she expected."

"Thomas, I'm sorry to hear that," I said, and for the first time probed my feelings about this man. The depth of them came as a shock. Yet he was old enough to be my father.

"You're a widow," Thomas said. "I've lost Gwen."

"Two more unrelated facts?" I asked.

Thomas grinned. "I'm a rich man with a country estate, house in London, another in Winchester not far from the cathedral. I've found no reason to stay in England these past two years, but I might change my mind."

"I thought only women did that," I said.

He'd been staring at our hands while he talked, but now he looked up. His expression was tense, and there was a new light in his eyes. Even his voice had changed.

"I've wanted you since I first saw you at that reception the other day. I willed you to come out on the terrace and you did. By the way, I'm talking about marriage," he said, as if it was an afterthought.

"I thought you might be, Thomas."

"You can't love me on such short notice, and I'm not an easy man, especially at sea," he confessed. "But I want you in my bed and across the breakfast table."

"Have I time to think about it?"

"Yes." Thomas took out his gold watch. "Five minutes."

Seeing England again, and being on the charity of the Fitzhughs, however well-meaning they were, no longer had any appeal.

"We'll be married," I told him.

CHAPTER 10

WITH A deep sigh of relief, Thomas snapped shut the lid of his watch, and put it away. "Will you excuse me for a minute?"

"Well . . ."

He strode toward the house from which we'd heard the lute and singing, and knocked on the door. When the tall Maltese boy answered, Thomas pressed bills into his hand and came back.

"Actually, I'm deaf as a post when it comes to music," he confessed. "You'll have to remind me to stand and uncover for 'God Save the King'."

"You bribed that boy!" I accused.

"Of course I did."

"You're a scoundrel, Thomas!" But I couldn't help laughing.

Taking my hands, Thomas lifted me to my feet. I was locked in his arms, then, and his mouth found mine. It was a dizzying kiss, and his hands slid down my back to press my softness against his hardness, but then he scooped me up in his arms.

"What are you doing?" I gasped.

"Carrying you," he said, striding off up the street as if he was unburdened. "We don't want the bride tired for her wedding, or her wedding night."

Thomas was breathing easily. "Sir Robert will marry us tomorrow," he announced. "I've already spoken to him and to Lady Godwin. Cedric has agreed to give you away. We'll make it a quiet wedding, in the chapel at the palace. Is there anything wrong with my plans?"

"You're sure of yourself, aren't you?" I pouted. Thomas kissed me.

"My daughter is a brat, but you don't have to get along with her," he said. "God knows, I don't. You and Edith Radcliff will be the only women aboard my ship for this voyage. She's a Bible-thumper."

"A—what?"

"Missionary to the heathen, off beyond Singapore somewhere. Plain sort of woman, in my opinion, but pleasant enough, and knows enough medicine to act as ship's doctor."

We'd reached the palace gate, and Thomas set me back on my feet. "What else do you need to know?"

"Do you love me?"

Thomas gave me a quizzical stare. "Now, how would I know a thing like that on this short notice? We've time to find out aboard the *Nancy Freeman*." His second kiss and embrace was more hungry than the first one had been. "Now, my daughter would ask a silly question like that of a man."

"What's her name?"

"Judith."

"I may like her."

"That you may," he admitted. "I do myself, some of the time."

The gateman had answered our ring, and the wrought-iron gates creaked open.

"Good night." Thomas gave my bottom an affectionate pat. "We'll be married late tomorrow afternoon. Agreed?"

"Yes, but it was nice of you to ask."

"Sir Robert and Lady Godwin have arranged a little reception after our wedding," Thomas told me. "No more than a few hundred people. Good night, Jeanette."

He strode off toward the harbor, whistling off-key. I wondered if I'd be able to break him of that habit!

* * *

Lady Godwin fussed over me before the wedding as if I were her virginal daughter. When we'd said our vows privately, and Cousin Cedric had claimed his bride's kiss, I found Thomas hadn't exaggerated. There were easily two hundred people for the wedding reception!

Again I was the center of attention, the women less guarded and speculative this time.

Our bridal suite had a breathtaking view of the harbor.

Since the night before, I'd been in an agony of indecision. How well versed in sex should I appear to be when we went to bed? Would Thomas expect me to be shy and tentative the first time we coupled? Or had he guessed I'd be no neophyte?

Then the recollection of my wedding night with Hippolyte intruded on my memory, and there was a twinge of fear that Thomas might turn beast as soon as we reached our wedding chamber. This was a fruitless worry.

"I'll retire to the adjoining room while you undress, Jeanette," he said, and his voice caressed my name.

Lady Godwin's gnome of a seamstress had somehow managed a frothy white satin nightdress for me, trimmed in chantilly lace. When Thomas came back, stripped to his drawers and with a

140

glass of champagne in each hand, I'd just slipped it over my head.

We toasted a happy and contented life.

"I feel damned silly in these drawers," Thomas said ruefully. "Mustn't offend my blushing bride, with all of me in full sight, I told myself."

"Thoughtful, Thomas, but you do look a bit silly," I said.

"Thank you." With an ironic bow, he turned his broad back and dropped the drawers.

When Thomas faced me again, his muscular body reminded me of Jamie's. He must have sensed the general direction of my thoughts because he said, "Each of us reminds the other of someone else, Jeanette."

"True, but am I that transparent?"

"We'll answer that another time." Thomas smiled, and his eyes forgave me. "Now, then, to the business at hand," he said in a brisk voice. "That's a most charming nightgown, my darling, but it isn't transparent, and don't you find yourself a bit overdressed?"

"For what you so obviously have in mind, sir, I do," I said.

Thomas glanced down. "It does speak for me, doesn't it?"

"I'd say so." Turning my back, as he had done, I lifted the satin gown over my head and dropped it to the floor.

I heard the sharp intake of his breath.

Hands clasped at the nape of my neck, I slowly turned to face Thomas.

"Magnificent!" he breathed.

I touched the smooth mound and asked, "Do you mind? They were preparing me for life in a harem."

A blush darkened his face under its tan, and I loved him for it. Sinking to his knees, he kissed me lightly there, murmuring, "Mind? I do not."

I was lifted in his strong arms, and stretched on the bed very gently, as if Thomas was offering a sacrifice to Aphrodite—and so he was, I discovered.

"Slowly and gently, first," I heard him tell himself.

It was with a blissful sigh that I relaxed, to let him have his way with my body, but I couldn't control a shudder of pure delight when Thomas finally entered my intimate shrine.

He used me as one might a fine musical instrument, gently coaxing crescendos from it, each more thrilling than the one before, finally reaching a fortissimo climax.

Instead of exhaustion, I only felt refreshed, and eager for him to take me again.

Thomas paced to the window to light a cigar while he admired the night view. "I'm not handy enough with words to make the proper comment," he said over his shoulder, in a husky voice. "Will you forgive me?"

"Only on one condition."

"And what would that be?" he asked.

"That you finish that cigar rather quickly, and come back to bed. You've inspired me, Thomas."

The cigar cut a fiery arc in the night.

It was my turn, and with my lips and trailing fingertips, soft pressures here, firmer ones there, denying him, offering, only to withdraw, then offer again.

"You vixen!" he finally gasped.

"Slowly and gently, Thomas," I mocked him.

"How much of this do you think a man can stand, woman?"

"We'll soon know, won't we?"

"Yes!" His hands reached to cover my throbbing breasts.

I'd finished teasing.

The night was too short. Together we watched a blazing red sun come up out of the blue sea, while a soft morning breeze ruffled the harbor's water.

My head was on his shoulder. One hand felt the strong beat of his heart.

Thomas kissed my hair. "Why do you wear it so short?" he asked.

"A whim of mine," I lied. "Would you like it longer?"

"I think I might."

"Then you shall have it, Thomas. I'll be your Rapunzel."

He chuckled. "Not quite that long, darling."

"That's the second time you've called me your darling," I said.

"Do you mind?"

I sighed. "Only if you don't call me that again, my very dear husband."

"And that," Thomas said, touching the tip of my nose with a finger, "is the first time you've called me husband. I rather like the ring of it."

"Do you now, husband?"

"Yes, darling."

I sighed again. "Was the night too long for you, Thomas?" I asked. "Neither of us got much sleep, I'm afraid."

"It was too short," he said.

I sat up. "I've just remembered something."

"What is that?"

"How hungry I am," I said, and added, when his glance was inquiring, "for *food*."

"Oh, yes, food," Thomas mused. "We do need to keep our strength up, don't we?"

"We most certainly do!"

Thomas rang for our breakfast.

Before it came, I remembered to slip into my nightdress.

Thomas pointed out the ship taking Bliss and Ishmael to Senegal. "Their sailing was delayed," he explained, "but I got them safely aboard. I had to trust Jenkins with knowledge of the diamonds."

"So you know about them?"

He nodded. "Bliss told me. She loved you, you know. Will you miss her?"

"I did, but I don't now."

Edith Radcliff wasn't as plain a woman as Thomas had led me to believe. Eyes that were a rather startling shade of violent were her most arresting single feature, but her long body was full-breasted, and her waist narrow.

Edith was tall for a woman, and crowned with dark auburn hair she wore coiled on either side of her head. Her complexion was pale, nearly sallow, her mouth wide, but sensitive.

When we were introduced, she gave me an unsmiling handshake, and I sensed shyness in Edith that she disguised with her brisk manner.

"Very pleased to meet you, Mrs. Townsend."

I'd just come aboard the *Mary Freeman* and Thomas was busy getting her ready to clear Valletta's busy harbor.

"I'm glad to know you, and it's Jeanette, please, since we're to be shipmates," I said.

"Of course." Edith had a warm smile. "I congratulate you for finding a fine husband. Some of us aren't that fortunate and must remain spinsters, but God knows what's best."

"Thomas says that you're a missionary," I said.

"A medical missionary," Edith explained. "I also preach the gospel to the heathen, in my own poor way, but a soul needs a sound body."

145

"I agree with that, Edith. Where did you study medicine?"

"A doctor friend taught me all that I know. Women are not encouraged to study medicine in our merry England, you'll understand." She made a face. "We're only supposed to cook, bear children and, if delicate, swoon at every opportunity."

I laughed. "It was much the same in Haiti, and I do know something about England." I told her of my mother and of my schooling. "Where are you going?"

"To join a small mission in China." She was eager to talk with me, but we were in the men's way here on deck. "Will you come to my cabin, Jeanette, before we get knocked overboard?"

"Yes. I'd like to hear about your work," I told her. "There's much I don't know about missions."

Edith's cabin was small but neat and not cramped. There was a shelf above her bunk for medical books and a Bible, a washstand and, in a cubicle, a lavatory.

"Dr. Phelps has started a small mission in Whampoa," Edith explained. "I've agreed to come out and join him in his work. I'll be the only white woman of good character in Whampoa, Dr. Phelps writes. It's a wonderful opportunity, don't you think? To be useful, I mean."

"Where is Whampoa?" I asked.

"It's the treaty port for Canton, on the Pearl River."

"What made you decide to be a missionary?" I asked.

Edith was thoughtful. "I don't suppose it was any one thing in my twenty-seven years of life. My father was a vicar in a small country parish, and my mother died when I was twelve. I was their only child, so I tried hard to take her place. I learned to like the quiet life and serving people."

There were other reasons she'd chosen her way of life, I knew, but we were still acquaintances, and not yet friends, so I didn't press.

Thomas wasn't as much a changed man aboard his ship as he'd led me to believe. At least as far as I was concerned, he wasn't. His first mate, Bob Dillard, was competent enough to conn the *Mary Freeman* during the early days of our voyage, so the captain had plenty of time to enjoy his new bride.

I sketched my past lightly for Thomas, and there were no probing questions or signs of jealousy. I skipped over Jamie. I wasn't ready to share him with anyone.

On a fair, calm day we slipped through the Strait of Gibraltar, and started down Africa's bulging west coast, standing well out to sea with a sharp lookout for pirate sails.

We didn't put in at Dakar, and that was just as well. Bliss was part of my past, and now had her fate in her own hands. But I couldn't put out of my mind the brief interlude we'd had aboard the *Salem Witch*. It had somehow been a moment of sweetness, rather than depravity, or so it seemed to me. I could better understand what drove handsome Celia and delicate and shy Marianne to seek the lesbian pleasures that got them expelled from Miss Wentworth's in disgrace.

Try as I might, satiated as Thomas kept me those first few weeks at sea, I couldn't still warmness in my loins when Edith and I were alone. Once or twice, I caught her glancing at me, when she thought I was unaware, in such a way that it made me wonder if she didn't want to taste my body. This only added warmth to my loins.

A long sea voyage becomes a succession of uneventful days and nights, and boredom soon sets in. I had much less reason to become bored, especially during the nights, than Edith had, closeted with her medical texts, or making endless rounds of the deck. Yet I began to become bored, despite lusty Thomas. It was then a new dimension crept into our lovemaking.

Under the flick of Madame Phyrigia's ivory-handled lash, I'd learned the various bizarre positions well, and other secrets to please a man. Thomas must have known more about my ordeal as a slave of Barbarossa than I told him, because he gently encouraged me to apply my new knowledge.

I did so, shyly at first, then more boldly as he

responded, and we filled our nights with many Moorish and Arabian pleasures.

"We British are just too damned prudish about sex," he told me, after one of our more strenuous efforts. "It must be the bloody climate."

He learned that he didn't have to apologize for fingermarks in surprising places on my fair skin—not too often, for Thomas had no sadistic streak in his nature, but often enough.

Boredom fled when I could ponder during the days aboard the *Mary Freeman* what new delights the night would bring.

CHAPTER 11

THE *Mary Freeman* was coursing south with a
bone in her teeth, out about 150 miles from the
Ivory Coast of West Africa, when the forward
lookouts sighted the wallowing ship that flew the
flag of Portugal upside-down. I'd just joined Thomas on the quarterdeck, with a mug of rum-laced
tea, to find him talking with Edith.

Edith was too seasick to leave her cabin the
first week of the voyage, but now she was up and
around the ship.

Thomas barked an order at the young Dutch
helmsman. The sinking ship was about five miles
to windward, so bringing the *Mary Freeman*

around, on a direct bearing with the sinking ship, was no problem.

Thomas studied the ship in distress through the glass, then told Edith and me, "It's a blasted Portugee slaver!"

"Are you going to help them?" I asked.

"No, we just let them all drown," Thomas said in a sarcastic voice.

"But you hate slavery and slave ships," I said.

"Don't be a little fool!" he snapped. "We don't ignore anyone's distress signal. That's the first law of the sea. What about the blacks stacked like cordwood beneath her decks?"

"Well, I just asked." It was the first time Thomas had chastised me.

The *Mary Freeman* was leaping through the water, with wind-driven spray wetting her decks.

Thomas focussed on the slave ship again, then swore, "Damn them! They're lightening ship by tossing blacks overboard."

I took the glass, and saw two husky white men snatch up a naked black woman by her arms and legs, to throw her among the bobbing heads that already surrounded the ship. But now they'd sighted us, signal flags fluttered, and the jettisoning of their human cargo stopped.

"They're screaming for us to hurry," Thomas said. "Anybody but a stupid Portugee would know if I crowded on more canvas in this wind I'd drive my ship under."

Bob Dillard reported. "Get the whaleboat ready to launch," Thomas ordered.

"Aye. I'll need six men to man her in this sea."

"Arm them with pistols. You'll find yourself in a dangerous situation out there should they unchain their black cargo. And get this, Dillard. You take command of the situation the second your feet touch her deck. I want every black in her hold aboard the *Mary Freeman* before we take off the master and his crew. Shoot anyone who interferes."

"Aye, sir." From his expression, I gathered that Bob Dillard approved of this order.

Thomas turned to Edith and me. "You women clear the wardroom to serve as an infirmary. Get a steward to help you. This close to Africa, we won't have too many sick blacks, but there's sure to be some."

"I'm praying there won't be too many," Edith said, beginning to roll up the sleeves of her dress.

"You'd better pray we don't take any aboard with the plague," Thomas said darkly.

Other passengers aboard were six men sharing the ship's steerage, Welsh miners bound for Australia to prospect for gold. They were surly and sometimes quarrelsome among themselves. Now they waited on Thomas in a tight-knit group.

"You wouldn't be about taking nigras off yon ship, would you?" their husky ringleader asked.

Thomas stared him down before saying, "Get off my quarterdeck, and take your friends, sir."

"Now, there, governor. We're meaning no harm," the man whined. "It's our health that worries us."

Thomas turned his back, seized a belaying pin, and said over his shoulder, "Clear the quarterdeck, and that's an order."

The ringleader's jaw set stubbornly. "We ain't your crew, governor. We be passengers."

Before Thomas could whirl around, and lay the belaying pin on the side of the miner's skull, Edith stepped between them. "How very fortunate, Mr. Grice," she said. "Mrs. Townsend and I need the help of you and your men."

"They ain't *my* men. In Wales . . ."

"But they will follow your lead, won't they?" Edith broke in. "Yes, I'm sure they will. Come along. We need you in the ship's wardroom."

That was the first time I saw Edith Radcliff exert her qiuet authority in a dangerous situation, and, as another woman, I was proud of her.

Below decks she took command. Somehow she'd learned the name of every man. "Put that bench over here, if you please, Mr. Grice," she would say. "Now, Mr. Llewellyn, please move that table, and get the cots set up."

She sent me with a steward to bring up her slender supply of medicines and the medical books. We broke into the linen locker for sheets and blankets. Within half an hour, despite the tossing of the ship, we'd cleared the wardroom and had a neat infirmary.

Edith stayed below when I returned to rejoin Thomas. She had the miners sitting around a table and was serving them sandwiches she'd sent the steward to bring.

"God will bless you for wanting to help me with any patients," she was telling them.

Then she began reading appropriate passages to the chewing, spellbound men from the small Bible she always carried.

The whaleboat had returned with its first pitiful cargo. As each naked, shivering body was handed up, Edith's miners carried it on a litter to our infirmary. Every cot was occupied, with children laid two to a cot, when the whaleboat pushed off for the sinking ship again.

I found myself in charge on deck. Some of the respect Edith commanded had rubbed off on me.

"Those are the worst, Mrs. Townsend," Dillard called up from the whaleboat. "You have twenty-five head, with fifty to come."

Two more boatloads before it was the turn of the crew. The slave ship's decks were nearly awash. No heads bobbed in the water, I noticed. All who were thrown into the sea before we came must have drowned.

I stayed by the starboard rail, watching the rescue and waiting to take some child or woman by the hand. I couldn't forget the apprehensive faces of our litter cases.

Torn from their friends and families by their own kind, sold to the white man, packed in the filthy hold of a slave ship in tiers, shipwreck was a new and unfamiliar terror to them.

Dillard had finally done his work, and the slaver had gone down. Groups of men, women, and children lay on our slippery decks. Their stench was overpowering!

The crew of the slaver and their captain were bunched around Thomas on the quarterdeck. Some sort of argument was raging.

Dillard and his armed men stood in a loose circle around the group.

I saw Thomas stab a finger at the swarthy, bowlegged slaver captain, and heard him shout, "This is my ship, and she goes where I send her, mister!" He lowered his voice, but I could still hear him. "We'll put your cargo ashore where they'll come to no further harm, and that's final. We've food and drink enough on board to carry you and them for three days."

I went to the wardroom to see how I could help Edith.

During the next forty-eight hours, Edith and I existed in hell. Without the assistance of the Welshmen, we couldn't have made it. There were two babies to deliver, dying children to comfort, a madwoman to contend with, and stinking black flesh to bathe.

Edith, hollow-eyed and staggering with fatigue, bore us all up. Because of her example, I couldn't shirk even the nastiest jobs. I saw Thomas only once, when he came to see how we were managing.

"How are you getting on, Jeanette?" he asked, munching a sandwich Edith had given him.

"As cheerfully as possible." My heart cried for his gaunt face with its bristling beard. "Are you all right?"

"Aye. We've rigged awnings for the others on deck, and posted guards. We'll put them on the beach somewhere in the Bight of Benin. That way they'll be safe from the slave pens."

"Will they get home?" I asked.

"Most of them won't." Thomas was hoarse. "The ones who don't starve will be captured; to be enslaved by their own kind if they're lucky, to be gutted and roasted on a spit if they're not. It's a hell of a thing."

"Then why did we save them from drowning?" I asked.

"The Portugee thought we did it because they were his property."

"Weren't they? He paid for them. They'd be better off returned to him, wouldn't they?"

"What the hell would you have me do, woman?"

"I don't know."

Edith joined us. "Mr. Townsend, we've exhausted the ship's store of medicines, as well as my own."

"Do what you can," he said wearily. "Accra is our nearest port. If we put in there, I'll be arrested for stealing his slaves from the Portugee."

"You must be very tired, Thomas," Edith said. "Can't you get some rest?"

"Doesn't your Bible say there's no rest for the wicked?" he asked. "Among the crew there may be some quinine, and break out all the rum and whiskey you can use. That's the best I can do. Now I've got to get back to tending my ship."

When he was gone, Edith said, "I envy you your husband, Jeanette." She brushed a strand of hair away from her forehead. "I loved a man like him once."

"Why didn't you marry him? Did he die?"

"No." She smiled. "He married another woman. I've forgiven him for it, but that decision cost me many hours of prayer."

"I'm sorry, Edith," I said. "I couldn't pray for any man who deserted me for another woman."

"With you, Jeanette, that occasion would never arise," Edith told me.

"My first husband was murdered—by a slave. He deserved to be killed. A man I loved was murdered, too. I'll tell you about it sometime." I was as tired as Edith was. "Why are we talking like this?"

"Because we're tired and silly women. Come on, there's still work to be done."

* * *

After he had put the blacks ashore, with all the provisions we could spare, Thomas set the Portugee captain and his crew adrift in an extra boat off the port of Accra.

Part of the mixed cargo aboard the *Mary Freeman* was consigned to Walvis Bay in Southwest Africa just above the barren and dangerous stretch of land called the Skeleton Coast.

"It's rightly named," Thomas told me. "No safe anchorage for the length of it until you reach Capetown and Table Bay. Storms off the South Atlantic pound it and try to drive ships on the many uncharted reefs. If you get ashore after a shipwreck, there's desert and savages."

"Can't we stay well away from it?" I asked.

"No. Too far offshore, and you're bucking the Benguela Current and adverse winds. Anyway, we're not well enough provisioned now to lose any time at sea. My charts are better this voyage than the ones I had the last time I came this way. We'll raise Table Mountain, so don't worry."

We were one day out from Accra when my head started aching. It wasn't my time of month yet, but I thought the strain of nursing the blacks had been too much—that this would be an early period—so I didn't worry about it. Only when my headache became too intense to bear did I go to Edith.

I found her in her cabin, studying a medical

text. "Come in and sit down," she invited. Then she looked at me more closely. "You're looking feverish, Jeanette."

I felt my forehead. "I guess I am. It's my headache I've come about, though. Is any medicine left that will help? It's killing me."

"Let's take your temperature." She got up and thrust a thermometer under my tongue, then her cool fingers were on my pulse. "I don't like this, Jeanette."

"I wish someone else had my head," I told her and giggled. "Could you use another head, Edith? Take mine."

She pushed me by the shoulders to lie down on her bunk. I remember her concerned frown and her cool hands undressing me.

My head had stopped aching. "You can have my head, but don't steal my husband," I said. "What about my body? Do you want it?" Her features were hazy and blurred. "Bliss had it— my body, I mean—and I was taking her body . . ." I tried to sit up, and Edith let me—but just long enough to slip a fresh nightgown over my head. ". . . taking her body," I rambled on, "but someone came. Who was that, Edith?" She put a cold cloth on my head. "What happened to Hippolyte?"

"Hush, dear, you're delirious." Edith's cool fingers covered my lips.

She was gone from my fever dreams, then. So

was Thomas, and the *Mary Freeman*. Bliss and I were children again.

We were running through a field filled with flowers, toward a river filled with silver water, and I was very thirsty.

"The worst is over now, Thomas." Edith's voice? Yes. "Her fever broke an hour ago. Now I have to keep her warm."

He asked a question.

"No," Edith answered. "What she's been forced to endure would have killed me—or any other woman. I can assure you of that."

"No word now of what she's told us in her delirium," Thomas cautioned.

"My dear, you know me better than that by this time." Edith was scornful. "Get back to minding your ship. She may be your wife, but Jeanette is my patient."

I kept my eyes closed, and waited awhile before I spoke. "May I please have a drink of water, Edith?" I asked when I opened them.

She greeted me with a tired smile. "Hello, there. You've been away awhile." She brought the water and sat on the side of the bunk while I drank it. "You've been a very sick girl."

"What day is this?"

"I've lost count. Don't worry about it. The ship is out of danger, and we'll soon reach Cape-town—and a hospital if you need one by then. I don't think you will," Edith said. "It's more likely that I will."

"Are you sick?" I asked.

"No, just tired."

I thanked her for taking care of me.

"It was my Christian duty to bathe you, change you, coax food down your gullet, and listen to you rave," Edith said, half-seriously. "By the way, you have a beautiful little body." Her eyes widened. "Now, why should I say a thing like that?"

"Because you noticed."

She met my eyes, then looked quickly away. "We have to change your nightgown—the one you have on is soaking wet. Do you think you can manage, or should I help?"

"Please help. I'm weak. I don't think I can do it myself."

"All right. Sit up." Edith was all nurse. "Careful you don't bump your head on my bookshelf."

She had to help me sit up and get out of the sweat-soaked gown. "We'd better bathe you," she said. "The steward just brought hot water, and I was about to do it, but Thomas came down."

"How is my husband?" I asked.

"As tired as I am. We went aground off the Skeleton Coast, and only his seamanship saved us all from drowning." Edith's hands, bathing my back, were lazy comfort. "When we reach Capetown next week, the ship will be laid up for repairs. Turn yourself over, Jeanette."

I managed, but it took all my strength.

"You've lost weight, dear, but you're still a beautiful woman," Edith said, and pressed my thighs apart to lay a gentle hand on my womanhood. "Did it hurt when they . . . plucked you down here?"

Tired as I was, I didn't want Edith to take her hand away, but I closed my eyes and said, "It's hard to remember now."

"I'm still a virgin," she said.

"I'm sorry."

CHAPTER 12

FORTUNATELY FOR US, this year the Dutch were on England's side in the fight against Napoleon, and Table Bay was filled with merchant ships and men-of-war flying the British flag. By the time we reached the Cape of Good Hope, and Capetown a day's sail beyond it, I was almost fully recovered.

The *Mary Freeman*'s bows had been breached when she ran aground along the Skeleton Coast, so the ship had to go in drydock, before taking aboard hides, dried fruit, wine, and brandy for the run to India and the Far East.

It was a good feeling to have my land legs

back again, and to breathe Capetown's cool flower-scented air after sweltering in the tropics. While the ship was being repaired, Jan de Witt, the shipping agent for Thomas's company, invited us to stay with him in his home. Jan included Edith in his invitation.

"You will not, please, look down your nose at the way I live," he told Edith, when he found out she was a missionary. "In England, so much fuss about abolishing slavery!" Laughter shook his heavy paunch. "Nonsense. We Dutch are not so dumb. We are the practical people. The Bantu and Kaffir need harsh masters—it is all they understand."

Jan was a tall, square-shouldered man with hair so blond it was almost white, and a ruddy complexion from drinking Holland gin.

"You justify slavery by the Bible, I suppose," Edith said.

"*Ja.* Sometimes." His deep blue eyes twinkled. "I do when it is with a missionary I argue. Him." Jan nodded toward Thomas. "We talk the economics of it, but it is always the same. Slavery there will always be, those of you who pity the cheeky black devils will always be with us, too."

Jan de Witt's home was a sprawling white structure, high on the slope leading to Table Mountain, and set in the midst of extensive gardens tended by dozens of black slaves.

"Count the Cape Coloreds running loose on the grounds, and you'll see what Jan means by your disapproving of the way he lives," Thomas told Edith when we'd arrived at his home. "Part Kaffir, every one. Jan won't have a Bantu on the place."

He'd found mothers for his children among the many girl house-slaves. "He breeds his own harem stock on an upcountry farm," Thomas explained. "Just as you or I would breed horses."

"Or dogs," Edith said.

"Yes, or dogs," Thomas agreed.

"What does he do with the boys his *mares* produce?" I asked.

"Sells them to Arab slave-traders. There's a great demand for well-trained boys in Egypt and Arabia. Jan used to be a trader himself, before he got into shipping."

"And you do business with him," Edith accused.

Thomas grinned. "I'm a practical man. Jan is the best agent I have."

Capetown and the home of Jan de Witt was Edith's first encounter with the reality of slavery in civilized surroundings. Our experience aboard the *Mary Freeman* had let her glimpse, and me, too, the raw beginnings of life as a slave. But I'd lived among slaves all my life, and owned one.

Until my brief experience as Barbarossa's slave, I'd accepted slavery as a way of life. Yet now I had to examine my conscience. I'd been outraged to think Barbarossa was going to sell me—a *white* woman—into a Moorish or Arabian seraglio, and not as a wife, but as a concubine.

Word of the uprising on Haiti had reached Capetown well ahead of me, and had sent a shudder of terror through the colony. I learned that Dessalines had been assassinated. Christophe was the new king. The plantations were in ruins. Nobody was doing anything about it.

Jan de Witt was outraged. "You see what it comes to, this foolish talk of liberating slaves," he taxed Edith and Thomas at dinner one night. "You French were too lax," he accused me. When he'd swallowed a tumbler of gin, he went on. "We know how to deal with insolent slaves down here."

I couldn't resist saying, "That's what the planters on Haiti thought, and see what happened."

The Dutchman's face flushed a deeper red than it already was. "Laxity—that's what gives them the idea they can best their masters! It's the fault of you French."

Thomas was watching me from across the table, but I could tell nothing from his face as he twirled the stemmed wineglass. It was only an hour since we'd finished dinner, and Jan's gin bottle was almost empty.

Edith watched me, too, from the end of the table. She moved her head from side to side, as if to say, "Watch yourself—the man's drunk."

I'd been trying to answer Jan's probing questions about the uprising on Haiti, without relating too much about my own experiences. But I seemed to know less about what had happened than he did.

"Years ago you should have killed off every slave on the island and started importing more docile tribes," Jan told me. "It would have been a practical solution, *ja?*"

Thomas lit another cigar. What kind of diplomatic remark did he want me to make?

It was just then a slender, large-eyed black girl who couldn't have been more than twelve or thirteen, entered the dining room with a fresh bottle of the sweet yellow Dutch gin. When she reached to set it down on the table, Jan somehow jarred her elbow, and the gin spilled into the lap of his white linen suit.

Without a word, he reached out to dig fingers into a breast, twisting it to force the girl to her knees, then slapped her to the floor with the other hand.

There hadn't been a cry from the child, and there wasn't now. She got up and scrambled from the room. Thomas had half-risen from his chair, a pulse throbbing in his forehead. Edith stared at Jan, open-mouthed and pale from shock.

Intent on talking with me, Jan mopped at his lap with a napkin, oblivious to Edith and Thomas.

"Not practical, you think?" he asked.

The child returned with a wooden face, no tears in her eyes, and set another full bottle of

gin before him. Jan reached for the bottle to fill
his glass.

Thomas had settled back in his chair, but that
pulse still throbbed. Edith stared at the candles
on the white tablecloth.

"We French are too frugal to destroy our own
property, Herr de Witt," I said.

"*Ja!*" Jan laughed heartily. "Your wife has
a fine sense of humor," he complimented Thomas.

"Hasn't she?" Thomas said in a tight voice, and
pushed away from the table. "If you'll excuse
me, I'm tired tonight, Jan."

"I am, too." Edith rose.

"Good night, Herr de Witt," I said.

"*Ja.* We must talk again."

He was pouring another glass of gin as we
filed out of the dining room.

Edith told us goodnight and went to her room.

Alone in our guest room, both Thomas and I
were silent as we undressed. My emotions were
boiling, so I broke the silence when I flung my last
garment into a corner of the room, and exploded:
"That *stupid* Dutchman!"

"It's all right," Thomas said. "Jan will make
it up when he takes the girl into his bed tonight."

My head jerked up because I was too angry to
appreciate that it was an ironic remark. "Does he
save a little virgin for *you* when you come down
here?"

Thomas sat on the bed, turned me over his

knee, and smacked the right cheek of my bottom, and then the left.

I struggled to my feet. "Damn you!"

I made a fist, and with all my strength, hit him in the face.

Thomas didn't blink. "I don't understand," he said in a quiet voice.

I buried my face in my hands.

"I'm sorry, Jeanette."

"You couldn't!"

"Understand?"

"Yes!"

"I'll sleep on the couch in the dressing room," Thomas said.

There was cargo for European merchants in the port of Dar es Salaam on the African east coast. From there we'd cross the Indian Ocean.

Thomas and I had slept apart only that one night, but our marriage had changed. Neither of us ever spoke about my reaction to his playful slaps. I'd taught Thomas myself that from some pain a woman derives her sexual pleasure, but how could I explain Jamie, and my first night aboard the *Salem Witch?*

I didn't love Thomas enough to try. The ghost of Jamie slept with us.

Dar es Salaam is a stinking Arab-dominated slave trading center. Lithe young Arab girls, with their budding breasts, and stripling Arab boys, are traded to savage African nobility for their sons and daughters.

"God must have forgotten this place," Edith said after we'd gone ashore while the *Mary Freeman* was unloading cargo.

We'd just seen a line of black children, chained neck to neck, shuffle past to go aboard an Arab dhow. Within days they'd be playthings in Arabia, the more aggressive boys castrated to make them docile, the girls left to the mercy of harem wives when the sheik tired of their charms.

Only the two of us—and Thomas—had taken notice as the sad procession filed past. We were in the busy market square. It was a cacophony of shrill bargaining for chickens, eggs, goat meat, and dates. At the other end, a naked and shivering Arab girl child was being offered for sale to bored blacks.

"You'll have to cope with girl slavery in China, Edith," Thomas said. "For the poor, girls are their stock in trade."

"I often wonder what it must be like to *own* another person," Edith mused. "Can you tell me, Jeanette?"

"It's hard to describe." I remembered a pang of anger when Bliss asked me to set her free. *What right had she to ask that?* "Let me think about it, Edith."

Bliss belonged to Ishmael now, and in my heart, I was jealous.

Thomas knew. I could tell by the expression

on his face. *Was he jealous of my feelings about Bliss?* I didn't dare ask, and another strain was added to our marriage.

I've heard of a Chinese torture. The victim is stripped and bound, and then the executioner begins to inflict tiny cuts. There isn't too much pain until there are so many small wounds that the tortured one begins to bleed to death. Our marriage was becoming like that.

At Dar es Salaam, Thomas loaded Mozambique coffee and brandy aboard the *Mary Freeman* for Bombay, and took aboard an East Indian woman and two young girls as deck passengers. We assumed they were her daughters, and the widowed mother was taking them to India and her family.

In a secluded niche on the forward deck, Thomas had an awning rigged, with canvas panels to give the family some privacy. The woman set up housekeeping with a charcoal brazier and a chamber pot. She and the girls stretched pallets on the deck, under the awning.

The woman was of an undeterminate age, with golden loops in her ears and a scarlet caste mark between her plucked eyebrows. She was thin, almost to the point of emaciation, with pointed little breasts poking the front of her sari.

One of the girls, and I judged she might be sixteen or seventeen, was fat with breasts like two gourds. The other was younger. She was a slender, brown-skinned little thing with a saucy air that reminded me of Bliss. Her bright almond eyes sparkled.

The older sister was obviously dull.

Two days out from Dar es Salaam, I'd fashioned a rag doll for the younger girl, and asked Thomas if I could take it to her.

"Go ahead," he said. "Look around up there, too. I want to know everything that goes on aboard this ship, and right now I suspect that I don't."

I stumbled into a situation that nearly cost me my life.

With a cheerful hello, I ducked into the deck tent with my offering, and found that I'd intruded into a scene straight out of the Marquis de Sade. The dullard had the naked younger girl's arms pinned above her head while the East Indian woman squatted tailor-fashion between the girl's splayed thighs. There was a slender, pointed knife in her hand. With it she was about to mutilate the gagged girl.

Throwing down the rag doll, I screamed and grabbed the woman by her hair, kicking the knife out of her hand, and then found myself wrestling with a tigress.

Reaching for my throat, the woman drove a bony knee up between my legs. Searing pain washed my body.

I'd captured her wrists with my hands, but she had the strength of a man. She butted my breasts with her head. As we spilled out of the tent, the older girl joined the fray. She caught me from behind, a fat arm around my throat.

The woman scrambled for her knife. Unable to spit the gag from her mouth, the sobbing younger girl had scuttled to a corner of the tent and huddled there, knees drawn up.

The woman had her knife. The fat girl's choking hold made my head swim and drained my strength. I kicked with my feet to keep the woman and her knife away, but she crouched, hissing, and waited for an opening.

On deck for a breath of air before going to bed, Edith joined the melee. Wrenching the fat girl away from me, with a shove she sent her sprawling on the deck, then turned to the half-insane woman.

"Now, enough of this nonsense!" she said with determined authority. "Give me that knife." She held out her hand. "Do it right now."

With a shudder that wracked her thin body, as if it was a small tree in a high wind, the woman straightened, then offered the knife, but an accusing torrent of words burst from her lips.

In a hoarse whisper, I told Edith what I had found.

The woman was calmer now, trying to explain. When she realized we couldn't understand a word she was saying, the woman called the fat girl to her, made her squat on her heels, thighs open. She jerked up the girl's sari.

By the light of the glowing brazier, we could see that she'd experienced female circumcision at some time, but the incisions were healed.

Edith had removed the younger girl's gag and held her to her breast. "She was trying to do that to this girl," Edith said.

"Oh, my God! We can't let her!"

With the woman following us, mouthing shrill protests, we took the sobbing younger girl to Edith's cabin. Edith was examining her when Thomas knocked and came in.

"Now what's this all about?" he said. "Mrs. Jamshed tells me you've stolen one of her daughters, and she wants the girl back."

The girl was calm enough to talk. A stream of words burst from her lips, tears rolling down her small face.

"I understand." Thomas raised a hand, and said it again, this time in her language. He turned to Edith and me, his face a hard mask. "Our Mrs. Jamshed is a whoremistress," he explained. "She bought these two girls in Dar es Salaam, and is taking them to Bombay." He flushed. "You seem to have saved this one from a ritual circumcision, Jeanette. She thanks you."

"We must do something, Thomas," Edith said.

Now the woman crowded into the small cabin, while the fat girl, owl-eyed, watched from the doorway. Edith stood between her and the younger girl, cowering on her bunk, eyes wide with fear.

"I'll care for this child, Thomas," she said.

"You'll have to buy her from this woman. If you don't, we're in trouble when we reach Bombay."

Edith didn't hesitate. "Ask her how much she wants for the girl."

CHAPTER 13

OUR PASSAGE from Dar es Salaam across the Indian Ocean, and up to Bombay, was a slow one, plagued by listless winds that barely filled the *Mary Freeman*'s sails, and torrid heat. We were fortunate when the ship logged 60 miles in a twenty-four-hour period.

Thomas armed the crew, and we kept a sharp lookout for the triangular sails of a dhoy. We were in a shipping lane frequented by lascar pirates. Twice dhoys came near us, but each time sheered off, intimidated by the cannons Thomas kept rolled out, ready to fire. He'd been across this ocean many times before.

Edith's brown-skinned charge was named Santha. She had been sold into slavery by her mother
after her father had been knifed to death by an
Arab trader in the Dar es Salaam marketplace.
She was grateful to me for her rescue, but she wor-
shipped Edith. Now that she was safe from Mrs.
Janshed and her knife, Santha bubbled with good
humor. She showed appreciation for my rag doll
gift, but didn't seem to know what she should do
with it.

Santha finally decided it was some kind of
Christian religious symbol and set it on one of
Edith's bookshelves to worship.

Both of us set out to teach her English, with
the help of Thomas, when he could spare the time.
Santha was bright and an eager learner. Before
we reached Bombay, Santha could read a few of
the simpler passages from the Bible, and chatter-
ed all day in a mixture of English and Hindustani.

"When we reach Bombay, what are you going
to do with Santha?" I asked Edith. "I don't suppose you can take her with you to China."

"There are a few Christians in Bombay," Edith
said, "and the East India Company has allowed a
mission. I'll have to place her with a good Christian family, or leave her in the care of missionaries."

"You won't get your money back that way," I
teased.

"My money? Oh, didn't you know? Thomas

paid Mrs. Jamshed for the child. So she is his ward and yours, Jeanette."

Thomas hadn't told me this.

Mrs. Jamshed seemed to bear Edith and me no ill will, once she was paid back Santha's purchase price. The few times I met her on deck she bowed respectfully and touched the crimson caste mark on her forehead.

The dull older girl had been a prostitute in Dar es Salaam, and being taken to India would probably improve her lot. When Edith finally convinced Santha that my rag doll had no religious significance, the older girl was delighted to have it as a plaything. She was never without it for the rest of the voyage.

From the Indian Ocean, the *Mary Freeman* slipped into the Arabian Sea and began tacking into the teeth of the northeast monsoon. Rain squalls washed her decks every day, but there was no relief from the humid heat. Thomas stayed on deck most of the time as we slowly approached Bombay. He caught snatches of sleep when he could, many times on a cot he'd had set up on the quarterdeck.

I grew more restless, bored and hungry for his caresses every day, but knew tacking the *Mary Freeman* into adverse winds, and rain squalls, was anxious business.

More and more of my time was spent with

Edith and Santha. Because Edith's cabin was too small, I took Santha to sleep in my larger cabin, but during the day Edith's cabin was a schoolroom.

The girl had a sly sense of humor. She was always comfortable, regardless of how hot it was, in her sheer sari, rolled and tucked under her arms to leave the shoulders bare.

"English woman . . . women . . . bad in their heads," she told us one particularly hot afternoon, her almond eyes sparkling with mischief.

"Now why do you say that?" Edith asked.

She fingered Edith's high-necked dress and made a wry face. "Too hot." She ran her palms down her sides. "Sari is always better."

"The child has a point," Edith admitted. "I'm sweltering in this dress and all my undergarments."

"Let's get Mrs. Jamshed to make us saris," I suggested.

"Now, that is a good idea," Edith said. "Where do we find the cloth?"

"I was rummaging in the ship's slopchest the other day, looking for a shirt that would fit Thomas. There's part of a bolt of Irish linen in there, enough for two saris. I'll get it."

Mrs. Jamshed was delighted with our order, and by the end of the day we had loose-fitting, cool saris. "Now what do we wear under these things?" Edith asked me.

"What Santha does, I suppose."

"Nothing?" I'd shocked Edith.

"They aren't transparent."

"But the men and Thomas—they'll know we're naked under our saris," Edith said. "It isn't a proper thing to do, Jeanette."

We were in her cabin. Santha was taking an afternoon nap in mine. I began to peel off my heavy dress.

"You be proper," I said. "I'm going to be comfortable."

With a trilling little laugh, Edith began to undress herself, too. I couldn't help noticing that a naked Edith, with hair streaming down her back, had a beautiful body, and I felt the faint prickle of desire. I'd been too long without Thomas.

There was a slight sway to the ship as she came around to make a fresh tack. It caught both of us off balance, and we sprawled on Edith's bunk. For a moment, we lay facing each other, naked, our bodies nearly touching.

From her eyes, and the intent expression on Edith's face, I knew she was experiencing the same prickling in her loins and breasts as I was, and it cost me effort to roll away from her and stand up.

Edith lay on her back, motionless, eyes fixed on my nakedness. She made no effort to cover herself with her hands.

It was a fragile moment.

I turned my back, reached for my new sari, and

wrapped it around my body. When I'd adjusted the roll under my arms, I turned back.

Edith was still as she was, but now she'd closed her eyes, and her lips moved in silent prayer.

"Let me help you with your sari, Edith," I said in a low voice. "Here. Come."

I reached a hand to help her.

As she came to her feet, the ship lurched, and our bodies touched, breast to breast.

When she was steady on her feet, I moved away from Edith, with my heart pounding and pulses racing, and watched her stoop to pick up her sari where it had fallen.

When she had it on, Edith said, "This *is* comfortable. Naughty but very nice." She spoke faster than she usually did, and in a shriller voice. "My poor father, if he could see me now!" She was avoiding my eyes. "Prim and proper Edith, decked out like a dancing girl, or one of those *houris* that Mohammed promises his followers in paradise." Her eyes finally found mine. "Thank you, Jeanette." Edith's voice was normal now. "I pray and offer my continence to God, but sometimes my flesh betrays me."

"You're a very desirable woman, and as hot-blooded as I am," I told her. "If Thomas stays away from me tonight, I'll find him, and damned if I care where it is. This *is* our honeymoon."

"You're fortunate to have a Thomas."

"I know. But what about you?"

"May I be frank, Jeanette?"

"Please be. We're very good and warm friends, I think. Both of us should be honest with each other."

"I'm unnaturally attracted to you. It started when you were ill and I was your nurse." She bent her head, covering her flaming face with both hands. "Don't ask me how, but I know the ways women make physical love to each other. I've never geen involved with another woman, understand that. And now . . ."

"You want to be?" I said, when she hesitated.

Edith's hands dropped to her sides, and she stood very straight. Her eyes flashed defiance—of me or her passionate desires—and she said, "It would be a great sin against your marriage."

I wanted to lock her in my embrace and conquer that throbbing body, as Bliss had conquered mine, but knew that if I did, our friendship would be gone.

"Edith, what you want is to be taken by a man," I said. "It will happen. There's too much passionate woman under that sari to go unfulfilled forever."

Edith nodded dumbly.

Thomas was surprised by the urgency of my desire, that night, but said nothing.

A wealthy Parsi, Chandra Chatterji, was Thomas's shipping agent in Bombay. He was a dark little turbaned man with flowing white robes, and was waiting on the dock when the *Mary Freeman* was warped in by half-naked, sweating rowers, and tied up.

Mr. Chatterji showed a wealth in gold teeth when he smiled. "Is good to see you again so soon, Captain Townsend," he said, bobbing his head, then shaking hands.

"Good to see you, Mr. Chatterji. This is my wife, Jeanette, and that is Miss Edith Radcliff." Thomas wiped the sweat from his forehead. "The monsoon must be late this year."

"Very late. Our farms are parched, and there will be famine if the rains don't come soon. But let us discuss more pleasant matters. I have for you some of the best white sandalwood and some fine ebony."

From Thomas I learned that sandalwood was in great demand out in the Orient; not only for carving inlaid boxes, walking sticks, fans and combs, but also to be ground up and made into fragrant candles for Buddhist altars and shrines. It was also used, Thomas told me, to make cosmetics and medicines.

Coolies began loading the long, thin logs immediately.

Mr. Chatterji entertained us the few days we were in Bombay at his country house, away from the teeming streets of the city, the swarming flies, and hordes of untouchable beggars.

Mr. Chatterji had become rich as a native employee of the powerful East India Company, the rulers of India. His country house, which was really a small palace, was on a breeze-swept hill near Poona, east of Bombay. In the carriage that took us there, I saw elephants for the first time, stacking tree trunks near a small, muddy river.

Santha was delighted with the elephants, and the men crouched on their necks, and wanted to ride one.

Mr. Chatterji had been too polite to ask why she was with us, but before we arrived at his house, Edith explained.

"Before we sail, I must find a proper home for Santha, Mr. Chatterji. I'd thought of a Christian mission, but perhaps you have a better idea?"

Mr. Chatterji pursed his lips. "Here in India, to be a girl is not a good thing. She has no father to pay a dowry when she marries?"

"No father," Edith said. "Her mother is in Dar es Salaam, and sold her into prostitution."

Mr. Chatterji frowned. "That is bad, but what else can a poor family do with girls?" He shook his head sadly. "You English think us heartless, but there is only so much food."

"Mr. Chatterji is blessed with three fine sons," Thomas said. "Isn't that correct, sir?"

"Oh, yes. They are all away at school just now. The house seems very empty."

"Do you have daughters?" Edith asked.

"Our only daughter died of the fever when she was nine," Mr. Chatterji said. "Very sad."

We passed through the village of Poona and

started up the hill toward the white house that crowned it. Mr. Chatterji had fallen into deep thought and glanced at happy Santha a dozen times.

Mrs. Chatterji greeted us. She was a frail little woman with gold-rimmed spectacles and gray hair, but her robes were the finest blue silk. There was a fountain and shallow pool in the entryway, in which golden carp swam lazily. Santha was fascinated. She scampered over to lean her elbows on the rim of the pool, and watch the fish.

Mrs. Chatterji studied the rapt child, then asked Thomas, "Who is the little one?"

"Temporarily, our ward," Thomas said. "Miss Radcliff hopes to find her a good home before we leave Bombay."

"Is this so?" Mrs. Chatterji was interested. She glanced at her husband. "Would you please decide for me, Chandra, whether I may adopt this child? She is enough like our dead daughter to be a reincarnation. Perhaps she is, and that's why she has come today."

Mr. Chatterji mopped his brow. "These women!" he said to Thomas. "Submissive to their husbands, always if they are good wives, but how they get their way with a man!"

Mrs. Chatterji patiently awaited an answer to her question.

Mr. Chatterji clapped his palms together. "I have decided," he said. "Santha becomes our adopted daughter. How much was it you paid for her?" he asked Thomas.

"Forget that." Thomas grinned. "One day soon there will be a dowry."

Mr. Chatterji slapped a palm to his forehead. "If we adopt her, that is right. There will be many money-hungry suitors for the daughter of Chandra Chatterji. Well, I shouldn't complain, so long as my wife has a companion."

We were warned not to walk alone in the lovely gardens surrounding the house. A servant armed with a snake-stick would always accompany us.

"The servant respects my orders never to kill a cobra because that would be very bad," Mr. Chatterji explained to Edith and me. "Who knows what he was in another life? With his stick he will keep you ladies from harm."

Edith and I decided we'd admire Mr. Chatterji's gardens from a safe distance!

Away from the ship for a few days, Thomas became an ardent lover. We couldn't seem to have enough of each other, sometimes even in the afternoon, when we made excuses to retire to our room.

There was a strange, new intensity in his lovemaking. At times he'd spend himself on my body in almost frantic haste. Other times Thomas transported me to a lingering ecstasy, prolonging our union until I would cry out for him to take me.

Whatever there was to say to each other, we said it with our bodies, and stillness lay between us. It was a strange interlude.

Our next port of call, after Bombay, was Ceylon, the island off the tip of the Indian Continent. The monsoon rains had just begun when we left the harbor to head down the west coast of India. They came in long gusts, sweeping the decks and splattering the sails. Favorable winds took us along at a pace that satisfied Thomas.

Deprived of Santha's company, Edith was morose and stayed in her cabin, studying, for most of this passage.

The fourth night out of Bombay, we sailed into the maw of a typhoon. With all sails furled, Thomas ordered a sea anchor over the side and had the ship battened down to ride it out.

The bare poles moved the ship through the water enough to provide steerage. She'd ride up on one wave crest, only to plunge into the next trough, with tons of green water sweeping her from stem to stern. The whaleboat was smashed to splinters and carried away. The crew manned the pumps around the clock.

Thomas weathered the storm on deck, tending the tortured ship, while I lay on the bunk in our cabin, saying Hail Marys. Each new plunge the *Mary Freeman* took, I didn't think she would be

190

able to throw off the water, and rise again. But she did.

One heavier sea smashed the porthole in Edith's cabin, so she joined me for the duration of the storm, and we prayed together.

Two men were lost overboard before the typhoon blew itself out. We were about fifty miles off course, but aside from the whaleboat, there had been remarkably little damage to the ship or its cargo.

The ship's carpenter made repairs, and Edith moved back to her cabin. We'd been too frightened by the storm to say much to each other.

CHAPTER 14

MY FIRST glimpse of Ceylon was the peak of Adam's Mountain, from which the Ceylonese believe the Lord Buddha ascended into heaven. It is a strange land of plains and ridges, tumbling rivers and dense jungles where the primitive Veddas live, much as they have since the Stone Age.

Thomas hoped to replace the two crewmen lost overboard during the typhoon, and to sign on ten additional sailors while we were anchored in Colombo's harbor.

"Reaching for Singapore from here, and then Whampoa and Canton on the China Coast, we're entering the most dangerous waters in the world," he told me. "As well as tea for England, we're taking aboard two hundred casks of opium. Malay pirates have their own grapevine in these waters, and if they think they can board us before we reach Singapore, they're certain to try."

The opium would be carried to Whampoa and loaded aboard junks there for the trip up the Pearl River to Canton. "The mandarins still think they can keep us barbarians out of their precious country," Thomas told me. "They also try to ban the opium trade, and there will be some kind of war about that one of these days. They'll find out Clive's East India Company is more powerful than all of them together."

He told me how Clive had conquered India for the British crown, using native mercenaries called sepoys who were hired by the company.

"I'd guess it's the only country in the world to be conquered by a private company's army," Thomas said. "To all intents and purposes, the company rules India and Ceylon today."

It was only in 1802 that Ceylon became a crown colony after the British drove out the Dutch.

The glassy-smooth harbor of Colombo was painted red by a flaming sunset when the *Mary Freeman* entered it. Seven tall, fat Indiamen— company ships—swung at anchor.

Some of these company ships would sail in convoy for Chinese ports, loaded with opium, while others would return to England with cargoes of Ceylon tea. I began to realize, as I never had before, the power and might of Britain. Napoleon's grandiose plans to bring her to her knees would fail. I was proud to be able to call myself a British citizen. Mrs. Thomas Townsend.

Edith was over her moodiness about losing Santha by the time we reached Colombo. Thomas was busy loading his ship and discharging part of the mixed cargo for Colombo merchants, but he appointed Bob Dillard to escort Edith and me for sightseeing and shopping while our ship was in the harbor.

We visited the Buddhist temple, and Bob told me he knew of seamen who'd shaved their heads, donned yellow robes, and become followers of Buddha when their ships came to Colombo.

"Considering forecastle conditions on some of these windjamming merchant ships, and bucko mates quick with their fists and the whip, I can't say I blame them." he said. "Whalers are the worst—especially American ships—but some of ours are pretty bad."

Edith and I were fascinated by the Sinhalese. Both men and women dressed in long skirts, pinned back their long hair with tortoise-shell combs, so at first glance it was hard to distinguish the brown-skinned men from their small-breasted women.

"We seem to be going native," Edith said, after we bought colorful silk saris in the bazaar. "If I report to Dr. Phelps with bare shoulders, he'll probably pack me off home!"

In a sense, what she said was true. I know I'd found a new freedom when I discarded dresses, skirts, and blouses, as well as most of my undergarments, and put on a sari. Most important, however, I was comfortable.

"Orientals scoff at the way European women try to disguise and bury their sex," Thomas said the first time he saw me in a sari. "They think all of you are somehow deformed, and for that reason ashamed of your bodies."

He said the question he was most often asked by Oriental men was what we wore in bed!

We sailed from Colombo for Singapore on a Friday, which happened to fall on the thirteenth of the month. There was some grumbling among the crew about this, but Thomas had heard ashore that the East India Company was soon going to monopolize the opium trade with China.

Thomas wanted to be well out to sea before that happened, and had chosen Singapore as our gateway to the South China Sea to avoid the island of Penang, where the East India Company had trading rights.

The sultan of Johore ruled the island of Singapore, but was friendly to British ships, and Thomas had heard it would one day soon become another crown colony.

"Those casks of opium will pay for this whole voyage, if we get them to Whampoa," Thomas told me.

With the Welsh miners no longer aboard, Thomas had decided not to make any Australian ports this voyage.

"I'm anxious to begin the return voyage to Liverpool," he said. "I want to spend more time with my new wife, without a ship to worry me."

"Maybe your English friends won't like this half-French woman you've married," I teased. "What will you do with me then?"

"Take your clothes away and lock you up in an ivory tower." Thomas grinned. "I don't want my English friends to like you too much!"

"You'd be jealous?"

Thomas rubbed his jaw and gave me a speculative stare. "Every man is jealous of the woman he loves, Jeanette."

"You do love me then?" I was in a coquettish mood. "You weren't sure just after we were married on Malta."

"Who was Jamie?" he asked.

I started, as if Thomas had touched a raw nerve. I'd never mentioned Jamie to Thomas, and had resolved I never would.

"How do you know there was a Jamie?" I asked.

Thomas looked away, and there was an expression on his face I'd never seen before. I know

197

now it was pain, but I didn't then. I thought it was rejection.

That expression was gone as quickly as it had come, and Thomas grinned. "Once upon a time, before Gwen, I thought I loved a Eurasian girl. Her father was German, her mother Javanese. Ting Lao was her native name."

"Was she beautiful?" I asked.

"Very."

"Blonde?"

"No, but she had her father's blue eyes," he said.

"What happened to you and Ting Lao?" I asked.

"Nothing. I kissed her good-bye and sailed back to England," Thomas said. "Gwen and I had known each other since we were children."

"Poor Ting Lao!"

Thomas kissed me, and then we made love. But our marriage had received another small cut.

In our hurry to get away, we sailed from Colombo shorthanded. Thomas didn't sign the ten extra men he wanted or replace the crewmen washed overboard during the typhoon.

The Strait of Malacca, between Sumatra and the Malay Peninsula, is the western sea gateway to Singapore and the South China Sea. There's no way for a ship sailing east to avoid this narrow strait, so it's the favorite hunting ground for Malay pirate junks.

It is 1572 sea miles between Colombo and Singapore through the Strait of Malacca, and Thomas estimated that we would be at least three weeks at sea, crossing the mouth of the Bay of Bengal before we rounded Sabang Island off the tip of Sumatra, then entered the strait. After that he thought it would take us another week to reach the island of Singapore.

Two days out from Colombo, the gally caught fire when the cook spilled hot grease onto the cook stove.

Caught in the flare-up, the Chinese cook who had been aboard the *Mary Freeman* for the last three voyages bolted over the side of the ship when his clothing was set on fire.

The galley was gutted, and many of our food stores were destroyed.

Bob Dillard urged Thomas to turn back for repairs and supplies, but my husband had a stubborn streak. He'd set sail for Singapore, and that was where he was going.

The atmosphere aboard ship began to change. On cold rations, the grumbling in the forecastle began to increase, and the crew went about their work sullenly.

The repairs to the bows of the *Mary Freeman* that had been made in the Capetown drydock began to leak. The pumps had to be manned two, four, six, and finally eight hours each day. This put an additional strain on the crew. The men doing the exhausting work of pumping weren't available to set and trim sails, so the ship's progress was slowed.

In a fierce monsoon squall, the rudder was carried away. The *Mary Freeman* wallowed helplessly for two days while temporary repairs were made. A jury-rigged rudder slowed the ship's progress even more.

We were five weeks out of Colombo before we sighted Sabang and started limping down the straits for Singapore. The *Mary Freeman* had a worried captain, a nearly mutinous crew, and I had an inattentive husband. All of Thomas's time and attention was devoted to his ship, and I was unreasonably jealous.

I was in a dangerous mood, and I knew it, but I couldn't help myself. I began to understand why only a few captains will take their wives to sea.

Edith and I were thrown together constantly. We couldn't associate with the crew, even if we had wanted to do so, and except for pleasantries, we avoided the mate, Bob Dillard. What happened between us, finally, was inevitable.

It happened one night after we were into the strait. It was suffocatingly hot, so I came on deck about midnight for a breath of air, and found Edith amidships, staring out to sea. There were double lookouts fore and aft, but our part of the ship was deserted.

I joined her.

"Where does all this heat come from?" she

asked in a listless voice. "I dream of England and cold fogs!"

Edith's hair flowed down her back. She wore a thin, loose robe. She'd been crying, because her face was still wet with tears. I touched her shoulder, and the flesh beneath the thin fabric was burning.

"Do you feel all right?" I asked. "You're hot and you've been crying."

She didn't shrug away from my touch. "I don't have a fever," she said. I could see only her profile. Edith snuffled. "Jeanette, come down to my cabin," she said. "There's a bottle of wine I've managed to chill." Her laugh was nervous. "Can you imagine *me* trailing wine out a porthole tied to a cord?"

In the closeness of her cabin, she went on. "I never tasted anything but communion wine until I was eighteen, and then my father didn't know."

It was rich Madeira. The wine wasn't exactly chilled, but it was cold.

"So much my father didn't know," she mused.

"My father slapped me once," I said.

"Did he? What had you done?" Edith asked.

"I didn't want to marry a man."

"I suppose you had your reasons."

"That seems so very long ago now, Edith."

She sighed. "Everything does. I've been on this damned ship forever."

It was the first time I'd heard Edith swear, and I laughed delightedly.

"This damned ship!" she said again.

"I'll drink to that."

We finished our wine.

"All right." Edith spoke as if she'd just made up her mind about something.

Rising from the edge of the bunk where we'd been sitting together, Edith turned to face me and opened her robe. She wore nothing beneath it.

"Will you make love to me, Jeanette?"

The quick intake of my breath must have answered her question, because the robe fell around her feet, and eager hands were helping me take off my sari.

Edith didn't lie when she said she knew how women make love to each other. My first shocked surprise was the fierceness of her kisses and her probing tongue.

Hands stroked me, caressed, searched, and found quickly.

"My dear!" she gasped.

I responded. There was no way I couldn't because Edith took me with the strength of a demanding man, and then took me again.

It was a shattering experience—more so for me than for Edith, because when I was sobbing, limp and exhausted, she rose to pour us what remained of the wine.

The lamp was out. In the darkness of the cabin I couldn't see her face, only the white glow of her naked body as she stood there, offering me wine.

"I'm not ashamed," she said.

I touched her hip. "I'm not, either."

We finished our wine again before she stooped to pick up her robe. "Will you sleep with me?"

"No."

"Do you hate me?"

"No, I don't. Should I?" was my question.

"I don't know."

"I just don't want to lose you as a friend," I said.

She took my face between her palms, bent and kissed my forehead. "You never will," she promised.

The next night, the *Mary Freeman* was ghosting through the strait, driven by a light but steady wind. The moon had set, and the sky was overcast, so it was dark as pitch. On the port bow, we were passing Malacca, at the narrowest part of the strait.

The ambush had been well planned and was perfectly executed. Two small junks slipped out of the night, bracketing the *Mary Freeman* before our lookouts could sound an alarm. Kris-waving Malays swarmed aboard.

They should have been able to carry the ship, but because Thomas was on the quarterdeck and alert, with Bob Dillard at his side, they didn't. But they thought they had.

I awoke when the junks bumped the *Mary Freeman*. The pilots had put their craft aside so skillfully, however, that I didn't recognize the sound. If I had, I might have bolted the cabin door—even barricaded it. As it was, I simply wrapped myself in a sari, brushed hair out of my eyes, and started for the quarterdeck to ask Thomas what had happened.

A man loomed ahead of me in the dark passageway with a scarf tied around his head, I do remember that much, and I saw the naked blade of the kris in his hand just before the fist grasping it struck my jaw.

That's all I remember of what happened to me aboard the *Mary Freeman*. There wasn't time to be afraid.

A bucket of fresh seawater struck me full in the face, and I gasped awake, to find myself sitting on a strange deck, bound back to back with someone else. Still uncomprehending, I stared at the grinning, dark faces of the men surrounding us. They stood in a close circle and I could smell their sweating bodies, but it was a slightly different smell.

"Jeanette?" It was Edith's weak voice.

I knew, then. We were alone aboard a Malay pirate's junk!

"I'm conscious," I told her.

They'd tied us wrist to wrist, elbow to elbow.

"What will they do to us now?" she asked.

There wasn't as much fear in her voice as I

thought there would be. Edith was resigned, but not afraid.

I was too stunned to be afraid. My head throbbed, and my jaw ached like fury.

"I don't know yet," I said.

I could hear the creak of the junk's rigging, and the passage of water along her hull, but the men around us weren't making a sound. It was eerie!

The scene was lit by smoking torches somehow fixed in the rigging, and their red-orange light was reflected from the sweating faces. They looked like so many disembodied masks!

Gargoyle masks.

"They were driven off and didn't get the ship," Edith said.

I was naked. I wondered about Edith, and I turned my head. So far as I could see, she was, too. Our tormentors were waiting for something —or someone—and I wished it would happen— or he would come—because I was sure we would be killed.

I wanted it over with. I tried to be thankful they hadn't taken the ship, but I knew it was going to be a harder death for us because they hadn't.

The circle parted. Through the opening stepped a Malay with a hideously scarred face. Part of his scarred nose had been cut off, and one side of his face was drawn up with scar tissue so that side of his mouth always grinned.

"You English ladies comfortable?" he asked in a high-pitched, mocking voice. His accent was surprisingly good.

I stared up at him without trying to answer. He slapped my face with a bare foot. "Answer!"

"No, we're not comfortable," I said. Now my head rang as well as throbbed.

My remark drew a cackle of laughter from the Malays and what I supposed was a grin from my disfigured questioner.

"You're comfortable *now*." It was a vicious emphasis, his implication unmistakable, and I felt Edith shudder.

But she said, and said it cheerfully, "I do believe they intend to torture us, Jeanette."

CHAPTER 15

THE FIRST fear of women in our position is that of rape. When we'd been cut apart, and willing brown hands strung us up by our wrists to the rigging, side by side, I realized our captor intended to spare us that ordeal—at least for a while. With two white Englishwomen with whom he could amuse his crew, disappointed because they hadn't taken the *Mary Freeman,* the man intended to make the most of the situation.

They'd triced us so that the balls of our feet just touched the deck, so close that our hips brushed whenever we moved.

The strain on my arms and back was bearable.

I gritted my teeth and waited, but nothing else happened. I could hear Edith draw in short, gasping breaths. I looked back over my shoulder. The Malays had squatted in a comfortable semicircle, no longer smiling, but with eager anticipation printed on their faces. I looked back over my other shoulder, but couldn't find the disfigured one.

Eyes shut tight, Edith was whispering a prayer. I couldn't pray. I was too angry with God and too afraid of the pain I knew would come.

In that moment, I remembered the pitiful broken bodies Bliss and I had seen back in Port-au-Prince, and asked *their* forgiveness!

The leader had soaked the lash of the two-handed whip in brine. I heard the hiss of it a split second before pain exploded in the small of my back. Edith's was a shrill scream; mine was a yell of pain.

His second stroke caught us both across the buttocks. I thought mine had been cut in half! I'd bitten through my lips, and blood was salty in my mouth, but I didn't yell.

Edith had fainted. I realized this when they dashed her with a bucket of brine that splashed on my back and buttocks. With a yelp, I bumped her body.

The laughter of the men sounded like the cluck of hens and the crowing of roosters.

They were cutting Edith down, and when the kris sliced the cords binding her wrists, she slumped to the deck with a moan, then fell back, unconscious again. How I envied her!

Why couldn't I faint?

I shut my eyes and tried, but it was impossible.

Edith lay on her back, arms and legs flung wide, and a squat Malay stood over her, loosening his loincloth. The others were cheering him on.

I'm ashamed, but I was glad of this diversion because fresh waves of pain were radiating from my back and buttocks.

I was glad too soon.

The clever one with the whip aimed his third stroke to catch me between the thighs, and up across my belly.

I was in too much new agony to hear the first fusillade of pistol shots. But when the *Mary Freeman* slammed into the junk, my arms were nearly jerked from their sockets!

Edith's scream and my yell probably saved our lives. Blundering in the darkness, Thomas would have passed the junk. As it was, he heard us and rammed her astern, so the crew, poised in the *Mary Freeman*'s bows, could swarm onto the junk's high stern deck.

I do know he would probably have found me dead if I'd been lashed again.

Thomas cut me down, carried me back aboard our ship, and cradled in his arms, while Bob

Dillard rescued Edith after blowing out the brains of her rapist.

Before the Malays could rally from that first rush, our crew was back aboard, and our ship sheared off. The shattered junk was spilling her crew into the water as we sailed away.

Thomas accomplished all this without losing a man. Only six crewmen were wounded.

Our cabin was the infirmary. Bob Dillard handled the ship while Thomas nursed Edith and me. While he treated our welts with a soothing ointment, Thomas swore at himself under his breath for being taken by surprise.

He spooned laudanum into our mouths to ease our pain and skillfully bandaged my bleeding where that last lash caught me.

Thomas forced enough brandy down our throats to make us half-drunk before he was content to leave us.

Thomas had tucked us in, and we were face down, side by side.

"You two try to get some sleep," Thomas said before he left us.

When he was gone, Edith spoke for the first time, her voice thick from the laudanum and brandy. "I'm no longer virgin, Jeanette, but I don't think he finished raping me." She paused, then said, "I was too frightened to be very brave."

I tried to make sense from what she'd said, but wasn't successful.

"I fainted," Edith told me, as if I didn't know.

"You were lucky," I muttered. "I couldn't manage to do that."

We never again spoke about what happened to us aboard that Malay junk.

It was two weeks before I could sleep on my back, and three before I could let Thomas make love. During that time he cared for me as if I were a child, with a tenderness and concern I didn't know any man could show.

"I nearly went insane when I thought I'd lost you," he told me. "I couldn't have lived with myself if that had happened."

"You know that you're spoiling me, don't you?" I said. "Not that I really mind." I patted his cheek. "As soon as I'm well, you'll get your reward. Be patient."

Thomas grinned. "That isn't easy." His hands cupped my breasts and gently massaged them. "Heal quickly," he whispered. "I'm not a very patient man."

"You're making me a very impatient woman when you do that," I said, "but please don't stop."

Our shared experience created a new bond between Edith and me. Any barrier between us left by our interlude in her cabin dissolved.

In boarding school, from other books, and French novels we smuggled into the dormitory—

books which I sometimes read to the other girls because of my better command of French—I knew agout the ménage à trois, or three-way love between a man, his mistress, and his wife.

I'd always considered this a most disgusting custom. Now I found myself having second thoughts, and I sensed Edith was having much the same thoughts—subconsciously at least.

I wondered what Thomas would think if I asked him.

In her cabin one night, just before we reached Singapore, Edith and I were drinking wine while Thomas was on deck guiding the *Mary Freeman* through the treacherous waters. For the first time I was well enough to make love, and he had promised to save the rest of the night for me.

"Don't tire yourself too much this watch," I told him. "You're about to be rewarded for patience."

Thomas gave me a leering grin. "Batten down your hatches, girl, and reef the mainsail, because I'm coming into port in more ways than one."

"I'll be your most willing pilot," I promised. "So batten your own hatches. It's been a long, hard voyage."

Edith was moody that night. I'd said nothing about my assignation with my husband, but I was restless, and I guess I had a glow she recognized, because she said, "We three have been cooped up on this damned ship too long!"

She tossed down her wine like a veteran toper.

"You've changed, missionary lady," I told her.

"You've noticed?" she said archly.

"Wouldn't I have to be deaf, dumb, and blind if I hadn't noticed?" I said. "You drink a little, swear a bit, wear a sari that doesn't disguise your womanly attributes, and we've made love."

Edith raised her refilled wineglass to study the wine's color. "For a woman, was I a good lover, Jeanette?"

I closed my eyes. "Very good."

She kissed me lightly on the lips. "Thank you for that."

"But you lied to me." I challenged.

"Yes, I did," she admitted frankly. "I was fifteen, and very lonely. She was headmistress of the school where my father sent me, and beautiful, I thought. I waited for God to strike me dead."

"Are you still waiting?" I teased.

Edith's laugh was husky. "No."

The ship's bell struck. "Thomas will be waiting, Edith," I said. "This is one night I don't want to keep him waiting too long."

She raised her glass. "Do your duty as a wife, but don't forget me."

"I never will," I promised.

Edith sighed. "I wish I could join you."

"So to your other sins we add reading French novels?"

She flushed, but said, "I first read the Marquis de Sade when I was eleven."

The three of us would be many weeks aboard the *Mary Freeman* after she cleared Singapore. I'd learned by experience that Thomas wasn't the inhibited Englishman I'd once thought, early in our marriage.

I found I was no longer thinking, could the ménage à trois happen? How and when was the direction of my thoughts now, because I was finding that I loved Edith as well as Thomas, each in a different way.

The island of Singapore, Thomas told me, would someday be the busiest port in the world. "When we British get control, and we will," he said, "we'll be in control of the entire Far East. There's a port that's forbidden us now, but I've seen it. They call it Hong Kong."

"What does that mean in English?" I asked.

"Perfumed water. Hong Kong is the port we must have to open up southern China to British trade, and we'll have it, sooner or later."

Singapore was crowded with shipping from all nations when we sailed into the beautiful harbor. The *Mary Freeman* would be laid up for three weeks. The leaking bows would have to be repaired, and the galley rebuilt before Thomas took her out into the South China Sea. Thomas had no shipping agent in Singapore to offer hospitality during our stay, but he rented a house the landlord reserved for shipping masters.

It was a lovely dwelling, built in the Chinese architectural style, with blank outside walls, but a court and fountain inside. Each room was entered by way of the court. Beside the central fountain, there was a small bathing pool in the court. Cooking was done in a separate building.

The landlord kept the house staffed with dozens of Chinese servants, men and women.

It was a sturdy compound, built entirely of teak, with no windowpanes—only mats that could be raised or lowered.

I don't know where the servants lived, but they were always there when we wanted them, never when we didn't.

After weeks of cold rations aboard ship, we were introduced to Chinese cooking by our chef, who was from Canton. Pork prepared in a dozen different ways, and with as many different piquant sauces, was our main dish.

Edith and I were introduced to bean sprouts as a vegetable, pickled radishes and onions, and a variety of rich gravies. Native wine had a delicate flavor, and was made from rice, to be served cold or hot. Fat carp were wrapped in herbs and roasted, to be served whole, as was roast pig.

To my surprise, here in Singapore, Thomas smoked an opium pipe every evening after supper. "I don't make it a habit," he explained, "It is one way for a man to relax, however, after a long, hard voyage."

He would retire to a special room, and the houseboy would bring his pipe to him, while Edith and I bathed in the pool. With the servants gone, we didn't bother with clothing of any kind for our nightly plunge. Each of us knew the other's body as well as her own.

We were only curious at first about opium smoking, but soon became anxious to join Thomas, if he could be persuaded to invite us.

Edith and I had discarded our saris for heavy silk Japanese kimonos. To our surprise, Thomas immediately donned the man's kimono we bought for him as a joke, and always wore it when he was in the compound. He somehow managed to be dignified and virile-looking, even in a kimono!

The cool night air of Singapore, blowing in off the ocean, is soft as velvet, and heady as wine. It was the night of the full moon, and Thomas had been down at the harbor all day on ship's business. Edith and I ate alone. As soon as the servants were gone, we dropped off our kimonos and plunged into the pool.

"I feel as if I'm *alive* for the first time," Edith said when we were both breathless, hanging onto the edge of the deep pool. She gave me a chaste kiss with her wet lips. "Could we make love in the water, do you suppose?"

"We'd drown, ninny!"

"Lovely!"

"Let's try."

We could embrace and sink, then spring apart and kick off the bottom. It became a children's game with us there in the moonlight.

"We're two porpoises," Edith said. "Let's be them."

Sporting like porpoises in the small pool was our next game. Tired of it, finally, we sat on the edge of the pool, kicking our feet in the sun-warmed water.

I looked up and saw Thomas standing in a moon-shadow across the pool. "Peeping Tom!" I laughed and pointed a finger at him. "Shame!"

"Didn't you know he was there?" Edith asked in a matter-of-fact voice.

Thomas was taking off his clothes. Edith's hand found mine and cradled it between her breasts. My arm slid around her slender waist. It was thus we watched a naked Thomas plunge into the water for his quick swim.

When he had finished, the three of us, un-ashamedly naked, retired to the special room and found that the houseboy had prepared three opium pipes tonight. No words were spoken.

Our ménage à trois that tropic night had the quality of an erotic dream, as I'm sure that Thomas, or Edith—perhaps both of them—intended it should.

Senses heightened by the sweet opium smoke, all normal inhibitions asleep, we became three people, each intent to give pleasure to the other two.

It was a mirrored room, walls and ceiling, too, and the sensuality of three twining, naked bodies was greatly heightened by the flashing visual images above and all around us.

We lost all sense of time. There was a yesterday, and there would be a tomorrow, but *now* was a week, a month, a year.

There was no bed in the room because the floor was a soft, tufted mat. Edith and I were handmaidens to Thomas, sharing him between us, then Thomas and I caused her gasping raptures of sensual delight, before Edith and Thomas shared me.

Edith and I made love while Thomas rested. Then it was the three of us again, his appetite revived and heightened by our display, and thus it was all night, until dawn crept into the room and birds sang again.

Empty of passion, finally, the three of us lay on our backs, Thomas sandwiched between my body, and Edith's, strands of her long hair trailing across his chest.

"I've dreamed, but I never guessed," Edith sighed.

Thomas kissed her, then me, before he rose and left us.

We listened and heard his plunge into the

pool, and spatter of water on the tiles, the sound echoing in the courtyard. There was the surprised trill of a bird.

"Don't be jealous of what we've just shared," Edith said. "Thomas loves only you."

"You and he planned this, didn't you?" I wasn't accusing, but I did want to know.

"No. Some things just happen, Jeanette."

The two of us joined him in the pool.

Thomas was able to replace the crewmen lost overboard in the typhoon from among sailors ashore at Singapore, and we took aboard a new Chinese cook. Rajah Muda Hasim on Borneo was at war with the headhunting Dyak tribesmen, and had requested that Thomas bring him weapons. On previous voyages, the two men had become good friends. So our next port of call would be the Sultanate of Brunei, before reaching for Whampoa and Canton.

CHAPTER 16

BRUNEI IS a bite into the jungles of Borneo on the west coast, occupied by the Malays and their sworn enemies, the Dyaks, a primitive tribe. To reach it we had to cross the southern end of the South China Sea.

As soon as we sailed, Thomas was busy with his ship again. My role could have been that of the jealous and neglected wife, but I was learning. I had Thomas teach me to handle the shipping accounts and ship's log. Instead of dull and tedious, I found this work fascinating. Thomas was surprised.

"I didn't know that I'd married a useful wife,"

he said, grinning: "How did you get this way?"

"Miss Wentworth had some advanced ideas about young women," I told him. "She thought how to hold a teacup, and carry on coy conversations with eligible young men wasn't enough education."

"Cheers for Miss Wentworth."

"Wasn't Gwen useful?" I asked.

"My wife didn't have your head for figures," he said. "Anyway, she never sailed with me because of her health, and in England I hire bookkeepers and accountants in dozen lots. Dillard should do what you're doing for me, but the lad is a much better seaman than he is a scholar."

"You and Gwen must have been very lonely, with you at sea most of the time."

"In command of a ship, you're always lonely," Thomas said. "Gwen had her charity teas, and women friends, and then there was our daughter. She had a good life."

"Was she pretty?" I asked.

Thomas hesitated, then said, "Sometimes."

As she had after losing Santha, Edith stayed in her cabin with her books, as I did in mine. We were friendly when we met on deck, but there was a distance between us now that there hadn't been before. We were afraid, I suppose, of what we now knew about ourselves.

Strangely, I felt closer to the core of Thomas

than I ever had before, and could feel no jealousy of the part of him I'd had to share with Edith. I was too honest to deny that in a perverse way I'd wanted it to happen. I'd even wondered how *I* could bring it about!

The harbor of Brunei was empty when we dropped anchor, and began lightering to the beach guns and gunpowder. The town itself was a cluster of thatched huts on the edge of a dense jungle, except for the teakwood fort that was Rajah Muda Hasim's palace.

Muda Hasim inherited his jungle kingdom when his brother was murdered by Dyaks. A Moslem Malay, he also fell heir to his brother's harem, and kept a seraglio that contained twenty wives.

We were invited to a palace banquet by Muda Hasim, to show Thomas his appreciation. Edith and I followed Thomas up the muddy road to the palace gates, keeping the respectful ten paces behind the lima, as decreed in the Koran. Behind us marched an armed bodyguard of six sailors and Bob Dillard.

Thomas himself was armed with two pistols.

"I wouldn't be showing Muda Hasim proper respect if I came to his banquet without my bodyguard," Thomas explained, "aside from the fact that I'd be a damned fool to trust the man."

"You've said he was your friend." I was puzzled. "What kind of friends do you have?"

"We are friends," Thomas insisted, but added, "We're as friendly as a Moslem and Christian can be, that is."

A dozen evil-looking guards were slouched by the two massive teak doors that opened into Muda Hasim's compound. Wearing scraps of uniform, they were armed with flintlock muskets.

"Deploy your men here," Thomas ordered Dillard, when we were a scant twenty yards from the gates. "Stay alert, and if you hear shots inside, rush the gate."

"Aye, sir." Bob Dillard looked worried. "Are we expecting trouble?"

"No. Just a pleasant meal for the ladies and me, with a bit of entertainment afterward, but you never know what's liable to happen on Borneo," Thomas told him. "I know good men who thought they knew what was going to happen, but aren't around to tell about what actually happened."

"I'm properly scared." Dillard grinned weakly. "Have a good time, sir."

"Do you suppose I could plead a headache and go back to the ship?" Edith whispered to me, only half-joking.

"If it were too dangerous, Thomas would have come alone," I whispered back, and hoped I was right.

Once inside the gates, Edith and I were pleasantly surprised to find ourselves in a long, narrow courtyard, with a profusion of sweet-smelling flowers, and a large, shallow pool filled with lazy carp. In a flowing white robe and slippers, the rajah himself came to greet us.

Tall for a Malay, with piercing black eyes set in a thin brown face, he carried himself as a prince should. Ignoring us women, as a good Moslem should, he greeted Thomas with a bow, then shook his hand.

"Allah be praised." There was a ready quality to his high-pitched voice, and the smile that seemed to be fixed on his face never reached those piercing eyes. "I am honored that you see fit to bring your wives to my poor banquet." His English was almost unaccented. "Come. My miserable cooks have prepared the meal that it is certain will be tasteless."

Thomas didn't bother to explain that both of us weren't his wives. "Why confuse him?" he said afterward.

We followed Muda Hasim down the courtyard and into the banquet hall. This, like the court, was long and narrow with a dais at one end. On the dais was a round couch with pillows. It was here that Muda Hasim would lounge while two of his younger wives fed him.

There was a couch for Thomas on his right hand. Muda Hasim clapped his hands, and servants placed a couch for Edith and me to share across the table from Thomas.

At the other end of the table, near the door, there were places set for Muda Hasim's wives who weren't serving him. After we arrived, they filed in and took their places, chattering among themselves like so many magpies.

To judge from the tone of their voices, there were some scandalized comments when they saw Edith and me at the head of the table with Thomas, but a sharp clap of Muda Hasim's hands stilled that topic of conversation.

His wives ranged in age from mere children to elderly women with drooping breasts and seamed faces. All wore ankle-length, wrap-around skirts, but were bare from the waist up. There seemed to be some significance in the number of combs a wife thrust in her hair.

The youngest wore only one or two tortoise-shell combs, and these simple ones. The young women, however, had as many as three or four of more intricate design. One older woman had a dozen! The least number any of the older women had was five. And these combs were inlaid with pearls and gems.

Thomas surprised me by being fluent in the Malay dialect Muda Hasim spoke. Neither Edith nor I had any idea what the men were discussing, except that Britain and England kept cropping up. Thomas spoke forcefully, Muda Hasim asked polite questions through that fixed smile, but I sensed that whatever Thomas was telling him was being taken with more than one grain of salt.

After a while, Thomas must have had the same idea, because his tone changed, his gestures became less abrupt, and this conversation was punctuated with laughter.

Kava was the only drink served—a sort of beer fermented from peppers. The roast pork had a not unpleasant smoky taste, and the baked yams and taro root were delicious. For the first time Edith and I tasted breadfruit.

I'd heard many discussions about this Polynesian fruit back on Haiti. Planters scoffed at the English effort to bring breadfruit trees to the West Indies as food for slaves. I expected it to taste like bread. Actually, I learned that it gets its name from the shape and size of the fruit. The taste was too bland for Edith and me, but it was nourishing.

Entertainment after the meal was staged in the courtyard by a troupe of black Melanesians, boys and girls. Music was furnished by three drummers, each drumhead tuned to a different pitch, and the dancing was lighted by smoking torches.

Muda Hasim's chattering wives sat cross-legged to watch. Servants brought us chairs.

Boys and girls danced naked, with palm oil rubbed into their black skins so that their bodies glistened. The dance started slowly, to the beat of one drum, boys in one file, girls in another, but quickened in tempo when the second drum joined in. Boys and girls danced toward each other, only to draw back. From gestures and inviting looks exchanged, I realized this was some sort of courting dance.

The third drum contributed its higher-pitched throb. Now the pace was frenzied, bare feet beating a tattoo, slim young bodies writhing. The drummers increased the beat.

The wives, no longer chattering among themselves, were intent on the dance, as was Muda Hasim. The two files merged into one file, then shattered apart as each boy claimed a partner.

What had been an erotic dance became an orgy! Girls, thrown to the ground, were mounted by boys, and boys, on their backs, bounced the girls astride their bellies—all this lubricious movement in time with the wild and frenetic beat of the drums!

Torchlight reflected from their oiled young bodies, and the sound of flesh on flesh, as well as the gasps and groans of erotic pleasure, heightened the madness of this scene.

I glanced at Edith, just as she looked to see how I was reacting, and our eyes met. Her face was swollen and flushed, lips parted, and I knew that her blood was as hot as my own.

The drums stopped. The pumping, writhing lithe black bodies froze in a tableau of lust, then parted, boys grinning impishly at their rapt audience, girls smiling.

Muda Hasim clapped his hands, and gourds of kava were given to the sweating dancers and drained in a few gulps. Then, in two files, hips twitching, they disappeared into the darkness at the other end of the courtyard.

"It's time we leave," Thomas said in a quiet voice.

"Allah be praised if you and your wives have found some small enjoyment in my poor entertainment," Muda Hasim leered through his fixed smile. "Perhaps you would like to see three of my boys perform with one of the girls? Privately, of course."

"Some other time," Thomas said. "We have to get back to the ship, rajah."

"They show some talent, these four," Muda Hasim urged.

"You have honored us too much, rajah. The bringing of guns was only a poor favor, and not worthy of such hospitality." Thomas was actually smirking! "I am always your friend and your servant."

With a side-glance at Edith and me, Muda Hasim suggested something to Thomas in his own language.

Thomas flushed before he answered.

Still smiling, but with disappointment reflected in his eyes, Muda Hasim showed us to the gate. He and Thomas bowed their farewells.

On our way back through Brunei to where the ship's boat waited, I asked Thomas, "What was that last thing he said?"

"He offered me four of his women—or boys, if

I preferred them—to show you two the sensual delights of his earthly paradise," Thomas said.

"I don't understand," Edith said.

"It would have been a swap," Thomas explained. "I would lend him you two wives, and get his women or boys for the rest of the night."

"Now I understand," Edith said. "But what could a man do with *four* boys?"

Thomas grinned. "You might be surprised."

"Do you think he could handle *four* women all at once?" I asked Edith.

She giggled.

Thomas glared at us.

"What were you discussing with Muda Hasim at the banquet?" I asked Thomas when we were alone in our cabin. "It had an interesting sound to it."

"We British need Brunei. Malay and Chinese pirates operate out of bays and coves all along the Borneo coast, bribing the Dyaks with guns to leave them alone. He hasn't any navy. I was telling him that he should ask us into his sultanate."

"Do you think he will?" I asked.

"Sooner or later he'll have to," Thomas said. "He's not convinced yet, however. What concerns him immediately are the pirates."

"Because they're arming his enemies?"

Thomas shook his head. "It's not that at all.

Only a few of the pirate captains are paying what he considers a proper tribute. He wants us British to make them pay up."

"I don't understand," I said.

Thomas laughed. "Stop trying. People have gone crazy trying to understand how the Oriental mind works. I like you sane." Raising my chin, Thomas kissed me, his lips lingering on mine, before he said, "But we're wasting the rest of this night on idle chatter. I have a better idea."

"So have I, Thomas," I confessed.

We sailed with the tide the next morning for the treaty port of Whampoa, twelve miles down the Pearl River from Canton.

I remember the passage to Whampoa as a series of velvet tropic nights, and long, lazy days when the now-familiar creaking sounds of the *Mary Freeman* underway, and the rush of water along her hull, were muted music.

We exchanged greetings with an Indianman, outward bound from Whampoa after discussing cargo, and learned there had been another riot.

"To the Chinese, we're barbarians, blue-eyed foreign devils," Thomas told me when I asked about the riots. "The mandarins let us use the treaty ports only because they're afraid of what we might do if they don't. Sailors get drunk and rape a Chinese woman, or kill a coolie with their horseplay, and hell breaks loose. I've seen one such riot in Macao. I hope I never see another!"

"Is it dangerous for the missionaries?" I asked.

"Very. Dr. Phelps is a fool to bring Edith out here. Do you know what the Japanese did with the Jesuit priests on their island?"

"No."

"Crucified every last one of them," Thomas said in a grim voice. "Sooner or later, something like that is going to happen to these missionaries trying to make Christians out of people who had the printing press three thousand years before Christ."

"Do you suppose Edith knows the danger?" I asked.

His eyes softened. "I doubt it. I know Dr. Phelps wouldn't have told her. He's a bible-spouting old fool who can't see the end of his nose. I've met him once or twice."

"Shouldn't we warn her?" I asked.

"I spoke to Edith about the danger when you were sick," Thomas said. "I even offered her passage back to England, should she change her mind. I don't think I frightened her."

"How long will we be in Whampoa?" I asked.

"Two weeks, three, maybe a month. It depends on their harvest of the tea crop this year. We have to wait until sampans bring it down the river."

I groaned. "Do we have to live aboard ship all that time?"

"No." Thomas grinned. "I own a compound on the outskirts of Whampoa, near the mission, as a matter of fact. I use it when I lie in here, and so do my captains. It's important *face*."

"Face? What is that?" I asked.

"*Face* for an Englishman is owning a compound, staffed with dozens of servants. If I stayed aboard my ship to save money, I'd lose face. Then no self-respecting Chinese merchant would have anything to do with me."

"You mean you've bought and *own* a compound way out here?" I said. "You're full of surprises, Thomas."

"You'll have to get used to the idea that you didn't marry a beggar," Thomas said.

"It's going to be hard," I told him, "but I'll try."

Thomas grinned and gave my bottom a sharp slap. "You just do that."

When we'd anchored off the mouth of the Pearl River, half a dozen jabbering Chinese pilots swarmed aboard to bargain with Thomas. He dismissed them to strike a bargain with a seedy-looking Australian bantam of a man who was half-drunk.

"Why did you pick *him* to take us up to Whampoa?" I asked. "He'll run us onto a sandbar for sure!"

"Maybe," Thomas admitted, "but the rule of

thumb here is never trust your ship to a Chinese pilot. Some are honest, but others take your money and a bribe from the coolies who would pull you off a bar. That's happened to me just once. I don't intend to have it happen again."

BOOK THREE

CHAPTER 17

WE FOUND the broad stretch of the Pearl River that curves through Whampoa, dividing the city, was thronged with more than a hundred ships, of all nationalities, waiting for the tea harvest. Some, like the *Mary Freeman,* swung at anchor apart from the others, but most were lashed together, with walkways from ship to ship.

Both banks of the river, behind wide promenades, were lined with foreign warehouses, or *hongs,* the lower floor for merchandise, the upper one for living quarters and offices. These *hongs,* like the ships, were linked by walkways.

Slipper boats moved among the ships, selling

fruit and vegetables, chickens, pigs, and fresh fish. Singsong Chinese and Eurasian girls sold themselves from the flower boats.

On the promenade Chinese gentlemen, in their silk robes, carrying caged birds, mingled with drunk sailors, captains, foreign merchants, and girls and women of every nationality and color.

Urchins darted in and out of the crowd, pimping or selling souvenirs.

Whampoa itself stretched behind the promenades, a welter of houses that seemed piled one on top of the other, with an occasional stately pagoda rearing above the tiled roofs. The narrow, crooked streets were crowded with rickshas, sweating coolies trying to move as fast as the lounging foreigner—most times a drunk sailor —wanted them to go.

The windows of every house and shop facing the streets were barred with iron grillwork. Trickles of smoke from braziers, and the smells of cooking food, blended with sandalwood temple incense, and the stink of excrement, both human and animal.

There was a lame beggar on every corner, some eaten with leprosy. And with it all, anywhere in Whampoa, there was the smell of the river.

News of our arrival off the mouth of the Pearl River to pick up a pilot had been sent by carrier pigeon to Whampoa, and Dr. Phelps came aboard the *Mary Freeman* to welcome Edith, and see her to his mission.

Dr. Phelps was a tall, gangling man, with stooped shoulders and gold-rimmed spectacles perched on the bridge of his crag of a nose. Watery blue eyes were set too closely together, for my taste, and a full beard compensated for his thinning hair which he combed across the bald top of his head.

"Miss Radcliff, Miss Radcliff!" he greeted a startled Edith, reaching for her hands. "How was the voyage, my dear? The Lord be praised that you have arrived safely!"

The expression on Edith's face was stoic, as she avoided his grasping hands, welcoming Dr. Phelps with only a curt nod. "How do you do, Dr. Phelps?" Her voice was formal and stiff. "May I introduce my friends?"

If Dr. Phelps was taken aback, he didn't let it show. "Captain Townsend and I have a long acquaintance," he said, "but I don't believe I know the young woman."

"She is Mrs. Townsend," Edith said. "They were married on Malta."

"My dear chap!" Dr. Phelps gave Thomas's hand a vigorous shake. "May God bless your marriage!"

"Thank you," Thomas said. "How is it at the mission these days?"

Dr. Phelps's enthusiasm dissolved. "The Lord's work is always difficult in a heathen country such

239

as China," he intoned in a sad voice. "You captains, the merchants, and the sinful men who come off the ships, I'm afraid, don't set a good example. We try to teach these pagans Christian love and humility, but you undo all our good work."

Thomas let the sermonette pass without comment.

"I'm afraid I've come aboard your ship to ask a favor," Dr. Phelps went on. "In the recent riot, our mission suffered the fury of the mob. They didn't quite destroy it, but no quarters are immediately available for Miss Radcliff. I'm living in a tent until we can rebuild."

I thought that Edith silently sighed her relief.

"If she could enjoy the hospitality of your compound, Captain Townsend, the Lord will reward you," Dr. Phelps said.

"Edith is always welcome to share hospitality with Jeanette and me," Thomas said with unconscious irony. "Don't give the matter another thought."

"I'll come to see you," Dr. Phelps told Edith, "and we'll discuss the Lord's work that you've been called to do."

Biting her lips, and paler than usual, Edith sail, "Yes, please do that, Dr. Phelps."

He stooped to brush a kiss on her cheek before he left.

"That bastard!" Thomas said, when he was

gone. Then he laughed. "You've made a good first impression on your boss, Edith."

She fled the deck, leaving me alone with my husband.

"I see why you don't like Dr. Phelps," I said.

"That unctous bastard?" Thomas laughed. "He brought a wife and child out here, to let the climate kill them. It's too bad that Chinese mob destroyed only his mission."

I went to find Edith and found her perched on the edge of her bunk, her face still wet with tears in spite of the sodden handkerchief she was twisting with her hands.

I offered my handkerchief. "What's the matter, Edith?"

"The man we just met *couldn't* have written those letters I received! What am I going to do? I made a half-promise I'd marry him, and that's why he sent the money for my passage."

"You're coming back to England with Thomas and me," I said. "We can't leave you here with Dr. Phelps, and you've heard what he said about the mission."

"I can't go back," Edith said, in a resigned voice. "I've burned my bridges. I couldn't stand the humiliation."

I sat beside her, my arm around her slender waist, and kissed her wet cheek. "You taste salty," I said.

Edith laughed, with a catch in her throat.

I smoothed the hair away from her forehead.

"You can and will go back, Edith. There's nothing but danger for you here. Thomas has offered you passage home."

"He's told you that?" she said.

"Yes."

"It was while you were sick."

"I know."

"Jeanette, I have to stay here in Whampoa and do what I came to do. Not marry Dr. Phelps, perhaps, but nurse the sick. I have to have some purpose in life!"

"You'll have time to decide," I said. "There are sick people back in England."

Edith took my face between her hands, and kissed me on the mouth. "Thank you."

I returned her kiss and said, "You're very welcome, Edith."

Edith and I rode in one ricksha, pulled by an emaciated coolie, and Thomas rode behind us in a second one. Bringing up the rear was a third ricksha, piled with our baggage.

As our coolies worked their way through the narrow, crooked streets, hostile stares from the Chinese we met convinced me that they truly considered us foreign devils. Within a mile I learned why.

A staggering drunk American sailor was between the shafts of a ricksha, bellowing, "Gangway, you slant-eyed Chinks!"

The terrified ricksha coolie was huddled in the seat, clutching his pigtail.

Behind them came another ricksha, with three American sailors squeezed into the seat. They'd cut off their coolie's pigtail and took turns whipping him with it, laughing uproariously whenever he fell to his knees.

Springing out in thes road, Thomas brought the first sailor up short by grabbing a handful of his blouse. "American scum!" He punched the sailor to his knees, then kicked him away to face the other three.

They came at him with knives, in an ugly mood. Thomas had no weapon but his fists. While two faced Thomas, feinting with their knives, the third sailor circled to get behind him.

"Look out!" I called, and stumbled out of my ricksha.

The tall black man burst out of an alley with the speed and stealth of a big cat. With a kick to the wrist, Thomas had disarmed one of his assailants and was struggling with the other.

I screamed as I saw the American behind him raise his knife.

The black man caught his knife arm, twisted savagely, and I heard the bone snap. As the sailor went down, screaming pain, the black man kicked him out of his way.

Thomas stooped, lifted the man who still had a knife by rolling him over his bent back, then, still holding his arm, slammed him down in the road.

The other two ran, leaving their injured comrades.

With a wide grin, and a pat to Thomas' shoulder, the black man was gone as quickly as he'd come, disappearing into the Chinese crowd.

My heart lurched. Terrified for Thomas, it wasn't until he was gone in the crowd that I recognized Amos, Jamie's mate!

Thomas helped the man with the broken arm to his feet and lifted him into one of the empty rickshas. The other sailor was on his knees, then his feet, shaking his head. Thomas watched him climb in with the injured men.

"Chop-chop, back to shipee," Thomas ordered the cringing coolie without a pigtail.

Thomas turned to me, dusting off his clothes. Amusement crinkled the corners of his eyes. "You look as if you've seen a ghost, Jeanette." He helped me back into the ricksha beside Edith. "Chop-chop, more fastee," he ordered our coolie.

By the time we reached the compound, I was no longer sure that I'd seen Amos. I half-convinced myself that it was a trick of my imagination.

The compound was just beyond Whampoa's crumbling ancient wall, situated in a formal Chinese garden behind a high plank fence. The house was small, compared to the one in Singapore, and shaded by willow trees. There was a separate tile-roofed cottage in back with the servants.

Number One Boy at the compound was Mr. Woo, a dignified Chinese gentleman. Thomas had informed him when we would arrive, and the five other servants were lined up to greet us. There was a houseboy, a cook, a gardener, and two maids, Mi Ling and Su Lin.

The girls were tiny, with bound feet. Their almond-shaped eyes as black as shoe buttons. Mi Ling would look after Edith, Su Lin would be my maid.

Plaited bamboo formed the walls of the small house, and red tile the roof. It was furnished with intricately carved teak, mahoghany, and ebony. The kitchen and servant quarters were apart from the main house.

While Thomas inspected the gardens, and planned our supper with Mr. Woo, Su Lin bathed me with hot towels while I stood in a deep basin, then helped me dress in black Shantung silk pajamas.

"Velly nice, velly plitty, missy." When she smiled, her black eyes danced.

"Thank you, Su Lin."

"Missy like tea now?"

"If you please."

I joined Edith for the hot green tea served by Mi Ling and Su Lin, with rice cakes.

"There's a lot to be said for a Chinese hot towel bath," Edith told me, "but Mi Ling has convinced me that you don't wear white in China."

She was wearing a ruffled pink blouse and a black wrap-around skirt made of cotton that she'd bought in Singapore.

"Why not?" I asked.

"It's the color of mourning. She nearly had a fit when I wanted to wear my white dress."

Both of us were refreshed after the hot day and the ricksha journey from the river.

"I've pulled myself together since this morning, Jeanette," Edith said. "I haven't really given Lester Phelps a fair chance. I feel that I owe him at least that. With the trouble he's had at the mission, I don't imagine he was at his best this morning."

"That could be," I said, but I was experiencing a strange emotion where Edith was concerned.

The vision of her in Dr. Phelps's arms disgusted me! What would that beard be like in bed?

We sipped our tea, each of us lost in her own thoughts. There was a tiny court in the middle of the house, with wind bells. Dangling from strings, they tingled whenever a breeze fanned them.

"I suppose, in time, I could get used to that awful beard," Edith said, as much to herself as to me. "My father had one, but then we didn't sleep together."

Thomas joined us, and Mr. Woo brought him a scotch. He seemed to be preoccupied and absent-minded.

"We were talking about Dr. Phelps," I said.

"Hmm." Thomas tasted his drink, then tossed it down. He regarded Edith. "Mr. Woo?"

Mr. Woo refilled his glass.

"You shouldn't let him get his hands on you," Thomas told Edith. "I know his unctuous kind. Not that it's my business."

"You've known she promised to marry him?" I asked, surprised.

"Of course." Thomas held up his drink to study the color. "Out here a single white woman is fair game."

"That really wouldn't be a new experience for me," Edith said. "Englishmen aren't that much different from Chinese men."

"Take my word, there is a difference," Thomas said. "Different ships, different splices. This is China, not Sussex or Hampshire, and outside the treaty ports, mandarins and the warlords rule absolutely. Without the protection of a husband, women disappear. Macao is the marketplace for girls and women. The lucky ones are bought by a white slaver and shipped to a brothel."

"*English* women disappear?" Edith asked incredulously. "I can't believe it. China is supposed to have the oldest civilization in the world."

"English women disappear," Thomas said. "Dutch, French, Danish, even Portuguese women, disappear. I know of half a dozen instances. As I've said, the lucky ones are bought by a white slaver. The unlucky women fall into the hands of some mandarin or warlord. When he tires of her in bed, his Chinese women get the woman and provide their lord and master with entertainment."

Edith was wide-eyed.

"I think I'm going to be sorry for asking, but what kind of entertainment?" I said.

"With the Chinese, torture is a fine art," Thomas told me. "The women are particularly adept at it, and especially if a white girl or woman is their victim."

"If you thought to frighten me," Edith said, "you've just succeeded."

Thomas finished his drink. "Come back to England with Jeanette and me," he said.

"I'll think about it," Edith promised.

When we were alone that night, I asked Thomas if he wasn't afraid that the American sailors he'd assaulted might want to even the score.

"Sobered-up, I don't think they would," he told me. "The Americans aren't all that bad a lot. Those men were off one of the fur ships in the river."

"Fur ships?"

"Yes. There's a big market for American fur here in China. The Americans bring their furs here and take back tea, silk, jade, and art objects. A few Americans bring out sandalwood from the Sandwich Islands."

"Did you recognize the man who helped you?" I asked.

"No." Thomas shook his head. "An occasional whaler comes up the river. He was probably off one of them," Thomas said. "They ship some blacks for their two- or three-year voyages."

After sharing Thomas with his ship for the weeks we'd been at sea, I had his full attention that first night, and he had mine.

There was no way that Thomas and I could have enough of each other, there in the scented darkness. My hunger was as great as his. Before our sensuality was slaked, however, we had to rest our tired bodies, and I lay in the crook of his arm.

Thomas toyed with a strand of my hair. "It grows fast," he remarked.

"Fortunately. Thomas?"

"What is it now?

"I can't stand the idea of Edith in bed with Dr. Phelps."

"Then don't think about it," he said.

CHAPTER 18

MI LING and Su Lin were cousins, I learned, and
came from Wuchow up the Sinkiang River above
Canton. Mr. Woo had bought them away from
their families to help him serve the blue-eyed
barbarians. It didn't occur to happy little Su Lin
that she was virtually a slave. For the first time in
her life, she was getting enough to eat, wore pajamas that weren't in rags, and looked forward to
whatever marriage Mr. Woo might arrange for
her. It was the same with Mi Ling, Edith's maid.

They were Buddhists and reverently burned
joss sticks before the small statue of Lord Buddha
set up in the servant quarters. I learned that Edith

and I weren't the first mistresses they had served at the compound—evidently the other captains didn't go without female companionship when they went ashore at Whampoa—but I was their first wife.

"How much childlen?" Su Lin asked me, and held up one, two, three, four, then five fingers.

"None yet, dear." I said.

"Velly bad, missy!" Hugging herself, her eyes filled with tears. "Velly soon husband go chop-chop."

"I don't think so, Su Lin. We haven't been married very long."

She didn't believe me. "You old, Missy. Must have childlen. Not sons so you sell?"

"We don't sell our children, Su Lin," I told her, but I could see she didn't believe that either.

Edith was as much of an enigma to Mi Ling.

"The girl thinks I should be a great-grand-mother at my age," Edith told me exasperatedly. "She says a girl should start having babies when she's eleven or twelve. Boys, of course. Did you know that both of these children have a child?"

"No." The cousins couldn't have been more than thirteen.

"It's true. They were married off to old men. Mi Ling's husband died during a famine, and Su Lin's was beheaded for some trifling offense. I think he was accused of stealing a pig."

"What's happened to the children?" I asked.

"Their families kept them because they were

252

boys. I asked about their bound feet because I understand that peasants don't do that to their girls. The Lings and the Lins are some sort of petty officials in Wuchow. If Mi Ling and Su Lin come from good families, I cringe when I think what peasant life must be like."

With Edith and Dr. Lester Phelps, I visited the Methodist mission that was being rebuilt by coolie labor. It wasn't more than a mile from the compound, but was within Whampoa, a stark yellow brick building in a slum of bamboo shacks.

Dr. Phelps told us it had once been a jail and place of execution. "The wealthy merchant who sold it to us, God forgive him, didn't say that people had been tortured and beheaded here," Dr. Phelps told us. "It's unfortunate. These people believe that our building is haunted by the spirits of the dead."

The angry mob had stormed through the mission, breaking furniture and setting fire to some of the rooms. But most of their fury had been spent on the small chapel. Pews shipped out from England had been chopped into splinters, and they'd made a bonfire of the hymnals. Dr. Phelps was philosophic about the English hymnals.

"The orphan children young enough to learn English are too young to sing," he said, "and the older ones find English, with all our r's, too hard."

The room on an upper floor that was supposed to have been Edith's dispensary and hospital was burned out, as were two adjoining rooms that were being prepared for her.

Dr. Phelps showed us, with some embarrassment, the small closet where he'd hidden from the fury of the mob.

"I am afraid, when it comes down to it, that I'm not the stuff of martyrs, God forgive me," he said. "I flatter myself that I hid because it was God's will I should, since my work for Him here is barely begun."

My second impression of Dr. Phelps was much better than my first. The same was true of Edith. If it had been me, the pitiful condition of the mission would have been so discouraging that I'd have taken passage on the first ship leaving Whampoa.

Not Edith. "This is a challenge to us as Christians, isn't it?" she said to Dr. Phelps.

I saw the Edith who had organized the dispensary aboard the *Mary Freeman* and persuaded the Welshmen and me to help in her work of mercy.

Dr. Phelps's drawn and tired face beamed. "I see I have chosen well, Miss Radcliff. God be praised! With you at my right hand, Christ will prevail here in Whampoa."

"If you can send a ricksha, I'll come here to help clean up tomorrow," Edith said. We were in the wrecked room that would be the dispensary and hospital. "Were your medical supplies saved?" she asked.

Dr. Phelps nodded. "Our medical supplies

were well hidden. This time we had some warning there would be a riot. A drunken seaman defiled a Buddhist temple not far from here." He turned to me. "I beg your forgiveness, Mrs. Townsend."

"For what, Dr. Phelps?"

"For chastising your husband. I was taxing him with the sins of others. Captain Townsend is a good, fair man. We need more like him on the China run."

"May I tell him you said that?" I asked.

"Please do." He paused, then said, "He and I have had our differences in times past, but I am ready to forgive and forget if he is."

"I'm sure Thomas isn't the sort of man who carries a grudge," I told Dr. Phelps.

Riding in a ricksha back to the compound, Edith was in a thoughtful mood. She stared off into space, hands clasped in her lap. To visit the mission, she'd worn one of her severe, high-necked dresses, and the glow she'd been showing was gone.

"Tuppence for your thoughts," I said.

"For the first time since my father died, I feel I'm needed somewhere, Jeanette. I can use my skills here, healing the sick."

"How do you feel about Lester Phelps?" I asked.

"I don't know," she confessed. "His letters reminded me of my father—I know that now. The man himself . . ." She sighed. "I just don't know.

I wonder what he and Thomas quarreled about."

"I wonder myself," I said.

That night I asked Thomas. Edith had gone to bed early and we were alone. He'd just bought two boxes of fine Havana cigars from an American skipper who'd been in the West Indies recently and was in a comfortable mood.

"Phelps is on the side of the mandarins so far as the opium trade is concerned," Thomas said. "He came aboard my ship once and denounced me for dealing in the stuff. I nearly tossed him in the river."

"What do the mandarins have against opium?" I asked. "It's a good medicine for killing pain."

"The Chinese peasant uses it to kill the pain of living," Thomas said. "Crops are neglected and famine results. Hungry people are liable to blame their overlords, and that causes trouble for the mandarins. They have to buy more warlords, and support more troops."

"I can see why they don't want it brought into China," I said. "How do they try to stop the traffic?"

"By passing laws they can't enforce. There will always be opium smugglers. There is too much profit in the trade for us to stop. Anyway, peasants back in India will starve if the trade is cut off, and Indiamen will rot at the docks. If it comes down to it, we British will have to go to war to save the opium trade."

"You've mentioned that," I said. "It seems like an odd reason for a war."

Thomas laughed. "Wars have been fought, lost, and won for less reason. Take your Napoleon, for instance. He's spending French blood to buy thrones for his relatives."

"Thank you very much," I said, "but I'm a British citizen now, and he isn't *my* Napoleon. He left us to rot in Haiti."

The corners of Thomas's eyes crinkled. "Sorry," he said. "I was carried away." He laughed. "You have a bit of a temper, don't you?"

"Are you just finding that out?" I asked.

"I've always suspected it."

To change the subject, and because I wanted to know, I asked Thomas if he'd seen the man who helped him against the drunk Americans.

"No, I haven't," he said, frowning. "Why are you so interested?"

"He looked like someone I used to know back in the West Indies. A mate aboard a ship," I explained.

"What ship was that?"

"The *Salem Witch*."

Thomas drew on his cigar and studied me for a moment before he said, "The next time I go to the ship, I'll ask around about him. What was the name of this mate you knew?"

"He was called Amos."

"What shall I do if I find him?" Thomas asked.

257

"Tell him . . ." I had to think. "Just tell him that I've asked about him," I finished lamely.

If the man was Amos, and he'd somehow survived the mutiny, Jamie was dead.

I was torturing myself. For a moment, I wanted to tell Thomas about Jamie McCoy and what we'd had, and he might have understood—but that moment passed.

When we made love that night, I closed my eyes and unashamedly pretended that Thomas was Jamie, and we were back aboard the *Salem Witch*. The body of Thomas wasn't on mine, it was Jamie's, and I nearly called his name.

"When are you going to stop dreaming?" Thomas asked when we were finished, and lay side by side.

"What do you mean, dreaming?"

"Where do you go, Jeanette?" Thomas was angry. "Remember me? I'm your husband."

"I don't know what you mean, and stop talking to me like that," I snapped. "Did you know that sometimes you're impossible?"

"No, I didn't know that. Thank you for telling me. I thought I was a man who wants the woman he loves to think of him instead of someone else when they're making love."

"Leave it alone!" My anger now matched his. "You're not going to tell me how to think. Who do you think I am?"

His eyes narrowed. "Jeanette, I intend to find out, and right now. I started to do something once that I didn't finished."

"No, you don't!" Sliding off the bed, I bolted for the door.

A stride behind me, Thomas caught my hair. "Not so fast."

"Let go! Leave me alone!" When he let go my hair I turned on him. "Damn you, Thomas."

He caught my wrist when I tried to slap him. "I always finish what I start," he said. "It's time you found that out."

"Don't you dare lay a hand on me!"

Tucking me under his arm, Thomas carried me back to the bed. Settling on the edge of it, he turned me over his knee.

"I'll kill you!" I yelled.

The smack of his callused hand on my bare bottom rang out like a pistol shot.

"Thomas!"

"Shut up!" He smacked me again, harder this time. .

I kicked and squirmed and strained. I called him names I didn't realize I knew. French names and English names. It was no use.

Thomas was hurting me, but at the same time the warmth from my spanked bottom was heating my blood, and to my amazement, I wanted Thomas more than I'd ever wanted him before.

"Please!" Swearing hadn't stopped him—maybe begging would. "Stop, Thomas, please!"

There was a sharp rap on the door. "Jeanette?" It was the frightened voice of Edith.

Before either of us could answer, she pushed the door open. "My God!" A hand jumped to her throat. "What are you *doing* to her, Thomas?"

Dumping me off his knees, Thomas snatched a sheet off the bed and stood up. "Edith . . ." He didn't get any further.

I couldn't help it. I had to laugh at the sight of the two of them. Both Thomas and Edith stared at me as if I'd gone mad. A fourth person would have laughed even louder. The chastised wife was sitting there on the floor, completely naked and hugging her knees, with tears running down her face while she laughed.

"Edith, it's all right," I managed to gasp.

"Oh." She straightened her shoulders, and gathered the robe she was wearing closer around her. "Please excuse me. I thought . . ." Her face turned brick-red. "Never mind what I thought!"

She was gone, closing the door behind her.

Thomas helped me to my feet and wiped my tears away with a corner of the sheet.

"I'm leaving early tomorrow morning to go to the ship," Thomas blurted. "You explain this to Edith, if you can!"

"Coward." I was smiling.

"Jeanette . . ."

"Shut up, Thomas." I linked my arms around his neck. "Shut up."

Afterward, when I lay in his arms, both of us

satiated, I said, "Who was I thinking about *this* time, Thomas?"

"Me?"

"You had my full attention," I said.

Thomas sighed. "It took a bit of doing to get it," he told me. "What are you going to tell Edith?"

"Let me worry about her. I'll think of something. Right now my mind is somewhere else."

Thomas was as good as his word. He was up and gone from the compound before sunrise. Mr. Woo served our breakfast in the garden.

I joined Edith at the table and eased my stinging bottom into a chair.

"Good morning." She was going to be impersonal. "How did you sleep?"

"On my stomach," I said.

Edith paused with the spoon she was lifting halfway to her mouth.

"And very soundly," I added.

Edith took the bite, then laid the spoon aside and reached for a napkin. "I *did* knock," she said. She patted her lips with the napkin. "Twice."

"One thing sort of led to another last night," I told her. "I appreciate your trying to come to my rescue."

There was the hint of a twinkle in Edith's violet eyes. "I'll just bet you do!"

We both laughed, then finished our breakfasts. Dr. Phelps had sent a ricksha for Edith to take her to the mission. For the first time, I'd be alone in the compound all day, except for the servants.

In the middle of the day, a coolie brought me a note from Thomas. The Pearl River was rapidly reaching flood stage, so he would have to find a safer anchorage for the *Mary Freeman*. He wouldn't be back at the compound until tomorrow morning.

"Thomas sent medical supplies to the mission from the ship's supply," Edith told me when she came back to the compound this evening. "Lester was very pleased."

"That was a nice thing to do," I said.

"Knowing his opinion of missions and missionaries, I'd say it was. Further, he's promised to ask the other captains to do the same."

Edith was tired and hollow-eyed, but she looked content. "Lester asked me to marry him today," she said.

"Did you say you would?" I asked.

Edith brushed hair away from her forehead. "No. I asked him for time to think it over. He was very understanding."

The sound in the warm night was that of a distant thunderstorm, but it seemed to be coming from every direction. Without further warning, there was an earsplitting roar, and the bed was wrenched out from under me.

I was thrown on the floor. I tried to rise to my

hands and knees, but was flung down again, and the house was crackling as the plaited bamboo sawed back and forth, and roof tiles smashed down outside.

The roaring sound drowned any cries and screams. Unable to kneel, sit, or stand, all I could do was hug the floor and wonder if this was the end of the world.

The floor was moving in staccato jerks that rolled me from side to side. A roof beam crashed, and then another. There was the crackling sound of broken pottery, and through the window I could see a willow tree snapping back and forth.

Then the roar vanished in the distance, and there was the terrible stillness of death.

CHAPTER 19

I WAS on my hands and knees now. A slanted roof timber prevented me from rising further until I crawled out from under it. When I did, and stood up in the shambles of what had been a bedroom, there was no longer any roof. I was staring up at the stars. The walls were buckled at crazy angles. The bed had turned over and was upside-down.

The air was filled with acrid, choking dust.

The doorframe stood, but the partitions had been jerked away from it, and the door was flung down, ripped from its hinges. I thought I was deaf until I realized that as yet there was nothing to hear.

There was only that deadly silence.

Numbly I wondered if Edith had survived the earthquake, but was momentarily too dazed to do anything but wonder as I stumbled across the canted floor of the wrecked house, and into the garden.

Where the servant quarters had been was a mound of broken tiles and bamboo rubbish. Through the haze of dust I saw dim figures crawling and staggering from that heap of rubbish, and now I heard their sharp cries.

Edith!

Turning, I jostled into her. We stood back and reached to steady each other.

"That must have been an earthquake," she said in a small voice.

"I think it was." Neither of us made much sense yet. "Are you all right?"

"Yes. I couldn't sleep and was out in the garden when it started. It knocked me flat on my back."

"I was thrown out of bed."

"Missy!" The houseboy tugged my sleeve, his face wet with tears. "Come along chop-chop. Mr. Woo, him dead."

Both of us burst out of the cocoon of stunned inactivity. A flying tile from the roof had struck Mr. Woo when he tried to flee.

The bare foot of the gardener, still clad in a

pajama leg, stuck out of the house wreckage. A beam had crushed his chest before he was buried.

Su Lin was on the ground sobbing as she nursed a broken arm. There was a gash on her forehead, and blood trickled down her cheek.

Mi Ling had escaped the tumbling house unscathed, but terror had snapped her mind. Her only speech was animal sounds in her throat. Her eyes stared to see nothing as she wandered back and forth, hands tucked into the cuffs of her silk jacket.

Flames licked at what had been the kitchen. The little tongues of flames quickly became a blazing bonfire, belching black smoke to take the place of the dusty haze as it settled.

We laid the whimpering Su Lin on a garden bench. Edith eased her broken arm across her body, then covered the shivering girl with her robe.

The houseboy was gone. We never saw him again.

No lamps had been lit in the house, so its wreckage didn't burn. "See what you can do with Mi Ling," Edith ordered. "I'm going to dig in and try to find my medicine bag."

"All right."

Mi Ling didn't know me. She tried to jerk away from me, but I had a grip on her wrist.

"Mi Ling." I captured her other wrist. "Mi Ling, look at me. I'm Missy Townsend, Mi Ling."

The girl shuddered, and her eyes slowly focused on my face.

"It was an earthquake, but it's all over," I said, just as the ground beneath our feet shuddered.

Willow trees swayed slightly in the aftershock. It lasted only a few seconds, but an entire outside wall of the house crashed down in a cloud of dust.

I led an unresisting Mi Ling to where Edith, who'd found her medicine bag, was spooning laudanum into Su Lin's mouth. She nodded toward Mi Ling. "Is she all right?"

"I think so. She was just scared."

"We need water," Edith said.

"Where is the well, Mi Ling?" I asked.

She pointed down a path to a far corner of the garden.

The blazing kitchen sent flickering light to all parts of the walled garden.

The windlass to hoist buckets had splintered and fallen over to lay beside the bricked head of the well. I tried to lower a bucket by hand, but after a few feet it struck the rubble choking the well. We had no water.

I was immediately aware of the dust in my throat, and the fact that I was thirsty.

From this high point of the garden, I could see over the compound's front wall. I saw Whampoa as it stretched down the river. Hundreds of fires were blazing! Some were small, but others sent sheets of flame into the sky, lighting up the whole section across the river. Reflected off the surface of the river, the flames lit up the anchored ships with their twinkling lanterns.

It was a beautiful sight, but fearsome and terrible, too. People still alive, but trapped, were being roasted to death. I thought I could hear their faint cries.

"The well has caved in," I told Edith. "I can't get us any water."

She looked up from examining Su Lin's arm. "We crossed a stream coming here."

"But that must be a mile," I said. I was carrying the empty bucket.

"Mi Ling, there's another bucket. You get it and go with Missy Townsend. Chop-chop!" she snapped.

Mi Ling scampered back toward the well.

Edith's hand was on Su Lin's forehead. "This child has a fever. Hurry with that water. As soon as it's light, I'll have to set the bone in her arm."

Mi Ling and I stumbled down the dusty road toward the stream Edith had remembered. I'd borrowed Edith's dressing gown to throw over my nightgown, but my feet were bare and bruised. As I walked, the bucket kept hitting my knee. Looking back, I saw Mi Ling carried her bucket on her shoulder. I hoisted up mine to do the same.

I wondered where Thomas was and when he would come.

People on both sides of the road were clawing

at the wreckage of their homes. Women were wailing, and children were crying. Some of those digging in the wreckage sought treasured possessions, others some missing member of the family.

We weren't the first to reach the tumbling little stream. The banks on both sides were lined with men and women dipping out water, some in buckets, others in jars. One old man squatted by the stream on his heels and drank from it with a teacup. From the peaceful expression on his face, I judged he was unaware of the babbling commotion all around him.

We found a vacant place on the bank, but had to wade into the stream to fill our buckets. I'd just stepped back up on the bank, the filled bucket on my shoulder, when the woman attacked me.

She was elderly, about half my size, and looked frail, but she went for me with the fury of a scalded cat!

"She want your bucket, missy." Mi Ling watched our struggle, a bucket perched on her shoulder.

With one hand the old woman was trying to jerk the bucket out of my hand, while she clawed at my face with her free hand. All the time she spit at me what sounded like Chinese obscenities.

I slapped at her and kicked at her shins.

The water in the bucket had spilled over me when she snatched at it, and I was soaked. We'd stumbled back into the stream, and were fighting for the bucket in knee-deep water.

Mi Ling, her face impassive, watched from the

bank. I realized that she wasn't going to lift a finger to help me with the woman.

I caught the woman on the jaw with my fist.

She fell back, splashing in the water, and I'd knocked her loose from my bucket. A pig-tailed man came sloshing to her rescue, his face contorted with hate as he screamed Chinese obscenities at me.

Hatred glared at me from all the other faces looking my way from along the stream.

I filled my bucket, lifted it to my shoulder, and waded ashore.

Just as I joined Mi Ling, a pebble stung me between the shoulder blades.

"Let's get away from here!" I urged Mi Ling.

She trotted ahead of me, water spilling from her bucket. Somehow I managed to keep up with her pace.

"Why did that woman attack me?" I asked Mi Ling when we were back on the road.

"You foreign devil." Mi Ling said it as if she was stating a fact everyone knew. "You bring all this bad thing."

"Oh, fine!" I was wet, shivering, and every step I took hurt my feet. "Now I'm to blame for the earthquake."

Mi Ling paused so I could lead and she could follow a respectable distance behind me. "Yes, you foreign devils to blame," she said in a resigned voice.

I was too tired and winded, at that point, to

271

point out to Mi Ling that China had earthquakes before Marco Polo. I don't think it would have been much use, anyway. Mi Ling wouldn't have believed me.

Edith, alone, had set Su Lin's fractured forearm while we were gone. She had it bandaged, and the arm in a sling.

Edith had pallets she'd dragged from the ruined servant quarters laid out on the ground, with Su Lin stretched on one, sound asleep. With her nightgown in rags, she was busy trying to build some kind of shelter from the rising sun out of odds and ends.

I set my bucket down beside Mi Ling's and collapsed on a pallet.

"You look a fright, Jeanette," Edith said.

"Wearing all that dirt and soot on your face, you don't look good, either," I said.

Edith brushed at her cheeks with her hands, then gave it up. "It's a good thing we're not expecting company."

Thomas came striding through the compound gate, followed by a string of coolies in single file. When he saw the three of us across the ruins of the house, he beamed with relief.

Thomas stopped and gave orders to the coolies before he skirted the ruined house to join us in the back garden.

"What about the other servants?" was the first thing he asked.

"Mr. Woo and the gardener are dead. The

houseboy ran off and hasn't come back," I reported. "Su Lin has a broken arm. Mi Ling is all right."

The coolies Thomas had brought with him were already sorting through the wreckage of the house, trying to find our baggage, meanwhile clearing away the rubble.

Thomas was gaunt, with a stubble of beard on his cheeks, and his eyes were sunken. He held and kissed me. "Praise God you're alive," he murmured in my ear. "I had a hell of a time getting here," he told Edith and me. "Half the people in Whampoa are dead or buried alive. Crews from the ships are ashore. They're trying to help, but it isn't much use."

"Did you pass the mission?" she asked.

"We passed where it was." There was a stricken look in his eyes. "His boy told me that Phelps was killed last night. There were orphans in the building with an *amah*. He went after them just before the whole building fell in on itself."

Staring at Thomas, Edith raised a fist to her mouth, to bite at her knuckles.

"I'm sorry." Thomas spoke in a lame voice. "Lester Phelps was a good man."

Edith turned away from us, and walked to the garden wall. She stood there with her head bowed.

"He'd asked her to marry him," I told Thomas.

"Damn!" He pounded a fist into the palm of his hand. "Do something for her, Jeanette."

"The best thing I can do is leave her alone

273

right now," I told him. "Where are we going to get something to eat and a place to sleep?"

"We'll have to go back aboard ship. It's a long walk, but I couldn't find a ricksha."

"What about Su Lin and Mi Ling?" I asked.

"With Mr. Woo gone, we can't leave them here like a couple of stray cats," Thomas said. "We'll take them with us."

Thomas left some of the coolies he'd brought cleaning up the compound, after we'd buried Mr. Woo and the gardener at the back of the garden. The rest carried our trunks and luggage on the long trek through Whampoa to where the ship's boat was waiting.

At the compound, we were a good five or six miles from the promenade along the Pearl River. Thomas led the way. Edith and I followed him. I was no longer barefoot, but my abused feet were swelling in my shoes. It was high noon and the sun was merciless.

Behind us trailed the coolies.

Whampoa was coming back to life. Some fires were still burning, and smoke stung our eyes, but it hadn't taken the flames long to consume flimsy bamboo structures that had collapsed on cooking fires. There were heaps of smoldering ashes on every side.

The pagodas had survived the quake and the fires. They stood like teak sentinels over the ruined city. Yellow-robed priests were hurrying rice to the destitute. Some Chinese still wandered through the wreckage of Whampoa in a daze, but most were busy cleaning up and chattering cheerfully.

"This happens every so often," Thomas told us. "Like the phoenix, Whampoa rises from the ashes every time. My hat's off to the Chinese poor man and peasant. If we'd get rid of the damned mandarins for them, it would be a good thing."

The dead were being dragged into piles, stacked like cordwood. Soldiers already filtering into the ruined city would douse them with kerosene and set each pile afire.

Our strange procession interested nobody.

"Lean on me," Edith said, when she saw how badly I was limping.

"I'm all right."

Thomas stopped. "Want me to carry you?"

"I think you'd better," Edith said.

"No." I sat down in the dusty road and jerked off my shoes.

My swollen and bruised feet still hurt, but each step was no longer pure agony. When we reached the promenade, I saw that all the *hongs* had survived the quake. It was as crowded as usual with people out for their evening stroll.

Thomas lifted Edith and me down into the boat, and then Su Lin and Mi Ling. Bob Dillard was in charge of the boat. "Glad you ladies are safe," Bob said. "Captain Townsend was worried."

* * *

After what we'd experienced, it was good to be back aboard the *Mary Freeman* at her new mooring, farther up the river toward Canton. Thomas had anchored in sort of a bay, away from any of the other ships.

Only a few of the crew were on board. The rest were ashore in Whampoa.

Edith had been withdrawn since hearing that Lester Phelps was dead. She went to her cabin immediately. I sent to the galley for hot water so I could bathe and soak my feet.

Thomas ordered a tray of hot food brought to me, and one for Edith, before he went back to the quarterdeck.

"With so few of the crew left on board, we have to keep a sharp lookout for river pirates," Thomas told me. "You've had a hard time of it, Jeanette. Try to get some rest."

"Thomas, I never thought I'd say it, but it's good to be aboard again. This ship is getting to be my home."

Thomas laughed. "You've got saltwater in your veins."

Bathed and in clean clothes, I was refreshed. Instead of sleeping, I went to Edith's cabin to see if I could help with Su Lin and Mi Ling. She had the two of them tucked into her bunk and was brushing the tangles out of her hair. Both girls were sound asleep.

"They look like babies!" I said. Their faces

were smooth with sleep, and Mi Ling had a thumb tucked into her mouth.

"Don't they?" Edith laid aside her hairbrush. "They were frightened half out of their minds when we brought them aboard. They honestly believed that English and American sailors turn cannibal when they go to sea. They thought they'd be butchered and eaten."

We moved out into the passageway so as not to awaken the sleeping Chinese girls. "Where are you going to sleep?" I asked.

"Bob Dillard is getting me a cot from the ship's stores. How are your feet?" Edith asked.

"I soaked them in hot water and they're better. Have you ever tried to limp with both feet?"

Edith laughed. "No." She frowned and said, "What do you suppose we're going to do with Su Lin and Mi Ling? I wouldn't know how to go about arranging a Chinese marriage."

"I think we should return them to their families," I said. "Thomas can probably arrange it."

"So their parents can sell the girls again?" Edith was bitter.

"Mr. Woo took good care of them."

"He had an investment. I wish I could take them back to England with me."

"You're going back to England?" I asked.

Edith sighed. "What other choice do I have, now that Lester's dead? I looked forward to a new life in China, Jeanette. I would have married him to have it. I know that now."

"You probably would have had regrets," I told her.

"Maybe. But I can't know that. If I could, I'd stay in Whampoa and try to carry on his work here, but I know I can't," Edith said. "Damn! I wish my father had had a son."

"I don't, Edith. I couldn't love Thomas and another man at the same time."

Edith touched my cheek with her hand. "Are you so sure you're not trying to do that right now?" she asked.

"What do you mean?"

"I was your nurse when you were sick," she said. "Remember? I know about Jamie McCoy."

CHAPTER 20

How MUCH I'd told in my delirium I didn't dare ask Edith. Coming out of the coma caused by my high fever, I'd heard Thomas caution Edith about mentioning anything I'd said while I wasn't rational. How much did he know about Jamie? I felt that Edith and Thomas had conspired against me. It was another small cut. My resentment was aimed at Thomas, not Edith.

Why hadn't he questioned me about Jamie? Didn't Thomas love me enough to be jealous? Of course, I didn't ask myself what kept me from telling Thomas what Jamie had meant to me.

The answer wouldn't have done anything for my self-esteem.

Thomas had been frank with me when I asked about Gwen, and he'd mentioned his early love, Ting Lao, the Eurasian girl, quite casually. I thought he owed me that much frankness. After all, he was my husband.

And you're his wife. It was a small voice that spoke from my conscience, but it did speak.

I asked Thomas what we should do about the Chinese girls. "We can't carry them with us back to England," I said. "We can't turn them loose on the Whampoa streets. Is there any way we can get them back to their parents?"

"It would be very risky business to go up the river as far as Soochow," Thomas told me. "For you, Edith, or me, that is. The mandarins are very touchy about foreigners penetrating their country."

"Can't we send them with somebody?" I asked.

"Those girls with their bound feet are worth just about half their weight in gold in Macao, Jeanette. A mandarin or warlord would pay through the nose to get his hands on them. What Chinese could we trust?"

"I thought you'd know someone."

Thomas scratched his head. "No," he decided. "I don't know any Chinese I could trust with those two little virgins."

"Virgins? They've both had husbands and have borne a child."

"You don't begin to understand the wily Oriental," Thomas lectured. "There are doctors on Macao who are rich men because they can perform an operation that makes a harlot pass for a virgin. It's a favorite trick of the slave traders dealing in girls and women."

I shuddered, thinking about such an operation.

"For the right price," Thomas went on, "a bored Chinese can watch the operation performed. No, we can't trust a Chinese to get the girls back to their parents and children."

"Who can we trust?" I asked.

Thomas scowled. "I'll have to think about that. By the way, the man Amos you asked about?"

My heart jumped. "Have you found him?"

Thomas shook his head. "No. But I asked around as I promised that I would. He came off an American ship that brought in a cargo of sandalwood from the Sandwich Islands, and furs from America's northwest. The owner traded for indentured Chinese labor to work a plantation he's starting on the island of Hawaii. He sailed with a shipload of coolies a week ago."

"Who was the owner?" I asked.

"I wasn't able to find out," Thomas said.

"You're sure the black man called himself Amos?"

"Yes, but it's a common enough name, Jeanette. I couldn't find out from where he comes."

The tea harvest was late. Bored captains and their officers visited from ship to ship, renewing old acquaintances and drinking vast amounts of gin. Their crews patronized the grog shops and whores. In narrow streets behind the promenade, on each side of the river, grog shops jostled each other. In nearby streets, the prostitutes solicited business from behind barred windows. Pimps roamed Whampoa, many of them mere children.

A man could leave the forecastle and rent rooms ashore for only pennies a day. For a few cents more, he could hire servants and a woman for his exclusive use.

"Whampoa is one of the few ports in the world," Thomas told me, "where a sailorman can live like a king and not spend all of his wages."

Crewmen of the ships in the river didn't care if sampans never brought tea down from Canton!

Anchored there in the cove, for the first time I saw Chinese fishing with cormorants. A cord tied to one leg kept these large fish-eating birds from flying free. Another cord knotted about the lower part of their neck prevented the birds from swallowing any fish they caught. For hours I would watch these tame birds plunge into the murky river, to come up and disgorge flopping fish into their master's hands. Only at the end of the day would the fisherman untie the cord around the neck of his bird so it could feed itself.

Thomas gave only a few men shore leave every day. By holding nearly a full crew aboard at all times, and keeping the men well armed and disciplined, we were safe from the river pirates.

"Compared to the Malays and seagoing Chinese from Macao," Thomas told me, "these river pirates are bad children. They steal from and murder the weak, true enough, but the sight of cannon and trained men awes them."

Because of restricted shore leave for his crew, Thomas relaxed discipline to the extent that he allowed the singsong girls from flower boats to solicit the men confined to the ship. Among their number were some known to the men as sew-sew girls. As part of their service, they darned socks and sewed up rents in clothing.

The grace and cheerfulness of these pretty little Chinese girls amazed me. They lived with their mothers or husbands aboard the flower boat, and considered themselves skilled artisans at a difficult trade.

They were even respected by the men they served, as I found out when I heard a husky and usually surly sailor from the stews of Liverpool tell his mate, "It's better I would feel about humping with the maid if she didn't remind me so much of my wee sister at home."

* * *

Edith was like a mother hen with Su Lin and Mi Ling. She wouldn't let them associate with the singsong or sew-sew girls, or so much as speak to any of the crew. The girls under her care were as safe as if they'd been in a convent.

There were houseboats anchored along the bank of the Pearl River upon which the whole families lived. Instead of a small scrap of land, their living, such as it was, came from the river. Li Chien Nung was the father of such a famly. His grandfather and father had been born and died on the same houseboat where Li now lived with his family of a wife and five children.

Li was a stocky little man with a broad face and winning smile despite the fact he had no teeth. Beside his houseboat, Li owned a flat-bottomed sampan, and made a living lightering supplies out to the anchored ships.

Li knew Thomas from previous voyages and considered him a good friend.

"Your husband treat coolie and merchant Chinaman all alike," Li told me. "Not so other gentlemen from England."

Years of associating with Englishmen and Americans had given Li a good command of English.

Whenever Li would bring aboard supplies to us there in the cove, he and I would talk about his family, the weather, or China. He was too polite to ask me about Su Lin and Mi Ling, but

I knew he was burning up with curiosity, so I told him their story one day.

His eyes were moist when I finished. "So sad! Life in Soochow not so easy."

"Do you know the place?" I asked.

"Yes, Missy Townsend. Li been there many time. Carry Chinamen who die here in Whampoa so they can sleep with ancestors. Many Chinamen in Whampoa come down the river from Soochow."

"We want to get Su Lin and Li Ming back to their parents," I said. "How do you suppose we can manage that? Thomas tells me we're forbidden to leave this treaty port."

Li nodded. "Mandarins in Canton afraid to let you. Their peasants see you English so well-fed, so rich, not so good for mandarins."

I had the glimmering of an idea, but I knew Edith would never let the children go off up the river alone with Li. She'd become too fond of them. Until she'd seen them back with their parents and children, Edith wouldn't be satisfied.

"Li, could you get Su Lin and Li Ming up to Soochow if Edith and I came along?" I asked.

"No trouble, missy." Li seemed confident.

"No danger?" I asked.

"No danger, missy."

He was telling me what I wanted to hear, but Thomas had warned me about that when dealing with a Chinese.

"Li, now you listen to me," I said. "If anything

285

bad should happen to me or Edith, or to the girls for that matter, Thomas will cut off your pigtail. Do you understand?"

Without his pigtail, Li would have no chance of being hauled up into heaven when he died.

"Understand, Missy Townsend. Nothing happen to the wife of Thomas, or her friend. I swear this by my ancestors."

"We'll talk further about this," I told him.

That night I spoke to Edith about Li. "I don't know if Thomas would let us go to Soochow," I told her, "but if you're game, I'll ask him."

Since getting to know Su Lin and Mi Ling better, and talking with them about their families, Edith had decided the only place they should be taken was Soochow. Mr. Woo, she learned, had been a distant cousin, and the generous financial arrangements he'd made with their parents had kept their families from starving.

"Whatever Thomas says about you, I'm going upriver with the girls," Edith said. "Now I've convinced them they won't be served up to the crew, they're so homesick it makes you want to cry."

"I'll see what Thomas says about me."

My playing the humble wife didn't fool Edith. "You'll talk him into it," she said. "Find out when your Li Chien Nung can take us."

Later that night, I approached Thomas with the idea. I expected objections from him and was ready to do battle if I had to, but he surprised me.

"I'll make all the arrangements with Li myself," he said. "He's the only Chinaman I'd trust with the life of my wife. Li doesn't lie like the rest of them. We'll see about it tomorrow."

Li poled his sampan out into the river an hour before daylight. Su Lin and Mi Ling were ecstatic and Edith and I were almost as excited as the girls. I hadn't felt so adventurous since my parents put me aboard that Dutch ship to go to England.

Mist steamed from the surface of the river because it was a cool morning, but there was a fresh enough breeze to fill the sampan's lateen sail.

Edith and I had disguised ourselves by wearing floppy black pajamas, sandals, and white head scarves. From a distance Li assured us we looked like two Chinese women, and with the white head scarves, mourners. As well as Su Lin and Mi Ling, he was taking a wealthy Chinese from Whampoa up the river to rest with his venerable ancestors.

"Chinese—even mandarins—respect dead too much to bother us," Li assured me.

"What about the river pirates?" I asked.

"They respect dead, too," he told me. "All Chinese respect the dead."

Li had brought his oldest daughter along to

prepare food on the brazier in the covered half of the sampan, and talk with Su Lin and Mi Ling in their own language.

As the European ships swinging at anchor off Whampoa disappeared around a bend in the broad river, I felt as if I was entering a new-old world.

The banks on either side of the river, right down to the water's edge, and as far as the eye could see, were dotted with small thatched cottages made from bamboo or mud. The fields were a hodgepodge of narrow strips, and Li explained most farmers owned a number of these strips, some widely separated.

"In China parents, the children, the grand-parents, all live together under one roof," he explained. "The sons bring their wives to their family. Daughters who marry go to the other family."

The narrow, separated strips were the result of fathers providing land for more than one son.

We passed small villages. "Each village all one family," Li told us. "They are named for family."

The dead, he explained, must always be buried where they were born. Chinese who died in foreign countries were shipped back to China.

Thomas had told me something about this custom. "Taking coffins to China is a very profitable business," he said, "but sailors are too damned superstitious. A dead Chinaman comes aboard, and half your crew is liable to jump ship."

Li wove his way through the dense junk traffic of Canton. The city stretched out on both sides of the river, and looked as large as London.

We were above Canton on the Sinkiang River when Li tied up to the bank for the night. Edith, the girls, and I would sleep on mats in the covered half of the sampan, while Li and his daughter slept in the open, on either side of the Chinese gentleman's ornate coffin. Li selected a place along the bank that wasn't too close to other sampans tied up for the night.

Su Lin slept beside me, holding my hand, while Mi Ling drew her sleeping mat close to Edith's. The gently rocking sampan was like a cradle, and the fresh smell of the river, now we were above Canton, was delicious. I didn't awaken the next morning until Li had the sampan out in the river.

After the long reach to Singapore on cold rations, Edith and I were used to ship's biscuits and salted beef, so we'd stocked the sampan before we left the *Mary Freeman*, and brought along a dozen bottles of wine. To the amusement of Li and his daughter, we boiled the river water before we drank it.

Li took his food out of the river; fat fish that his daughter broiled on the brazier, mussels to be eaten raw with pepper, watercress, and even water lilies. They wouldn't touch our biscuits and salt pork, but shared their food with us.

There was a new sight for our Western eyes every day. We saw blinded water buffalo and oxen tramping endless circles to suck water from the river and spill it into irrigation ditches. Families, including the children just old enough to walk, stood in the shallow water of rice paddies, harvesting the crop. Sampans passed us loaded with tea for Canton.

Taoist and Buddhist pagodas were scattered along the river banks. Li was a follower of Confucius and looked down on Taoists and Buddhists alike. His was a philosophy, not an ignorant religion, he explained.

"Here in China, if you follow the Buddha, you try to live like him," Li told Edith when she mentioned Christianity. "You believe Confucius a very wise man, you follow what he says. Taoists try to be good people, too. But you Christians . . ." He shrugged his shoulders and spread his hands. "They tell me once this Christ a good man. Why did you kill him?"

Edith didn't try to explain. "I was told in England these Chinese are heathens," she told me. "Now I'm learning, by talking with Li, that we can learn a great deal from them."

It took us a week to sail the one hundred miles upriver from Whampoa to Soochow. We found that we had arrived at a bustling all-

Chinese city. Only a few of the thousand of people thronging Soochow had ever seen a European. For the first time since we'd come aboard his sampan from the *Mary Freeman*, Li was nervous.

"You English ladies stay on sampan," he said. "Me and the daughter ask until we find girls' families. Maybe you not safe here if mandarin finds out."

By questioning the girls, Li had learned that their fathers were merchants here in Soochow, dealing in silk and jade. They had fallen out of grace with a previous mandarin.

"That one dead now," Li told us. "This mandarin feed him bamboo slivers until he die."

But Li assured us that the present mandarin was a good fellow and had probably reinstated the Lis and Mings.

That evening, when Li and his daughter came back to the sampan, he was bubbling with good news. He'd located both families and found them prospering as they never had before.

"Did you talk with the fathers?" I asked.

"Me talk with fathers?" Li was shocked. "A houseboat man little better than the coolie. But I find a friend from Whampoa. He the Ming steward. I pay him to tell their fathers."

"What did the fathers have to say?" Edith asked Li.

"Tomorrow, maybe next day, someone come

to see if these girls their daughters. They think maybe Li lies."

"Or the *next day?*" Edith was incensed. "We go to all this trouble to reunite the Lins and Lings with their daughters, and now they make us wait, as if we were asking them favors."

"Only coolies hurry," Li said in a philosophical tone of voice.

CHAPTER 21

IT WAS the Honorable Ming who came the next day, carried in a red sedan chair borne by two sweating coolies. The sampan was moored to a short pier that jutted out in the river. The coolies set the curtained sedan chair down in the road.

Li's friend, the steward, had trotted behind the sedan chair. When he got his breath, he came out on the pier. The steward was a gray-haired Chinese, with Li's broad face. After a series of bows and the ritual exchange of compliments, Li told Edith and I we could show the girls to the steward.

The sedan-chair curtains hadn't moved.

Heads bowed, hands grasping elbows, Su Lin and Mi Ling stepped onto the pier from the sampan and stood before the steward. Cupping Su Lin's chin, he raised her face to study it, then did the same thing to Mi Ling. Without changing expression or saying a word, the steward paced back to the sedan chair.

He spoke a few words through the closed curtains. Turning, he beckoned Su Lin and Mi Lin to come. Eyes downcast, they hobbled to the sedan chair. Now the curtains parted.

The Honorable Ming wore a black skullcap. Long wisps of white hair dripped from either side of his nose. He spoke to the girls, his face stern. Su Lin answered, because she was the oldest.

Without a backward glance, the girls stepped into the sedan chair, the curtains shielded its occupants again, and the coolies picked up their burden.

The steward approached Edith and me while the coolies waited. With a deep bow, he presented each of us with a small package.

"Honorable Ming and Honorable Lin very grateful to you English ladies," he said. "Please accept small tokens of this gratefulness."

We thanked him.

When the sedan chair, with the steward trotting behind it, was out of sight, Edith and I unwrapped our gifts. In my hand I held an

exquisitely carved white jade figurine of Su Lin!
Edith's figurine was of Mi Ling.

Li sucked in his breath. "The English ladies
greatly honored. Very fine jade."

The steward had given Li a small package.
He sucked in his breath a second time when he
unwrapped a small bar of gold. "Self is honored,
too."

"Damn," Edith said. "I think I'm going to
cry."

The next morning, the steward was back. This
time he presented Edith and me with bolts of
finest silk, gifts from Su Lin and Mi Ling.

This time *I* cried.

Sailing with the river current instead of against
it we were back aboard the *Mary Freeman* within a few days. The tea harvest had been brought
down from Canton, and there was a frenzy of
shiploading. It went on all day, with streams of
sampans coming and going among the ships,
and all night lit by torches and lanterns. It was
a fantastic sight! There was too much excitement
for anyone to sleep.

Across the Pearl River from where we were
anchored was a ship flying the American flag.

Something about that ship was faintly familiar,
but I knew I'd never set eyes on it before.

Edith wanted to visit Lester Phelps's grave
before the *Mary Freeman* left Whampoa. "It's

the very least I can do for him now, Jeanette," she said. "He wrote me of an aunt in London, and a cousin in Birmingham. I'll have to visit them when we get back to England, and I'm sure they'll want to know where he was buried."

Thomas was busy supervising the loading of cargo for the return to England, and couldn't accompany us. We went to the promenade one morning with the crewmen who were off duty that day. As the men streamed away, looking for the nearest grog shop, to put them in the mood to seek out the nearest available woman, Edith and I strolled to the line of rickshas, coolies crouched on their heels between the shafts. To pull the two of us, we selected a husky coolie we'd watched other ricksha seekers disdain.

"The man may be feebleminded," Edith said, "but he still has to eat, and perhaps he has a family."

It was a hot morning with the sun just beginning to burn off the river mist drifting through the crooked dirty streets of Whampoa.

These streets were always crowded, but this morning it seemed to me they were more crowded than usual. Something else was different. By this time, we were used to an occasional hostile stare. It had ceased to bother us that every time we went ashore, someone was bound to spit when we passed.

By just being who we were, we offended the

Chinese, but we'd been in Whampoa long enough to know that and ignore the fact.

But this morning we drew a battery of hostile stares as our coolie lumbered through the crowds, and it seemed as if every other coolie spit in the tracks of our ricksha when we passed.

I first noticed the city's changed atmosphere, and said to Edith, "Every woman we see seems to have the same hateful expression on her face as the woman who tried to steal my bucket."

"I'm aware of something wrong," Edith said. "Do you think we should turn back?"

"We'd lose face if we did," I told her.

"Is this coolie taking us the right way?" Edith asked.

I'd made it as clear as I could in pidgin that we wanted to go to the mission. I thought our coolie had understood.

"He may be taking us a better way," I said.

"A different way, certainly." Edith pointed. "I know I've never seen that pagoda before."

"I haven't either." Because of the vast differences in architecture, it's impossible to mistake one pagoda for another. "Stop!" I ordered our coolie.

He plodded stolidly ahead, looking neither left nor right.

I couldn't remember the Chinese word.

"No go chop-chop," I said in a louder voice.

He glanced over his shoulder, gave me an idiot's grin, and increased his pace.

"Damn it, stop this thing!" I yelled.

Edith was having a laughing fit.

Our coolie broke into a fast trot.

I finally remembered the Chinese word for *stop*, and used it, as well as some other Chinese phrases I'd heard our crewmen use after a few trips to the beach.

When he skidded to an abrupt stop and dropped the shafts, Edith and I nearly pitched out on our faces. "We would pick this one!" I said to Edith.

With that idiot grin our coolie turned and waited for further instructions. Ashamed of yelling at him, I got out of the ricksha.

He'd turned up a narrow side street just before he finally understood we wanted him to stop.

"Mission." I launched into halting pidgin, asking if we were lost (he nodded cheerfully), did he know how to reach the mission from here (another cheerful nod), how long would it take? Still another cheerful nod!

"I don't think he understands a word you've said," Edith told me. "Come to that, I don't think I do either, Jeanette."

"Do you want to try him?" I asked.

"No thanks."

A sullen crowd of men and women had begun to surround us.

"Does anyone here speak some English?" I asked the impassive faces.

My glance around the circle of faces gleaned

stares of pure hatred, and suddenly I was afraid.

I pointed toward the river and, in pidgin, told the coolie to take us back to the promenade. He grinned and stood there, arms dangling at his sides.

More people were crowding into the narrow side street, and the circle had begun to close, those on the inside pushed by the curious outsiders.

Edith got out of the ricksha and joined me. "I don't like this," she whispered. "These people are in an ugly mood."

"I know it, Edith." I could feel the heat generated by their close-packed bodies.

There was no singsong chattering back and forth—just ominous silence as the two of us faced the grinning coolie. I'd become convinced nothing could wipe that slack grin off his face!

"Maybe he's deaf," Edith said.

I hadn't thought of that.

"Deaf?" I put my hands over my ears. "Can't you hear?"

Still grinning, he nodded.

"Is he deaf?" I asked the crowd.

I knew they understood my question, but no one answered, and a woman jostled me with her bony shoulder. Perhaps she'd been crowded, but my nerves were up on the ragged edge. I turned and with both hands pushed her away from me.

Our coolie was bright enough to recognize trouble when it was about to start. Snatching up the shafts of his ricksha, he plowed through the crowd of men and women, to disappear around the corner.

Instinctively, Edith and I stood back to back. "There's a shop on that side of the street." I'd noticed its barred windows. "We've got to reach it."

"If we push into these people, they'll tear us to pieces!" Edith said in a tense voice. "Can you make them understand we didn't mean any harm?"

"I don't think so."

"How did we get into this?" Edith sounded on the verge of hysteria.

Standing there, back to back, we heard a new sound off in the distance. It was a muted but angry hum I can describe only by saying it sounded like a million angry wasps. This abruptly changed the mood of the mob pressing in on us. There were angry mutterings of "foreign devils" and "barbarians"!

All this while, standing on the step of his shop, an elderly Chinese had been fanning himself while he watched us, occasionally turning to speak to someone hidden in the darkness behind him. The expression on his face was that of one watching some curious new game.

I smiled toward him and raised a hand in greeting. Covering his face with the fan, he bowed in the most polite manner, then resumed his role as a spectator.

The crowd had us hemmed in so close that the smell of their bodies was almost overpowering. I jerked away from a woman's clawing hand.

"Edith, come on!" I whirled and struck out at the nearest faces with my fists. The shopkeeper paused in his fanning to stare at this new development in the game he was watching.

I was shouldering my way into the people toward the shop and shopkeeper. Hands clawed, my dress ripped to the waist, but with elbows and knees I was making some progress. Edith was behind me, pushing.

A woman spat in my face. I raked her cheek with my nails and kicked her shins. A man grabbed for my throat. I thrust his hands away with strength I didn't know I had.

My dress was gone. Hands ripped at my undergarments. But kicking, hitting, and butting, I was closer to the open door of the shop. A hand shoved at my face. Grabbing the wrist, I sank my teeth into the fleshy palm.

The screeching Chinese, trying to pummel Edith and me, were packed so closely in the narrow street that they were striking each other.

The Chinese who'd been watching leaped inside his shop and was trying to push the door closed, but the surging mob sent him sprawling. Unable to get at us, some turned into the shop.

Whampoa's Chinese police, distinguished by their conical straw hats, glistening with black lacquer, carried six-foot-long staves. I saw someone wielding such a stave slashing his way through the mob toward us.

A blow knocked me to my knees. Edith stumbled and fell on me. Now they tried to trample and kick us to death!

Standing astride our fallen bodies, the man wielding the stave beat back the mob. I could hear the stave whistle, then strike flesh. Cries of anger turned to yelps of surprise and screams of pain.

"Come get more, you devils!" the man bellowed. "Let me break your heads!"

He'd put the mob to flight.

I curled up, hugging my knees as I sobbed for breath.

The man dragged Edith to her feet, then nudged me with his toe. "Come on, it's over. Get up."

He didn't wait for me to obey. I was hauled to my feet and stared into the tanned face of Jamie McCoy!

Jamie was as stunned as I was.

"Who are you?" Edith asked him. "If you hadn't come when you did, we . . ." She stared at me. "What's wrong, Jeanette?"

"Edith, this is Jamie McCoy."

"No!" A hand jumped to her throat. "But you're supposed to be dead!"

The three of us were alone in the street.

Jamie leaned on his stave. "I've been thinking

Jeanette was dead." He touched my cheek with his fingers. "You really are alive."

A group of shouting Chinese raced past the entrance to the side street.

"They're amok all over Whampoa," Jamie said. "I'm thinking we'd better find cover."

He herded Edith and me into the shop we'd tried to reach. It was a shambles. Smashed porcelain and ceramic littered the floor, and crunched under our feet. The shop owner was perched on a stool, blood dripping from his nose, the broken fan in his lap. His wife hovered over him, dabbing his face with a towel, while she made clucking noises. Neither of them paid any attention to us.

Jamie touched the man's shoulder with his stave. "Back entrance?" He pointed. "Alley?"

The shop owner sniffed and nodded.

"We'll be leaving the back way," Jamie told Edith and me. "We'll be laying low somewhere until dark. They run in packs today—and they're out for blood."

We'd found refuge in an opium-smoking den at the end of the alley behind the shop. Elderly Chinese sprawled on mats, sucking at the long-stemmed pipes, their eyes glazed. A girl-child rolled the sticky black balls, and inserted them into empty pipes, lighting the opium with a taper.

We could hear the shouting mobs as they tried to find foreign devils, and it was a blood-chilling noise, even muted as it was, but the opium smokers couldn't have cared less. They'd found earthly Nirvana.

The three of us huddled in a corner. Jamie had paid our fee, but waved aside the offered pipes.

"That Swede—Anderson—must have fixed the priming of that pistol because the ball only broke a rib," Jamie told us. "I let them toss me over the side so they wouldn't finish the job."

Amos had seen him thrown into the water and had dived in to save him.

"There was a sail yonder, Jeanette, remember?" he said.

"Yes. It had you worried."

"Aye. But that was a fisherman. We made for him, Amos towing me part of the way. He put us ashore on the north coast of Jamaica."

From there Jamie and Amos made their way to Charleston, and finally to Boston. "There I learned you were still alive from a Captain Briggs," Jamie told me. "Do you remember the favor you did him and his daughter?"

"Very well," I said. "It cost me."

"Aye." Jamie scowled blackly. "I can imagine it did."

Jamie had privateering profits in Boston, and with some of his money he bought a new ship, the one I'd seen anchored across the river.

"Young Decatur told me of your misadventure along the Barbary Coast," Jamie said. "And of

304

your marriage on Malta," he added in a bitter voice.

"Do you know Stephen?" I asked, surprised.

"Aye. We met in Baltimore. The boy is quite a hero these days."

"Why did you think I was dead?" I asked.

"I heard it from someone."

"Who?"

"Your husband."

"Thomas?" I was shocked.

Jamie nodded.

"No wonder he was so willing for us to take Su Lin and Mi Ling up to Soochow!" I told Edith. "Damn Thomas!"

"He told me you'd died of a fever along Africa's Skeleton Coast," Jamie said. "When I heard you were married in Malta," Jamie continued, "Amos and I sailed around the horn and out to the Sandwich Islands. I have a plantation on Hawaii now."

"Thomas told me you'd sailed back there with indentured coolies, Jamie."

"Your husband," Jamie said, "is quite a liar."

"He has every right to be." Edith was nettled. "Thomas was protecting his marriage. Don't you realize that, Jeanette?"

CHAPTER 22

EDITH'S QUESTION annoyed me. "What am I supposed to do—thank my husband for saying that I'm dead? I don't like anyone to say that I'm dead! How would you feel if Thomas said that about you?"

"Thomas doesn't happen to be my problem," Edith replied.

Jamie was stretched on his mat between us. He looked from me to Edith.

"I'm not at all sure about that!"

Jamie stared at me.

"What is that supposed to mean?" Edith asked hotly.

"Does the shoe fit?" I said.

"No!"

"I think it does," I told her.

"You're wrong, Jeanette."

"I don't think I am."

Jamie was amused. "Can anyone join this quarrel?" he asked.

"We're not quarreling," I said.

"Sorry." Jamie grinned. "It sounded as if you were."

"I think we were about to have a falling out," Edith said. "I'm sorry, Jeanette."

"I shouldn't have said what I did," I admitted. "My nerves are raw."

"I know what you mean to Thomas," Edith said.

"I think I do, too."

"Why don't you women try to sleep?" Jamie said. "We've a long and dangerous night ahead."

"I couldn't possibly sleep in here," I told him.

"I can't sleep, either," Edith said.

Jamie slipped his jacket around my shoulders. "Try to sleep. You, too, Edith."

The jacket smelled of Jamie and the sea. I gathered it closer and lay back. My whole body was sore and bruised, my hair a tangled mess, and I felt filthy.

By her regular breathing, I knew Edith had fallen asleep. I closed my eyes and took a deep breath. I was so tired!

* * *

Edith was still asleep when I awakened to find Jamie raised on one elbow, staring down into my face. "Hello." He brushed a kiss on my lips, and with a finger, lifted a strand of hair from my forehead. "You don't snore."

"I'm glad to hear that. Have you been awake all this time?" I asked.

"I'm used to standing watch."

I smiled up at him. "Over two women who were about to have a quarrel?"

"I've given your Thomas some thought," Jamie said in a serious voice. "It was a dirty thing for him to tell me you were dead, but I would have done the same thing."

"I don't forgive him so easily," I told Jamie. "It was a very dirty thing he did. And then he sent me off up the river with Edith. I might never have found out you're still alive."

"What difference can it make?" Jamie asked.

I touched a hand to his cheek. "I don't know yet, Jamie."

"Damn Thomas!" he said under his breath.

Edith stirred, to sit up, stretch and yawn. "I hurt all over!"

"In a few minutes, it will be dark enough to start for the river," Jamie said. "When your coolie told me the trouble you two were in, I had to knock down a Chinese policeman to get his stave. We'll have to stay out of their sight, too."

"You're really encouraging," I told him.

"Our coolie got us lost," Edith said. "Do you think you can find our way to the river, Jamie?"

"If I can't, we're in real trouble," he said. "I think the mandarin in Canton sent in his retainers to start this rioting."

"This is a treaty port," I said. "Why would he want to stir up trouble here?"

"Because it *is* a treaty port. The Chinese got along for thousands of years without us. Look around in here and see what the opium trade is doing. This is only one den. There are a million more, all over China. Now the Western powers are bickering about how to divide China into spheres of influence, and they'll do it unless we Americans stop them."

"That could mean a war," Edith said.

Jamie grinned. "I don't think you British are ready to tackle the United States again. My father died at Saratoga, or so my mother told me."

"My father opposed that war," Edith said. "He was very unpopular in his parish, and with church superiors."

"An uncle on my mother's side was a Tory," Jamie told her. "The last we heard, he was in Quebec, picking feathers out of the tar."

Edith laughed. "Father's parishioners didn't go that far."

I could see that Jamie McCoy impressed Edith. I never asked what she expected he'd be like, from what she'd overheard me say, but I knew one thing. I wouldn't share Jamie with Edith, as I'd done Thomas in Singapore. All of Jamie would be mine.

But I was married to Thomas, I remembered with a start. Now that he'd found me, how could I have Jamie?

The search for foreign devils to kill or maim had degenerated into an orgy of rape, burning, and looting when night fell. There was indiscriminate killing, too. Bodies were everywhere as we made our way through back streets and alleys.

I knew Thomas must be ashore searching for Edith and me, but we made it to the promenade on the south bank of the river without seeing him. It was just before dawn, but Jamie awakened a Chinese sleeping in his sampan and paid him to take Edith and me up the river to the *Mary Freeman*. He'd hail his ship from the shore and have them take him aboard.

"When do I see you again?" I asked Jamie. His jacket was still around my shoulders. "You'll have to come for your jacket."

Jamie searched my face. "How will it be with us, and you a married woman now?"

"I was married when we met."

"Aye, but that was different."

Edith stood apart, watching us, and she was interested. I didn't want to part with Jamie, and she knew it.

"When do you sail?" I asked.

"The day after tomorrow."

"Oh, so soon?" I asked.

Jamie turned his back to Edith and lowered his voice. "Sail with me, Jeanette."

I bit my lip. "Jamie, I don't know what to say."

"Do you love me?" he asked.

"Yes."

"I'll come for my jacket," Jamie said.

Thomas was aboard the *Mary Freeman.* "My God, where have you two been?" he asked when the sampan had carried us to the ship. Thomas needed a shave, and there were dark smudges under his eyes. "I took five men, and we went to the mission. We were lucky to get back alive."

"A mob tried to lynch us, and would have done it except for Jamie McCoy," I said.

Thomas went white under his tan, and a muscle under his eye jumped. His eyes burned into mine. "You've been with McCoy all this time?"

Edith spoke up. "He saved our lives yesterday, Thomas. It was a very close thing."

"I want to bathe, eat, and then sleep," I said.

Thomas followed me to our cabin. He snatched Jamie's jacket from my shoulders and threw it into a corner. "Damn you, Jeanette! Where did you go to meet him?"

"Jamie heard two Englishwomen were in trouble with a mob of Chinese," I said in a weary voice. "He knocked down a policeman, stole his stave, and got us away from a mob just before we were kicked to death."

Disbelief was written on his face. This was a side of Thomas I'd never seen before. My husband was seething with jealousy, and I knew he had reason to be—but how could he know that? The love I have for Jamie must be very obvious, I thought.

"A cabin boy is bringing hot water from the galley," Thomas said.

I'd removed my undergarments to examine the scrapes and bruises I'd earned fighting that Chinese mob.

"Where were you yesterday and all last night?" Thomas asked.

"With Jamie and Edith. Why did you tell him that I was dead?"

"You *are* dead to him."

Thomas took the pitcher of hot water from the cabin boy. He sat on the edge of our bunk to watch me bathe. "You'll not see McCoy again," he said.

I'd finished bathing and was toweling my damp body. Thomas seized me by the waist, his fingers digging into my flesh. "Do you hear me?"

"Jamie's coming aboard for his jacket," I said. "So I will see him again, Thomas."

"No." Letting go my waist, he came to his feet, and his face was livid. "No!"

"Be reasonable, Thomas. I've been through hell in the last twenty-four hours. I've met a man I thought was dead, and who thought I was dead, thanks to you. Now I need to sleep. We can talk later."

"There's nothing more to talk about. You're forbidden to see him again."

"All right, Thomas." Anything to be alone!

Thomas stormed out of the cabin.

Sleep didn't come easily. I wasn't treating my husband fairly, and I knew it in my heart, but there was nothing I could do to stem the love I felt for Jamie McCoy. All it had taken to arouse that love was a touch of his hand, a gentle kiss, the sound of his voice.

As Mrs. Thomas Townsend, I would have position in England, a solid home, money, but that no longer mattered. I knew nothing about the Sandwich Islands. Hawaii might be a cannibal habitat, or a desert island—but if Jamie was there, that's where I had to be. I'd have his child. We'd make love on the beach, in the moonlight, or on a couch in whatever sort of hut that served as our home. Maybe we'd have many children.

I wondered how Thomas would try to stop me from seeing Jamie again. Whatever he tried wouldn't succeed. I hadn't come all the way from Haiti to China just to lose Jamie again.

I finally slept.

* * *

The *Mary Freeman* was underway! I came wide awake in an instant. *Thomas was taking his ship down the Pearl River and out into the South China Sea.* He wasn't waiting for the tea sampans to come down from Canton. These were my first thoughts.

I dressed hurriedly. Maybe Thomas was only seeking a new anchorage. The ship's business always came first with him. From keeping his accounts, I knew how much it would cost him to sail without a cargo of tea.

I met Edith in the passageway. "Why are we moving?" I asked.

"I've been asleep," she said. "I was coming to ask you."

I brushed past Edith to climb the ladder to the quarterdeck. A sampan, with coolies bent to the oars, was towing the *Mary Freeman* toward midstream. Across the river, still swinging at anchor, was the American ship I now realized belonged to Jamie. She'd seemed familiar because it was another schooner, with the lines of the *Salem Witch*.

Our crew was setting the sails.

Thomas himself had the helm, with a stubborn expression on his face that told me his intention without me asking. The *Mary Freeman* was bound for the South China Sea and England. At this moment, and in his present mood, Thomas was capable of putting me in irons. Instead of the Australian, Thomas had a Chinese pilot on board, testimony that this was an impulsive action on Thomas's part.

Across the river, the American ship I now knew was Jamie's swung peacefully at anchor, and there was no activity on her deck. Yet Jamie must know that the *Mary Freeman* was heading downstream!

Why hadn't I stayed with him on the promenade?

"You're sailing without your tea cargo?" I asked.

Thomas didn't answer. Instead he called an order to one of the men aloft, and asked the pilot about downriver conditions. The Pearl was just a little below flood stage, he was informed. We'd have no trouble reaching the sea.

He would reach the South China Sea, however, without Jeanette on board, I resolved. How I would get ashore and return to Whampoa I had no idea, but I was going to do it. The less said to Thomas at this time, the easier it would be for me to escape the *Mary Freeman*.

Thomas had the right to do anything in his power to prevent me from joining Jamie. He'd been good to me as well as for me. Despite these things, I was cold-bloodedly scheming to desert him and run to another man. The Jeanette who married Hippolyte de Verlaine out of gratitude had come a long way. I didn't like my new self very well.

I was selfish, I was fickle, and I was desperate

to be back in Jamie's embrace, without more than a passing thought about what the future might bring. But, perversely enough, I'd doubted that Thomas really loved me since the interlude in Singapore with Edith. I say "perversely" because I'd wanted to happen what did happen. I wouldn't be honest with myself if I didn't admit to that!

Yet there it was. I didn't love Thomas as I should, or even enough, and there was doubt about the quality of his love for me.

It was two hours later, and I was in our cabin, thinking about escape, when the *Mary Freeman* came around sharply.

Thomas knocked, then entered. "We're going back to Whampoa." He said it tersely. "Will you go to McCoy?"

"Yes." I looked up at him, but could tell nothing about his face. "I'm sorry. I've been sitting here thinking of way to escape this ship."

"You would have found a way." It was a wry grin. Thomas sat on the bunk beside me and took my hand in both of his. "I shouldn't have lied to him."

"Jamie doesn't blame you. He's told me that. I don't blame you, either, Thomas."

"Bob Dillard will take the boat that puts you aboard his ship," Thomas said. "Do you know its name, by the way?"

"No."

"She's named the *Jeanette*." Thomas turned my hand and examined the palm, as if he were searching for something there. "You'll make better time in the boat than aboard this ship."

"You want me to leave now?" I asked.

"It would be better if you did, Jeanette."

"I think so, too."

Thomas turned my face between his palms, and kissed me on the lips, then the forehead. "I'll manage a divorce when we're back in England," he said in a resigned voice. "If he'll have you, you can marry your lover."

"Thank you, Thomas. You're a much better man than I deserve."

He got up, suddenly brisk, and there was a twinkle in his eyes. "You are exactly right about that," he said. "I should be beating you black and blue, but damned if I'll do it. Get packed and off my ship before I change my mind, and that's an order."

"Aye, sir!"

Edith came while I was packing. "You're leaving us?"

"Yes."

"Thomas told me. Can I help you pack?" Edith asked.

"No, thanks. I'm nearly finished."

"I'm going to miss you on the long voyage back to England," she said. "We've been through a lot of grief together."

"Haven't we? Edith, I'll miss you, too."

"I think you'll regret leaving Thomas for the Scot."

So Jamie was The Scot to her now, too.

Edith and Thomas. They were already closing ranks against me, the impostor. I felt better about going to Jamie.

"Good-bye, Edith." I kissed her cheek.

Edith firmly turned my face to kiss me on the lips. Without a word, she left me there in the cabin. She was on the quarterdeck with Thomas when Bob Dillard ordered the boat lowered.

CHAPTER 23

BOB DILLARD was puzzled and alarmed when I told him to deliver me to the *Jeanette*. It stuck in his mind that Edith and Thomas were banishing me, for some reason beyond his comprehension. "They'll change their minds," he reassured me.

"This is my decision, Bob," I told him. "I'm going to another man."

For the first time I wondered if Jamie would welcome me aboard his ship. It's one thing to ask a woman to leave her husband, something else when she does. *My God*, I thought, *we don't know each other at all!*

"You're making a bad mistake, Mrs. Townsend. I'm sure the skipper loves you, and that Miss Radcliff is only a passing fancy."

Bob Dillard had told me something I needed to know.

"They're more suited, Bob."

He gave up.

I needn't have worried about my welcome aboard the ship that was my namesake. Jamie was frantically trying to make sail when my boat came in view. When he lifted me over the side, Jamie whispered, "Jeanette!" and told me with his husky tone of voice that all my misgivings could be forgotten.

"What would you have done if you caught up with the *Mary Freeman*?" I asked Jamie.

"Damned if I really know," he confessed. "But I would have got you off her somehow—believe that."

I did believe him. In the days and months to come, I would learn what a reckless and impulsive man I'd chosen to love. In his own way, Jamie was as wild and unpredictable as the sea. I simply couldn't envision his leading the peaceful life of a planter.

When we were well started down the river to the sea, Jamie turned the ship over to Amos. "You'll be taking her most of this voyage," I heard him tell his mate. "You can handle our Polynesians better than I can. They consider you a black Melanesian, a man to obey before he has them for supper."

Amos had a way of grinning that wrinkled his whole face. "Don't you and Miss Jeanette make this big ship rock. Our Chinese will get seasick."

"We'll rock her if we can, you black rascal," Jamie said. "Just steer a true course."

God! How I wanted to be below in Jamie's cabin with the door bolted. I wanted to drink in with all my eyes his big body with its broad chest, and feel his arms lock me to him, with his mouth crushing mine. I was aflame with desire for Jamie. My loins were swelling with my need for Jamie McCoy.

Amos winked at me over Jamie's shoulder. He knew. It must have been printed on my face.

Jamie scooped me up in his arms. "She's your ship now for a while," he told Amos. "Let that Chinese pilot run her aground and I'll have your . . . ears," he finished.

We'd passed the *Mary Freeman* beating back upriver. Neither Thomas nor Edith was on deck. I hoped they were in each other's arms. Her body was almost as familiar to him as mine. It was a lovely body. I had a fleeting moment of homesickness for Edith's company.

Would Thomas spank her as he had me? I thought he might sometime. I remembered the expression on her face when she intruded on my spanking scene. It was envy.

The vision of Edith turned across Thomas's

lap vanished quickly with my urgency for Jamie, but it would be back.

"Take me!" I urged.

"My bunk is sour from being anchored in the heat too long," he apologized.

"Damn your bunk!" I pressed against him. "We have the floor."

"So on the floor it will be this time," Jamie said, his voice gone husky. He couldn't wait for me to unbutton my blouse and skirt. "I've a tailor aboard who will sew those buttons back on," he told me.

We made a savage sort of love on the cabin floor, and then retreated to his bunk, stripped of its sheets and blankets. He treated me tenderly this time, and I responded in kind.

"I love you," Jamie said.

"You've proven it," I told him, "but in a while you can offer additional proof if you like."

"Would you be loving me?"

"As often as possible," I teased, then swallowed the lump rising in my throat, to whisper, "Until I die I'll love you, Jamie, and if you're not dead first, I'll come back to haunt you with my love."

"We'll speak of marriage later," Jamie said. "Right now I've something else on my mind."

"I've noticed," I said.

In the following lazy days and night, Jamie and I explored the limits of each other's sexuality, but found companionship, too, of a sort I'd never experienced with anyone. He wasn't interested in anything about me I didn't want to tell him. On the other hand, I wanted to know *everything* about Jamie.

I had to know about his other women in a way I never felt toward Thomas. I'm afraid he indulged my curiosity more than he should have. Alice became my particular phantom rival. Jamie had met her in Bermuda after his rescue; she was the oldest daughter of the governor.

"What did Alice do for you that I don't?" I would ask.

Or I would say, "You've told me she cried when you left, but exactly how did you feel?"

"Forget Alice!" It was the first flash of Jamie's temper I'd seen.

I wanted to see Jamie really angry, and set out to provoke him. Alice was my weapon. I asked for details of Alice in bed. (I didn't get them.) I asked how she wore her hair, what she ate, what they talked about, where they went.

Finally, when we were in his bunk, I kicked down the sheet to reveal my nakedness. "I know you must compare me with Alice," I said. "Look your fill at naked Jeanette, and then tell me why you liked her breasts better than mine, or her belly, or her thighs. I want to know, Jamie."

He sat up. "Stop being such a jealous bitch, Jeanette!" Jamie's face was flushed with anger and there was danger in his eyes. "I'll have no more of it."

"What will you do, spank me as you did before when I was defenseless? Did Alice let you spank her little English bottom? I'll bet not!"

"Shut up!"

"You'll spank me if I don't?" I taunted him.

Jamie's eyes narrowed and his face hardened. "You can depend on it."

"Did your lovely Alice do *this* for you?"

Jamie's temper was off the leash. As he turned me over his thighs, and locked my wrists behind me with one big hand, I realized I'd perversely worked to achieve exactly what was about to happen.

I hope you like the way Thomas spanks, Edith, I thought.

The way he'd spanked me before was nothing compared to this time!

I won't beg!

Each cheek was punished in its turn. I wondered if the hard smack of his palm against my flesh could be heard all over the ship.

I'll never beg!

I chewed my lips, and I squirmed, but there was no way to escape that hand, and I really didn't want to. I was Jamie's to punish. It was somehow part of the dark side of my love for the man.

Jamie paused. "Had enough?"

"No, damn it!"

"You're asking," he said, and a blister broke under the blow of his hand.

I was on fire with passion! And I knew this was arousing him as much as it was me. I gritted my teeth. Jamie paused to catch his breath.

"Alice!" I yelled.

Jamie swung me up to sit in his bare lap. "You little devil, you *wanted* me to spank you!" His face looked swollen.

I didn't have to answer just yet. It would have been rape if I hadn't been so ready.

"Yes."

Jamie rose on an elbow with a puzzled frown. "Yes, what?"

"I wanted you to spank me, Jamie. I don't care a fig about Alice, or any other woman you've had. I really don't. You're mine now, and that's what really counts. Never leave me, Jamie."

"I never will, God help me," he promised. Then Jamie asked, "Did Thomas ever spank you?"

"No," I lied.

"Only me?"

"Yes."

"I asked about Thomas because I had a limey shipmate once who liked to use a whip on his wife whenever he came home from a long haul at sea. I've noticed the faint scar on your behind."

"A Malay pirate did that to me. I've told you how they carried Edith and me off, and how she was raped. Thomas didn't use a whip."

Jamie grinned. "Just his hand?"

I'd trapped myself in the lie. "I don't tell lies very well, Jamie."

"That you don't," Jamie said, "but never mind, there are other things you do well."

"Thank you, sir." I smiled up at him.

Jamie brushed a kiss on my lips. "I have to go on deck," he said. "Amos tries, but he can't steer a true course yet."

"You can't until you've salved me, brute!"

He shrugged. "Well, a few more miles off course can't matter."

We finally did reach Hawaii in the Sandwich Islands.

Jamie woke me up at sunrise the thirty-fifth day after we'd left China's coast behind us. We'd come five thousand miles with fair winds and only two rain squalls, but it wasn't the fastest passage between China and Hilo Bay. In a way, I suppose that was my fault. I didn't want to share Jamie with his ship anymore than I had to. And Amos never was able to sail a true course.

"I've a sight for you to see," he told me.

Rubbing sleep out of my eyes I followed him up on deck. From the bows, plunging through moderate seas, I had my first glimpse of Mauna Loa's craggy summit, more than thirteen thousand feet of volcano. Mist lay on the sea, waiting to be burned off by the morning sun, so only Mauna Loa's shoulders and truncated head rose above the mist. Smoke spiraled from her deep crater.

Tears stung my eyelids, then coursed down my cheeks. I didn't care. There was tightness in my chest and throat.

Jamie put an arm around my shoulders and drew me to him. "I cried the first time she welcomed me like this," he confessed. "The beauty she promises, Jeanette, spreads all around her, as you shall see." He blew a kiss to the mountain. "Watch over the two of us, Mauna Loa."

"You'd better make that three," I said.

Jamie took a long moment to consider this information. When he'd turned it over a few times, he asked, "Is it mine?"

"Yes, damn it. I can count."

Jamie grinned. Then he let out a wild whoop that must have awakened everyone aboard the *Jeanette,* and swung me in his arms until I was dizzy.

When he'd set me back on my feet, I braced against the rail. "Am I to understand you're pleased by this most recent development?"

"As punch," he said.

"Then I am, too. Is our thatched hut large enough to have a nursery?" He'd always referred to his plantation house as *my thatched hut.*

"I guess we'll manage without being too crowded," Jamie told me.

I didn't realize yet that Jamie could be the master of understatement.

I had one more question. "How often does Mauna Loa erupt, Jamie?"

"At long intervals. We leave this ship in Hilo Bay to reach our plantation by a sloop I own. It's behind Apua Point on the lower slopes of Kilauea, another volcanic mountain, but she's little more than four thousand feet. My Hawaiians tell me they used to toss a maiden into their maws whenever either mountain threatened to erupt."

"Did it work?" I asked.

"Sometimes. When it didn't, they decided to be more careful about choosing next time."

"How was she chosen?"

"By the elders, without consulting the young men," Jamie said. "It was an honor to be sacrificed to the mountains, so there was competition among the girls."

I laughed. "So next time they consulted the young men?"

"Yes." Jamie grinned. "But it turned out that the young men were more afraid of the girls' wrath than they were of a volcanic eruption."

Jamie's sloop was a small two-master with decks fore and aft, but open amidships. Leaving a caretaker crew aboard the *Jeanette*, and landing the Chinese in Hilo, from where they'd make their own way to our plantation, after visiting the other indentured workers in that town, we beat around the island to a small, shallow cove at Apua Point.

The house Jamie had bought was the palace of a former minor king. He'd died in an abortive foray across the island to war with another king. It was huge!

I've lost count of all the rooms in that thatched house that stood on a hill overlooking the cove where the sloop swung at anchor. A wide porch ran all the way around it. There were neither doors nor windows. Grass mats served instead.

Every room seemed oversize to me, but I knew the reason why. Jamie's Hawaiian workers had greeted us with an aloha song. Both brown-skinned men and women were magnificent!

Every man I saw was over six feet, and some were close to seven, without a lean body among them. They weren't fat, but their sleek bodies were solid flesh.

The women were tall, too, some matching the men in height. Here, too, their was no sign of fat. They came bare to the waist, wearing grass skirts, as did the men.

There was such easy informality between Jamie and his Hawaiians that I was amazed. I was used to slaves. Men and women garlanded me with orchid leis. The men patted me; their women kissed me.

When we were finally alone, to get ready for the luau scheduled that night, I said, "With a crew like that, why do you need Chinese workers?"

I was in a grass skirt, and bare to the waist, at Jamie's suggestion. Our grinning housewoman had just served us something made from rum we drank from hollowed-out pineapples with straws.

"My Hawaiians work like the devil was after them, when they want to, but that isn't too often. They prefer to swim and make love. Food is fruit they can pick from trees, and fish they can net by wading out into the sea a few yards. Some use a spear. So why work? They've never heard of slavery. They wouldn't understand it."

The smell of the fish and the pig they were roasting in an open pit drifted through our house.

"Do they dance?" I'd told him of the dancers we'd seen on Borneo.

"They dance," he said. "You'll see tonight. It's a language with them. These people were originally Polynesian, you know. Legend says they came here in war canoes."

"Speaking of war," I said, "they seem too happy to go around killing each other, yet you've told me the king who owned this house was killed in a war."

"They fight with the same zest they work and play," Jamie said. "It's a sport with them. If you want to kill a man, you send him word of your intention, and the game begins. Everyone bets on the outcome of the cat-and-mouse match. When it's over, everyone gets drunk and dances.

These people killed Captain Cook, you know. They were very friendly to him and his men when they first landed, but when he came back, they killed him. No one knows why."

I shivered. "Beautiful people!"

"They are just that," Jamie said seriously.

"How did you come to buy this plantation?" I asked.

Jamie chuckled. "I met the son of the late king in a poker game over on Oahu. That's an island north of here. We were playing with the master and mate of a whaler laying in for supplies. The son tried to fill an inside straight."

"You won all this in a poker game?" I was astounded.

"Sure. I'm a good poker player."

"Wouldn't that make him vindictive?" I asked.

"Why should it? He didn't want to grow a crop. He had a house. He was glad to get rid of the place. His favorite wife didn't like it."

Jamie was thoughtful for a moment, sipping his drink. "Jeanette, I'm going to sell our ship. I no longer need it to privateer. We'll settle down and raise a crop of sons and daughters. One day we'll own this whole island."

"You're going to miss the sea," I warned him.

"Maybe. But I'm getting no younger. I was about to buy a plantation called Great Oaks in Louisiana near Baton Rouge when I won this one. I was on my way to New Orleans to close the deal."

"I'm glad you got into that poker game!"

He could have said, "So am I," but that wouldn't have been Jamie McCoy.

"I fancied Great Oaks," he said. "It's on the river, with two hundred slaves, a haunted and haunting place. I was smuggling for Jean Laffite when I met the owner."

"How did you get out here?" I asked.

Jamie grinned. "I wanted to see the Sandwich Islands before I settled down. I'd never been around Cape Horn, either. I wanted to do that bit sailing."

CHAPTER 24

I DRANK kava again, this time with Jamie and his Hawaiians, washing down delicious baked fish and roasted pork. We ate from banana leaves with our fingers, in a ring around the charcoal pit. The women danced first, then the men.

This was lazy sensuality; fingers, hands, and arms sinuously telling a story while the hips and bellies of the women, who'd dropped off their grass skirts, left no doubt of what their arms were telling. They smiled and they laughed.

Jamie and I sat cross-legged on mats to watch. He was stripped down to a loincloth.

Each woman circled the seated men, dancing

before this one, then that one, until it was finally
Moana's turn. I hadn't been able to keep my
eyes off her. She was naked as the rest, with
long black hair streaming down her back, and a
flower behind her ear. She was taller than Edith,
and as muscular as a man, but her brown breasts
were heavy and firm. The rest of her large body
was exquisite.

With a glance, she questioned Jamie. He
nodded. Moana danced away from the Hawaiians
and approached us.

"I wondered when we'd get our solo perform-
ance," I said.

"Moana's our best dancer," he explained.

Eyes half-shut, lips slightly parted, Moana
knelt before us, and I could smell the not unpleasant musky odor of her brown-skinned body.
Still swaying from the waist, she lifted her breasts
in her palms, offering them to Jamie, and then
to me. I did as he did. I touched each of Moana's
breasts.

Moana turned back to Jamie, still on her
knees. She offered him her breasts more urgently,
eyes tight shut. My lover leaned forward and
kissed each brown nipple!

Somehow I knew it was a farewell kiss.

Slithering to her feet, eyes open now, and lips
smiling, Moana retreated from us, fingers, hands,
and arms eloquent, as the Hawaiians began to
sing.

"Do you understand them?" I asked Jamie.

"Yes."

"Tell me why they sing, and what they are now saying."

"If you wish."

"I'm not jealous, Jamie." And it was true!

"Moana is thanking their gods for having had love, and saying, although she's sorry it is gone, there are no regrets. They sing the words she's telling us with her gestures. Moana knows the gods will give her love again. She thanks them for that."

"She's lovely!"

"She thinks you are, too, for a white person. We seem a bit strange to them. They consider clothes are an unnecessary habit, and unhealthy. They think we don't make love often enough, too. Sex is as natural as eating and drinking to them. Missionaries go crazy trying to convert these people. They go to church as if it were another sort of luau; and if it gets warm, they simply take off the clothes the missionaries have made them wear."

"That must frustrate the missionaries."

"Not half as much," Thomas said, "as when they discover their converts have just added another god to worship. Moana over there is a devout Christian once a week. The other six days she placates the various Hawaiian divinities. We have a new missionary on Hawaii, some young fellow I haven't met yet. By this time, they all know it upsets a Christian preacher to know they also follow the Old Ways, and that's discourteous. So he doesn't know yet about Moana."

"When will he find out?" I asked.

"When he proposes marriage, I'd guess. It's on the grapevine that he's in love with her."

Our first Jamie was born there on Hawaii, and it was Moana who attended me. She made the delivery as easy as she could, but I was in agonizing labor for two nights and a day. The baby finally came when there was a sudden downpour of rain late at night, and lightning struck near the house.

Moana was sad when she laid the newborn child on my breast. "The gods decide this one will not be long here," she said. "They spoke as he came from your body. I am sorry, Jeanette."

The child was perfectly formed and alert— also very hungry.

"Superstition!" I jeered.

"To a Christian like yourself, yes. The Christ god no longer speaks in storms and other ways. I don't know why. Hawaiian gods still do. By now everyone on the island knows this child won't live long. For weeks they've known it would be born tonight."

"How could they know that? I thought he never would come!"

"Our gods spoke to them," she said with simple faith.

Our first Jamie lived just three weeks. On

another stormy night, he died in his sleep for no apparent cause. For two days Jamie was nearly mad with grief. I hadn't told him of Moana's prophecy, but it somehow prepared me for the loss of our child.

They said I was very brave. In my heart I was cherishing something else Moana told me that night my first baby was born.

"You will have more, Jeanette," she said, "but not on this island. You will be far away from here with your husband."

Moana married her missionary, and they sailed to Kauai, the northernmost Sandwich Island, where he went native and was made a chief. The next missionary sent out from London was an elderly man.

We prospered in 1807 as we never had before, and more money than we could use was piling up in a Hilo bank.

January 7, 1808, dawned like any other day, but stillness was in the air. That's the only way I can describe how that day felt. I found myself tense and nervous.

Jamie was unusually silent while we ate breakfast on the porch overlooking the cove. The sloop was gone on an errand to Hilo. The cove looked strangely empty. "When will they bring her back?" I asked.

"The day after tomorrow. Why?"

"I don't know." The sloop was often gone to

Hilo for supplies. "I just wish she was anchored down there."

A ground quiver rattled our dishes on the table. This wasn't so unusual that it called for any comment, but Jamie said, "Mauna Loa just said good morning."

The crater had been smoking more than usual for three weeks. "I hope she's a lady and behaves herself," I said.

"She can't bother us too much," Jamie told me. "Kilauea protects us from her lava flow."

This morning there were no wisps of smoke from her crater.

At ten o'clock, Jamie went to the Chinese barracks to discuss some plantation matter with his Chinese overseer. I went to a sheltered beach in the cove for a nude swim. From the Hawaiian women I'd learned to love swimming and diving. I couldn't match the least of them in the water, but for a white woman I was a strong swimmer. I could even dive down to the pearl oyster beds.

I'd learned from them how to make sounds like a porpoise if a shark wandered too near. They'd taught me the trick of hyperventilating before a deep dive, and then to go down with only the normal amount of air in my lungs. I'd fashioned my own goggles from shells scraped so thin they were transparent.

At ten o'clock I'd just been down to the pearl oyster bed. Mauna Lei, Moana's younger sister, was swimming with me. She waited on the surface, hanging onto her surfboard while she kept mine from drifting away.

A school of fish suddenly shot past me, swimming for the surface. Their panic seized me enough to start me kicking up. Just as my head broke the surface, fish shot into the air all over the cove, flashing in the sunlight.

The tide should have been coming in. Instead, a strong current was sweeping us out. There was too much beach about fifty feet away!

Mauna Lei's eyes were wide with panic. "Tidal wave coming!" she gasped.

We frantically fought the rush of water.

It was no use.

Then something happened I don't understand. A cold streak of current just under the surface caught us both in its grip and washed us up on the beach as though we were stranded fish! Mauna Lei was up and running without a backward glance.

I looked over my shoulder. A wave that seemed to block half the sky was rushing toward the cove. I dropped my board on top of hers and ran, too. We just made it to the house when the tidal wave hit the cove with its still-jumping fish.

There on the hill we were surrounded by a welter of angry water. It swept all around the hill, knocking trees and huts out of its path, and we were on a temporary island. Then it was running out, sweeping everything before it. I saw arms, legs, and heads of those unlucky enough to be trapped in the huts. Fortunately, most of the Hawaiians were in the fields.

Kilauea picked that exact moment to explode.

Jamie raced from the Chinese barracks and floundered up the hill toward the house. Kilauea stopped him in his tracks. He stared up at it, open-mouthed, as Mauna Lei and I raced around the porch to see what was happening.

Tattered streaks of white-hot lava floated above the angry crater, writhing like snakes. Huge boulders seemed to hang in the sky. The whole mountain blurred, as if shaking itself. That first explosive roar from Kilauea either temporarily deafened us, or there wasn't any sound for a moment.

Jamie reached the house just as the first of the boulders and stones began falling. As they began to strike all around the house, the mountain's shudder reached us. We went sprawling.

The gouts of lava fell back on the mountainside. One boulder smashed into the center of the house, setting the thatch on fire. The porch rocked under us like the deck of a ship weathering a storm. Then it was still.

One minor explosion followed another, each weaker than the one before, and Mauna Lei said, "She going back to sleep now."

We went into the house. I found an ankle-length muumuu for Mauna Lei, and one for myself. Jamie stayed on the porch, staring up at

Kilauea, and I'll swear he was never aware the two of us had been mother-naked.

When we returned, he didn't say a word, only pointed up to the rim of Kilauea's crater. It was cracked like a broken teacup. White-hot lava gushed through the crack, widening it, turning red as it flowed toward us, then black as the exterior of each stream cooled; but the rivers of lava cracked their cooling surface.

Determined, giant snakes, with an ever-changing red pattern on their backs—that's what they looked like. Volcanic gases mushroomed into the sky, but the prevailing wind swept them inland.

The lava streams spread out as they flowed. Trees burst into pillars of flame ahead of them. Time went out of joint. What seemed like minutes could have been hours, but the largest stream reached our hill, split to flow around it, finally sending up a sheet of steam when each kissed the cold sea.

Crackling and hissing, they began to congeal.

The crater was silent, its crack closed with cooling lava. Now Kilauea would sleep again, perhaps for a century. If her purpose had been to change the thrust of Jamie's life, and mine, she had succeeded.

We fled the house the next morning down the lane between the two lava flows and reached the beach just as the sloop hove to.

Jamie divided the plantation between the

Hawaiians and Chinese, releasing his Chinese from their indenture. We sailed the sloop to Hilo and were married there by the elderly missionary who'd replaced Moana's husband.

He was a cheerful, cricket of a man, with an unruly cowlick. He married us outside his church, under a tree, because it was too stuffy inside. Now I could call Jamie "husband," but I never did. He was my love and our vows didn't change anything.

Some headstrong impulse was driving Jamie back to Louisiana. Because of its French history, I was willing to follow him, but if he'd suggested we storm the gates of hell, I would have felt the same way.

I was pregnant again. I prayed that if this child was a daughter, she would find as great a love as I found.

Jamie obtained letters of credit on the American banks in New Orleans before we booked passage on a windjammer, homeward bound from China.

"We'll buy Great Oaks if it is still for sale," he told me. "If it isn't, we'll strike out and build our own plantation. We've money enough for slaves."

There was another reason I was so willing to sail for Yerba Buena from Hawaii. The lava flows had obliterated my first Jamie's grave. I considered that an omen, telling me it was time to move on. Moana's prediction was always half-awake at the back of my mind.

With the sloop sold, for the first time in his adult life, Jamie didn't own any sort of ship; it made him restive and thoughtful in turn.

Our windjammer was bound around South America's Cape Horn, and there was plenty of time to reach some South American east coast port to find another ship bound for New Orleans, but we debarked in Yerba Buena.

"I'd lead a mutiny if I had to spend another week on that damned ship!" he confessed. "A dunderhead for master, an idiot for mate, and as scurvy a crew as I've ever seen."

The working of the windjammer hadn't struck me as being all that bad, but the food was awful! Salted beef and ship's biscuit three times a day. I was glad to come ashore on the peninsula of Yerba Buena. It was a sleepy little mission town controlled by the brown-robed Franciscans, located on the most beautiful bay I've ever seen.

Jamie had a way wherever we went. We were lodged in one of the Franciscan missions until the next party started south along the mission trail to *El Pueblo de Nuestra Señora la Reina de Los Angeles de Porciuncula*.

My mouth popped open when Jamie told me that was where we were going.

He laughed and said, "You can just call it Los Angeles."

"What's the rest of the name mean?" I asked.

"The Town of Our Lady Queen of the Angels of Porciuncula," he said. "That last is a chapel of some sort in Italy."

From there we'd continue on down the mission trail into Mexico and eventually reach Vera Cruz where we could catch a ship bound for New Orleans.

We'd chosen a quiet time in the Spanish realms of North and Central America. Our convoy of mules and coaches was under heavy guard because a bishop was riding with us on his way back to Spain. Each mission along the trail was a day's ride from the next. The Franciscans showed us every courtesy.

We were in Vera Cruz just a day before an American ship sailed for New Orleans. She was heavily armed to run the gauntlet of Laffite's Baratarian pirates, but Jamie laughed at their precautions.

"Laffite is too clever to touch a ship that flies the American flag," he told her captain. "New Orleans is an American city now. He stays after the Spaniards, privateering for Cartagena, and sells his prizes to the Americans."

"I've heard rumors about one of his captains— Gambini. You seem to know a lot about Jean Laffite, and I've heard he isn't too bad a fellow, but what about Gambini?"

"The Italian." Jamie spat over the side. "He fawns on Laffite, then stabs him in the back whenever he can. But you can handle him and his crew. They skulk off Cuba, however, looking for slavers coming up from the Ivory Coast. Laffite's main business these days is trade in black ivory."

He told me in confidence later that Laffite would no longer pirate slavers, but didn't hesitate to deal in Negroes when his other captains did.

"What sort of man is Jean Laffite?" I asked.

"You'd find him charming," Jamie said, "but in a duel, he's as deadly as a snake. The best businessmen in New Orleans don't hesitate to buy from him, but he's headed for trouble with our American governor, Claiborne. That's why I got out of the smuggling game. Laffite has been too clever, too long. He and his brothers, Pierre and Dominique You, are headed for trouble. They're too damned arrogant these days."

We reached the West Pass into the Mississippi and sailed upriver just in time for me to give birth to Celeste at the convent hospital.

Great Oaks had been sold, but was up for sale again. "A damned Yankee bought it, a man from Vermont or somewhere up there in New England," the broker told Jamie and me. "He's been too quick with the whip to get much out of his slaves. Kills them off, damn him! He's into the banks here for $20,000. I can get you Great Oaks for a few thousand more than that."

"Buy it," Jamie said.

CHAPTER 25

THE TWINS were born in 1809. Jamie II was his
father again, in every way. Bliss was me. Celeste,
a toddler of one, was a mixture of our genes. Her
hair was sandy, like Jamie's, and her eyes were
clear hazel, like mine. Joyful one moment, she
was pensive the next, and always determined.

Celeste loved me as she should, but adored
her father and never resented the intrusion of the
twins into our life at Great Oaks. She was the
only child of ours who had a Negro wet nurse,
and from the time she could walk, she toddled
away from the Great Oaks mansion to the slave

cabins. Her playmates were always black. This worried Jamie.

"This isn't the time or place for a color-blind child," he told me. "Do something about Cee, Jeanette. Keep her away from our slaves. I've had trouble enough teaching them their proper place."

Cee was Jamie's pet name for Celeste.

"Having Bliss for a companion never hurt me," I said. "Celeste knows the difference between black and white. She just doesn't care about it."

"Well, damn it, I care. Colonel Carroll rode all the way over here yesterday because Celeste snubbed his youngster to play with the black kids." Jamie was exasperated. "We're having enough trouble being accepted here, without the Carrolls being down on us."

Colonel Carroll owned the next plantation up the Mississippi, The Columns. His son, Richard Carroll, was a handsome youngster, two years older than Celeste. They had the same tutor.

Jamie was changing. We'd found Great Oaks run-down, with all but seventy-five slaves sold off, and the remaining blacks in a sulky, sullen mood. Their former owner, from all I could tell, had been a sadist who was stupid as well. Morale of our slaves was at a low ebb. Jamie and I set out to raise it. We needed every hand, and fresh slaves, if Great Oaks was going to pay back our $25,000 investment.

Doubling their bacon ration helped, and we

granted each male slave with a family a quarter-acre plot where he could cultivate his own garden on Sunday, or after his field work was finished. Until we bought Great Oaks, they'd had to subsist on cornmeal gruel.

We repaired the run-down brick slave cabins. This was done before we did any work on the plantation's Great House. Jamie appointed himself overseer until we could find a suitable person. Our neighbors, especially the Carrolls, considered this below his dignity, and said so. Another Jamie would have told them all to go to hell. Mine at Great Oaks went out of his way to explain that being his own overseer was a temporary expedient.

Jamie made many trips to Grande Terre in Barataria Bay below New Orleans to buy fresh slave stock from the Laffites. By 1809 we had 150 slaves, all in good condition.

Jamie confounded our neighbors by plowing up the indigo and sugarcane acreage on Great Oaks, to plant that crop new to Louisiana, cotton. With the growing demand from British textile mills for this fiber, our neighbors soon followed his example, and Jamie's prestige rose. He was proud of this coup.

By 1810, Jamie the privateer, and sometime pirate, had become a respected Louisiana planter.

These American planters, I was discovering, were very little different from their counterparts I'd known in Haiti. They drank as much, gambled the same large sums they couldn't afford, and wenched with their female slaves. But this was a new environment for Jamie, and he wanted to be part of it.

"The first time one of our women has a mulatto child that even faintly resembles Jamie McCoy," I told him, when we first arrived at Great Oaks, "I'll hang you out to dry!"

Jamie began to drink a little more than he used to, and he gambled, usually winning, but if he ever went to a black woman on Great Oaks, I never knew it—and you can be assured I would have!

In 1810 Great Oaks showed considerable profit for the first time. Jamie still acted as overseer, and I kept the books. Jamie was one of the first to see the 1812 war with Great Britain coming.

"It will be fought mostly at sea, Jeanette," he told me. "I need a solid deck under my feet and a crew I can trust. We have no navy of consequence, so Congress must commission privateers—and that's one trade I know better than planting."

"You'd leave me with baby twins, and a one year old child to run Great Oaks?" I asked, with some spirit. "Think again, Jamie McCoy! If a war is coming, you stay out of it."

"It may not come," Jamie admitted, but there was a reckless glint in his eyes.

352

Early in 1811, Jamie finally found a man with whom he could trust our slaves. Clinton Scott came to Great Oaks asking if he could preach to our slaves. Jamie was in New Orleans on business. Reverend Scott talked with me.

"I'm down here from New York State, Mrs. McCoy," he told me. In his early thirties, Clinton looked much younger, with his flaxen hair and china-blue eyes. He had a snub-nosed, open face with a spray of freckles on his nose and cheeks. "Word among owners hereabouts is that you and Mr. McCoy are uncommonly good to your slaves. I want to help them, too."

We were in my small office off the drawing room of Great Oaks. The plantation's books were open on the desk before me.

"What is your motive, Mr. Scott?" I asked. "You don't look like a zealot to me, or a man touched with religious mania."

He flushed. "I'm neither, Mrs. McCoy."

"Do you have a degree from a divinity school?" I asked.

"No."

I knew a great deal about Clinton before he was shown into my office. Alicia Carroll, Colonel Carroll's young wife, and I had become close friends. Clinton had asked if he could preach to their slaves.

"No, damn you!" Colonel Carroll had bellowed. Too much whiskey and peach brandy made him an irascible man. "Ignorant blacks don't need to know about a white God!"

Alicia confided that she written northern friends about Clinton. I believe she was somewhat smitten by the man. As a result of her correspondence, I knew he had a medical degree from Yale.

"I'm curious why you, a medical doctor, want to preach the gospel to our slaves," I said.

"Mrs. McCoy, you've found me out," Clinton admitted. "What I've told you about wanting to preach isn't a lie, however. Both my grandfather and grandmother were bonded servants in Virginia. My parents died when I was quite young, and they raised me. From them I've learned of the hopelessness of the enslaved. Yet they are God's children, too, don't you agree?"

"I certainly can't disagree."

"Does it hurt if I give your slaves hope of a heaven, while I try to learn why some diseases are fatal to them, and only minor affliction for us whites? Or why diseases that are minor to them are many times fatal to us of the white race?"

"You won't learn that in a day, a week, or even a year," I said.

He nodded. "In a lifetime of work, I may get only a few slender clues, but I intend to spend the rest of my life on this research project."

"All the more reason you might make us the proper overseer," I said.

Jamie liked Clinton on sight, although I've

never known two such opposite men. We hired
him as our overseer. Within a month, Jamie was
gone to New Orleans to buy a ship.

"There's a fortune to be made bringing manu-
factured goods down from northern ports, carrying cotton to England, and English cargo to
northern ports," he told me, and I knew he was
right. "You and Clinton can run things here
without me." About that, Jamie was right again.
"And when war with England comes," he said,
"I've my ship and crew ready to twist the British
lion's tail."

This was more like the Jamie McCoy with
whom I'd fallen in love. A ship of his own was
integral to his self-esteem.

"Jamie, go to sea again," I urged. "Just don't
forget to come back to me."

"You'll not be objecting?" he asked, surprised.

"Would I try to keep a hawk in a cage?" I
asked.

Jamie's eyes were moist. He tipped up my chin
to stare into my eyes. "You have all the love for
a woman that a man like me can give, Jeanette,"
he said, and his voice was solemn. "Should anything happen to me, I want you to know that."

"See that nothing does happen to you!" I
scolded.

Jamie's ship, the *Corsair*, a swift three-masted
sloop, carried the war to England at sea, working out of Mobile until 1814. Getting wind of the

British invasion force anchored off Chandeleur Island, Jamie sailed up to New Orleans in 1814, just in time to combine forces with the Laffites and their Baratarians. Jamie had enlisted his crew from among the Baratarians, too.

These descendants of pirates of every stripe manned Jackson's cannon. As a matter of fact, most of his artillery at the Battle of New Orleans came through the swamps from Grande Terre.

Jamie lost his hatred of the British on Chalmette Plantation.

"The red-coated limeys never stopped coming, Jeanette." Jamie's face was haggard with the memory. "Our grape and canister ripped great bloody holes in their ranks. They would close up and come on with fixed bayonets. Mostly boys, not men. Dominique You was sobbing but he kept his cannon hot, and so did I."

This poured from Jamie's inner soul, and tears stood in his eyes. "It was a terrible thing to see and to cause. We couldn't bury them properly— there were too many—and rain washed them up from their shallow graves. The stench could be smelled in New Orleans."

I held his head to my breast. "It's happened, Jamie. It is all over now, and we're at peace with the British."

"It wasn't necessary, with the Treaty of Ghent already signed before the battle." His voice was hoarse and muffled. "Damn!"

"Listen to me, Jamie. If they'd routed Jackson

and gained control of the whole Mississippi Valley, do you think the British would have said, 'So sorry, chaps!' and sailed back to Jamaica? Would you? I wouldn't, and I'm only half-British."

Jamie was silent, thinking about what I'd just said. He raised his head to kiss me. "So the slaughter pen was necessary," he mused. Then Jamie did a very characteristic thing. "We'll not speak of this ever again," he said. "I've had my war, and I never want another, and there's the end of it, Jeanette."

"Come to bed," I said.

Jamie grinned. "That I'll be doing, and quickly. You've a long night ahead, woman."

"I thought I might have," I said, "so I brought the children to Alicia Carroll, and sent the house servants down to their quarters. Is there anything else you want to know?"

"Yes." He was fumbling with his buttons. "Why is it a man takes so damn long to get his pants off at a time like this?"

"Let me help." I grabbed, ripped, and the buttons pattered on the floor of the room. "There." I pushed him back across our bed. "You're about to be raped," I told him.

Jamie closed his eyes. "Have at it."

It *was* a very long night.

The years until 1825 were mellow ones, with Great Oaks prospering because of Clinton and me, while Jamie and his *Corsair* earned additional working capital with which to buy more land and slaves. We had 300 by 1825.

Celeste was a beautiful young woman of seventeen in 1825. Celeste McCoy was never a girl.

"That one was born a woman," Jamie insisted.

It was true. She was a solemn little thing at first, inspecting the world through those hazel eyes as if she expected to find its flaws. As my children grew, Celeste mothered the twins as much as I did, and always seemed years older than her age.

I've said she adored my Jamie, and she did, but there were never scales on Celeste's eyes. Hers wasn't blind adoration. She knew his faults as well as I did—maybe better—but where I loved him as much for them as for his strengths, Celeste set out to correct them. For her sake he stopped drinking so heavily.

Celeste was scornful about his gambling. "You waste good time gaming, Daddy," she told him. "Time you could spend with Mother and me, as well as the twins. You say how much you win, but never how much you lose."

"Cee, stop fussing," Jamie said. "I won a whole plantation once with my gambling. Your mother will tell you about that."

"She has," Celeste said, "and how you gave it away."

"You'll be showing your father proper respect," Jamie chided. "You've heard too many Clinton

Scott sermons, I'm thinking. Who are you to lecture me, girl?"

Celeste melted him with her smile. "Mother doesn't, and every man should be a little henpecked, don't you think?"

Jamie stopped gambling.

I resented Celeste from that time on. Whom did my Jamie love most? I learned there are different sorts of jealousy.

1825. Richard Carroll was courting Celeste, and the Carrolls wanted a match. Jamie didn't. But I wanted her married as much as Alicia wanted Celeste for Richard's wife. I told myself that was because, as her mother, I wanted Celeste married to the most handsome young man up and down the Mississippi, and The Columns with Great Oaks would be a fief upon which to build a Carroll-McCoy dynasty.

My real reason, of course, is that I wanted all of Jamie's attention, which I had in bed, but never the rest of the time.

"Richard Carroll isn't the man for Cee," Jamie insisted.

"And just why isn't he, McCoy?" I demanded to know. "They'll have beautiful children."

"Look at his father," Jamie said.

"Richard is Alicia's child, too," I pointed out.

Jamie scowled. "Aye, but Richard takes from his father the most."

"You're not going to like any young man who

comes to Great Oaks courting your favorite daughter," I accused. "Wake up, Jamie. Your blood and mine is hot. Celeste borrows from both of us. The girl's heart will take her someday where her head knows she shouldn't go. Unless she marries and settles down, that is."

"Let her follow her heart," Jamie said.

That was the last discussion we ever had about our oldest daughter.

We needed an educated slave to help me with the plantation books and accounts. Jean Laffite told Jamie that just such a slave was for sale at The Temple, the Laffite trading place in the swamp and bayou land that lies between that city and Barataria Bay.

Celeste had gone with him to New Orleans to buy dress and suit materials for herself and the twins. It was January 7, 1826 when word came up the river that Jamie and Celeste would be two days late returning to Great Oaks.

The next night I had a horrible dream. I was back on Haiti, and seeking Jamie, but there was a fog. Wind would blow a hole in the fleecy stuff, and I'd glimpse Jamie—but only his back, never his face. He was always moving away from me to disappear in the fog.

I cried his name and woke up calling it. I was soaked with cold sweat. The rest of the night I tossed and turned.

All the next day I was restive. Scott and I

were going over the accounts. "Mrs. McCoy, perhaps we should wait a day," Scott finally said. "Are you feeling well?" He laid his cool palm on my forehead, and it was the first time the man had touched me. "No fever."

The air in my small office was suddenly charged. "Are you sure I have no fever?" I asked, and he knew I wanted him to touch me again.

"Quite sure." He closed the account books.

I looked up and saw Celeste was framed in the doorway. She was the color of the gray fog in my dream, and her eyes burned out of a haggard young face.

"Daddy is dead," she told me. "Killed by Gambini in a duel! Oh, God damn it!" She saw neither Clinton Scott nor me. "I'm going to kill the Italian."

I felt as if the world had collapsed around me. Scott stared at Celeste, slack-jawed.

* * *

The funeral for Jamie McCoy was brief and private, as he would have wished it. There was no oration but there was a vast cluster of flowers from the plantation and from neighbors who'd known and admired him. Clinton Scott stood, stalwart, at my side. Celeste wept and then I knew how much she'd loved her father, though she'd fought him tooth and nail—very much as he may have fought his own father as a stripling striving for his place in the world.

361

I didn't weep then. That happened a few days later when I journeyed down to New Orleans and stood on the farthest dock reaching toward the Gulf. In my hand was a casket containing the ashes of the man I had loved so utterly. Wordlessly, I flung ashes, casket and all out into the waters leading to the sea which he had loved, perhaps more than life.

It was then that I cried, great sobs that racked my body until I had no more tears. I rose, went to my carriage, in which Celeste and Scott were waiting, and returned to the life that was left.

Rose of Passion, Rose of Love

Jeanne Sommers

"WE ONLY HAVE ONE TEXAS"

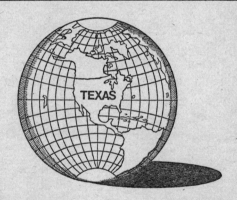

TEXAS

People ask if there is really an energy crisis. Look at it this way. World oil consumption is 60 million barrels per day and is growing 5 percent each year. This means the world must find three million barrels of new oil production each day. Three million barrels per day is the amount of oil produced in Texas as its peak was 5 years ago. The problem is that it is not going to be easy to find a Texas-sized new oil supply every year, year after year. In just a few years, it may be impossible to balance demand and supply of oil unless we start conserving oil today. So next time someone asks: "is there really an energy crisis?" Tell them: "yes, we only have one Texas."

ENERGY CONSERVATION -
IT'S YOUR CHANCE TO SAVE, AMERICA

Department of Energy, Washington, D.C.